REMO THREW UP HIS HANDS IN DISGUST

"Fine," he snarled. "Go traipsing into the jungle and reenact more scenes from Luzu Dawn for all I care. But I am not covering for you on this one."

Chiun's wrinkled face grew dark. "That is because you are a good son, Remo," he said with bitter sarcasm. "And good sons always turn like hissing vipers on their fathers in times of need. Tell your precious Smith whatever you want."

Scowling from the sting of Chiun's words, Remo turned to go. Something caught his attention.

Through a break in the shrubs he saw the shadowy image of a familiar face behind a tinted windshield.

There might yet be a way to salvage this. Of course, he'd have to do it without Smith's approval. And in that moment, Remo came to what he decided was the most well thought out decision of his life.

"Ah, screw it."

Folding his arms over his chest, he waited for the approaching government car to stop, ankle-deep in b̲u̲s̲h̲e̲s̲.

Created by Murphy & Sapir

THE

Destryer™

A POUND OF PREVENTION

A GOLD EAGLE BOOK FROM

W❖RLDWIDE.®

TORONTO • NEW YORK • LONDON
AMSTERDAM • PARIS • SYDNEY • HAMBURG
STOCKHOLM • ATHENS • TOKYO • MILAN
MADRID • WARSAW • BUDAPEST • AUCKLAND

First edition October 2000

ISBN 0-373-63236-3

Special thanks and acknowledgment to
James Mullaney for his contribution to this work.

A POUND OF PREVENTION

To my teachers at St. Leo's, who did pretty well considering what they had to work with.

And especially to Sister Eileen. I can't pinpoint the day, but I know it was in her fourth-grade English class that I decided what I wanted to do for a living.

To Joss Whedon for giving me something to do on Tuesdays.

And to the Glorious House of Sinanju,
e-mail: housinan@aol.com

Although currently under contract we will still entertain all serious offers. Tyrants and warlords must produce proof of current bank balance, two forms of picture ID and one letter of recommendation from nothing less than a European-level monarch.
(And remember: No shoes, no shirt, no assassination.)

PROLOGUE

In the glory days of the great Luzu Empire, on the fringes of what would one day become East Africa, before the final encroachment of Europeans, which would change the face of the continent for centuries to come, before the bloody Boer Wars and the countless deaths that they would bring, the people of the tribe of the mighty Luzu chief Kwaanga met in ceremony on the shores of the great azure sea.

The day was warm, not hot, the sky as clear as glass and as blue as the smooth waters of the sea that stretched out boldly to the horizon. At some distant point, sea snatched sky from the heavens and clutched it firmly to its undulating bosom.

In the center of the small bay—barely an inlet—a sleek, strange ship from some distant land lay at anchor. The wooden vessel bobbed lazily on the gentle waves that rolled toward the sandy yellow shore, where they became thin froth.

Out of respect for their parting guest, the females of the Luzu tribe covered their breasts with silks from far-off lands where dwelled men with slits for eyes and skin the hue of a lion's belly. The Orient. The place from where their honored guest had come. The place to which he would now go, never to return to the land of the Luzu.

The elders of Luzuland were dressed in flowing caftans and dashikis, the wealth of the empire reflected in their raiments. The young males were smeared in green and red paint and carried finely crafted metal-tipped spears—an honor guard for the man who had served them all so well for so long.

The recent news of the revered one's departure had been a surprise to all. Or perhaps not *all*.

Surely great Chief Kwaanga had known. It was he who had summoned the mysterious warrior from his faraway land to aid the Luzu. They had not been told because, as mere subjects, it was not their place to know. But Kwaanga had to have long known that the thin man with hands and feet as swift as an arrow in flight would this day take his leave of the Luzu.

The people had turned out at dawn. Hurrying to prepare for the ceremony, they were ready by midday. Just in time.

When the white-hot sun reached its highest point in the heavens, the great men arrived.

Chief Kwaanga strode in front, a powerful man with a broad, smiling face and flowing, colorful robes. This day, Kwaanga did not smile. Behind their chief, astride a huge black pony, rode the protector of the Luzu people.

The chief's horse had once belonged to the Spanish. It was a demonstration of both gratitude and humility that the chief should lead his guest like a common Luzu.

A hush fell over the people—ten thousand strong—gathered at the foamy shore.

The man atop the horse wore a ceremonial robe of a green deeper and more vibrant than anything the Luzu had ever seen. Upon his head bobbed an awkward hat of thin rice paper, stained black. The hat was too small for his head and seemed ready to blow off from the slightest breeze.

He was known as Nuk, the Master of Sinanju. He who had taken as seed a small band of warrior peasants and helped them to grow into a mighty empire.

Nuk did not meet the eyes of the crowd. As his pony walked closer to shore, he stared over the heads of the people. He looked beyond the land, beyond even the waiting ship in the harbor. He was gazing at a point where sky met sea, to distances the Luzu people could not perceive and to depths none but he could fathom.

A warm breeze came across the ocean, pushing landward. It disturbed silken robes and blew a cloud of fine sand inland. Passing through the multitude, the Master of Sinanju and Chief Kwaanga paid the wind no heed.

Where the men walked, the Luzu people parted.

Silently, proud black features glistening in the merciless African sun, the chief led the horse through the throng. At the shore, he stopped.

A small rowboat listed on the sand of the beach. Two anxious sailors stood near it.

A nation strong, the Luzu people crowded on beach and bluff.

Near the boat, Master Nuk slipped from the

pony's bare back, his wooden sandals failing to disturb even a single grain of sand.

The Master of Sinanju was tall but thin, his black hair lately touched with streaks of coarse gray. When Nuk turned to address the chief of the Luzu, his voice was loud enough for all to hear. He spoke in the language of their fathers.

"Sinanju would take its leave of you, fearless Chief Kwaanga of the Luzu," the Master of Sinanju intoned.

Before the lean man, whose face was the color of sand in shade, Chief Kwaanga drew himself up to his full regal height. The top of his head came only to the bridge of the Master of Sinanju's nose.

"I would grant you your leave, Great Master Nuk, he who graciously throttles the universe, from the fearsome House of Sinanju."

A nod that was not quite a bow passed between the two men. Afterward, Master Nuk looked out at the gleaming black faces of the Luzu nation. Though his words were directed at their leader, they were intended for his tribe.

"You are a wise and powerful ruler, O Kwaanga. Your people are brave and strong, your diamonds pure. You give your nation both physical strength and strength of character. The leader serves the nation and the nation, the leader. And Sinanju is honored to have served both." There was a hint of pride and sadness in the Master's hazel eyes. "Remember you this—though I now depart this land, if ever there comes a time when your people are in need of the services of Sinanju, you need but summon us. This is the pledge of Nuk, current Master of Sinanju, to you, Kwaanga of KwaLuzu.''

And from his robes, the Master of Sinanju produced a small ceremonial dagger. Its cudgel was of ivory, its blade the purest gold. It had been given to the Master by Chief Kwaanga. Master Nuk returned the small knife to the Luzu leader.

Accepting the blade, Chief Kwaanga found that a new symbol had been carved into the handle of the knife. It was a simple trapezoid bisected with a vertical slash. The symbol of the House of Sinanju.

"This is a sign of amity between our peoples," Nuk proclaimed. "Keep it always close."

With that, the Master of Sinanju lifted the skirts of his robes and climbed into the waiting wooden rowboat.

The two nervous sailors in attendance had eyes round like a Luzu, but their skin was neither that of the Luzu nor of the departing Master. They had skin as white as the clouds above Kilimanjaro and spoke in a tongue foreign to native ears. Once the Master was seated in the boat, green skirts arranged around his knees, the sailors pushed the tiny vessel into the gentle surf. Climbing aboard themselves, they began rowing quickly toward their waiting ship.

And as Master Nuk left that shore for the last time, a soft sound rose up from the gathered Luzu nation. The cheers grew in size and strength until the very air shrieked with joy. As the rowboat passed the anchor of the moored ship, great raucous ululations carried over the bay.

The Master of Sinanju did not look back as he scurried aboard the big vessel.

Chief Kwaanga did not see the Master clamber into the boat, nor did he wait with his cheering people as the ship put to sea. As soon as Master Nuk had climbed into the rowboat, the chief had mounted his own black horse. As his people shouted their joy and gratitude, he rode off alone. Away from the sea. Back to the seat of his empire.

The chief was quietly concerned. In the hollow place where dwelled his spirit, he wondered if the words spoken this day were merely for ceremony. If there ever came a time that the Luzu were in need of the Master of Sinanju, would the head of the ancient House of assassins truly take heed?

As the cheers of his people faded on the wind, Kwaanga returned to the heart of KwaLuzu, alone and with a deeply troubled heart.

The Mafia was represented.

The Cosa Nostra delegations from the United States and Sicily had insisted on a place of honor near the head of the table, and they still commanded enough respect to get it. Truth be told, everyone there knew the Mob's time had nearly come to an end.

Once rich and powerful, it had flourished before most of the men there were born. But that was before there was any real competition in the world. Now...

Now. Well, politeness did not allow the other delegates to speak of the hard times that had befallen the Mob of late. Now it was more out of respect for what it had been in the past that its demands were acceded to in the present. Like a doddering father too beloved by his family to place in a home, the Mafia was allowed its seat of honor.

An agent from the Camorra was there, as well. Looked down on for years by the more powerful Mafia, the Camorra was thought to have had been abolished by Mussolini early in the twentieth century. It had survived, but only with a fraction of the power it had previously enjoyed. It had experienced a resurgence of late, poised to make inroads in what had previously been purely Mafia territory.

Black Hand was there. This was the crime syndicate thought at various times in its history to be one and the same as both the Sicilian Mafia and the Naples Camorra, but which was never part of either. It was strong and stealthy, its leadership unknown. So complex were its transactions that its influence was impossible to calculate.

The current titans on the world scene were the powerful drug dealers. And from France to the Far East, from the Russian Mob in the north to the Medellín cartel in the south, all had sent representatives to this introductory meeting.

The promise of peace had brought them all there. But that had been shattered the moment Jamon Albondigas spied Russell Copefield, the ambassador for the Cali cartel.

"You are a fool who works for fools," Albondigas spit viciously. The La Cosina drug lord was pudgy with a dark brown complexion. Even in the chilly air-conditioned hall, he perspired like a Venezuelan stevedore. Crescent moons of sweat stained the underarms of his white, open-necked shirt.

"If you and your brothers cannot compete..." Copefield shrugged in a delicate shift of Armani. The Cali agent was a New York lawyer in his mid-forties. His weasel's face was tugged forward in perpetual condescension.

"Cali is *dead*," Albondigas snarled. "*We* are the new power. My brothers and I have buried you."

"We'll see who'll be dead at the end of the day," the American lawyer taunted with infuriating smugness.

Albondigas gripped the edge of the huge table. Furious eyes darted to the double doors.

The bodyguards and hired killers waited beyond. Albondigas had brought with him a hulking Paraguayan with arms as wide around as tree trunks and a chest as broad and muscled as the hindquarters of a charging rhino. If Albondigas called, the giant would break down the door. The other bodyguards would follow him in, guns blazing. In the ensuing bloodbath, they'd *all* be killed.

Albondigas's face twitched with barely contained rage.

The others in the room glanced anxiously to the head of the table for guidance. For a soothing voice. For *something* to stop this madness. But only silence issued from the most prominent chair in the big room.

"You are very certain of yourself, gringo," Albondigas hissed abruptly.

The softness of his tone was jarring. All eyes returned to Albondigas.

"I'm paid to be certain," Copefeld replied tightly. There was something in his voice, in his eyes. Like a cornered animal. Almost as if he didn't believe what he was saying. Yet he did not back down.

Albondigas clenched his jaw. Slowly, his gaze

shifted to the main doors. And as all watched, his lips pursed with jeering malevolence.

Before Albondigas could utter a single word, another sharp voice broke in. The English was clipped and precise.

"This is foolishness. We are not here to squabble. Stop this *now,* Mandobar."

Sham Tokumo of the Yakuza was looking to the head of the table, to their silent host.

The faces of the men were bland—deliberately willed calm to mask inner unease. Flat eyes focused once more on the world-famous chocolate-black face of Mandobar. Their host's eyes were unreadable; the mouth held an expression of puckered impatience.

Mandobar's reaction to the war of words surprised them all. There was a long sigh, followed by a very slight raising of shoulders. Utter helplessness.

"I did not believe it would come this quickly," Mandobar clucked unhappily. "Of course, I knew a conflict was likely inevitable. But here? Now?" The head shook, the eyes were sad and slightly downcast, as if lost in weighty thought.

Albondigas licked his lips. He glanced from the lawyer up to Mandobar.

Albondigas's temper was legendary. Yet no one seemed ready to prevent his calling his bodyguard into the room. Not even the person who had summoned them all there for this great meeting of the world's most powerful crime syndicates. For Albondigas, it was now a matter of honor.

With agonizing slowness, he pushed his chair

away from the big table. The mahogany legs groaned a sad protest across the dry, buffed-marble floor.

Across the table, Sham Tokumo was stunned. The Yakuza man could not believe Mandobar wasn't stopping this. Wasn't that what this whole plan was all about? Unity among these organizations? Tokumo didn't want to die because two squabbling idiots couldn't get along.

Albondigas was walking slowly to the door.

Tokumo glanced desperately around the gleaming conference table for someone to stop the madness. When Albondigas ordered his man to shoot, it would all be over.

Tokumo had not spent four months negotiating with the East African government to be slaughtered over some petty remarks not even related to the current meeting.

"Stop this, Jamon," Tokumo called, rising to his feet.

Pausing, the drug dealer turned. He stood in the middle of the wide, vacant room, as big as a large auditorium. The table was far behind him, illuminated by sheets of cascading light pouring in from a latticed network of skylights that filtered the ultraviolet from the burning African sun.

"Do not worry, Sham," Albondigas said blandly. "I am only stepping outside for some air. It has suddenly gotten foul in here." He began walking once more.

Tokumo spun to the Cali lawyer, who sat a few

seats from the Yakuza agent. "Apologize, fool," he hissed, whipping off his owlish glasses.

There were beads of perspiration on the lawyer's upper lip and forehead. Again, there was the sense that he hadn't expected a few ill-chosen words to go this far.

Tokumo saw a single bead of sweat form just beneath the neatly shaved hairline at the back of the lawyer's head. It slipped to the top of his white shirt collar.

Albondigas was barely a yard from the door when the Cali attorney called to him.

"The *business* day," Russell Copefeld called abruptly, his voice echoing in the big hall.

Albondigas turned slowly, eyes narrowed. The harsh sunlight, muted through the blackened glass, cast weird shadows on his burly form. He was so far across the huge room they almost needed binoculars to see the expression on his face.

"What?" Albondigas said, his tone flat.

"I meant to say 'we will see who is dead at the end of the *business* day,'" the lawyer offered, his voice suddenly going timid. "Rhetorically, there's a big difference. It wasn't a threat—it was a metaphor. For our healthy business rivalry. If you took it another way, it was not intentional and I *do* apologize, most sincerely."

Near the door, Jamon Albondigas weighed Copefeld's placating words carefully. It took him a moment to react. When he took a step back toward the table, Sham Tokumo felt the very air lighten. It was over.

"I accept your apology," Albondigas said tightly as he strode back to the table. "And I wish you dead, as well. In the healthiest, business-metaphor sense, of course."

As the others laughed, Albondigas resumed his place at the conference table.

When Sham Tokumo glanced at Copefeld, the Cali lawyer was mopping sweat from his tan face. Tokumo frowned at the man's strange behavior even as he felt relief that they could now resume the more mundane business before them.

At the head of the table, Mandobar had been a surprisingly silent observer. Not a word had passed the broad lips. Even now, that famous face remained unreadable. As though it could have been carved from a chunk of gleaming coal. But as Tokumo and the others returned to their papers and briefcases, a happy chuckle rose from the far end of the great table. When those gathered glanced up, they found that the stern mouth had melted into a broad grin.

Mandobar laughed a deep, rolling belly laugh. The black eyes sparkled, and the familiar laugh lines returned. It was the same face they'd all seen on newspapers and television screens since the nation of East Africa had been so abruptly thrust into the world spotlight some fifteen years before.

"Do you not see?" Mandobar happily asked the puzzled faces. "This was the first real test of our new union, and the crisis has been resolved peacefully. With *words*, not violence. Gentlemen, we have already succeeded. It is as I have promised. There will be no conflict here. The Republic of East

Africa will be ally to *all* of you.'' Mandobar looked to Albondigas and Copefeld in turn, eyes beaming.

Far, far down the enormous table, the Tadzhikistan representative began to applaud. Near him, the agent for the Sons of Belial started clapping, as well.

What began as a polite ripple quickly grew. Tokumo, Copefeld—even Jamon Albondigas joined in. Like thunder rumbling in across the vast Serengeti, the cheers grew and grew, echoing across the great hall.

And in the place of honor at the head of the table, Mandobar reveled in the accolades from this collection of the world's greatest purveyors of misery and dependence.

THE MEETING DISBANDED late in the evening. The cheers were long dead by the time Russell Copefeld crept alone through the shadowy compound near the darkened meeting hall.

The night was warm. Distant animals until now familiar only from PBS documentaries howled sad, desperate shrieks at the bejeweled African sky.

A line of neat bungalows to his right housed some of the delegates from around the world. Many others had been helicoptered back to Bachsburg after the meeting.

It was now long past midnight, and all of the tidy little houses were bathed in blackness. The only light Copefeld could see came from the cottage of the French delegate. A local brothel had been supplying prostitutes for the delegates since first they arrived at the secret VIP village. No doubt the French agent was at it again.

Copefeld didn't care about the Frenchman or his whores. Right now, all he was interested in was getting paid.

This cloak and dagger was ridiculous. Stealing around like common thieves in the dead of night. He'd be sure to let Mandobar know when they met.

There was nothing wrong with bank transactions. Hell, wasn't that what all of this was about? Untraceable cash, banks willing to look the other way at huge deposits and, most importantly, no tax man breathing down anyone's neck.

Copefeld was a great proponent of electronic cash. It was part of why he had convinced his Cali bosses to look seriously into this East African deal. A haven for crime that didn't care where the money came from? A fixed rate of graft with the local government locked in more securely than a United States government treasury note? Approval for the entire enterprise at the highest levels of government?

It was a sweetheart deal. East Africa was going to be a nation like none the world had ever seen.

Every country or state or city had its lawless suburbs. Many countries looked the other way at certain types of crimes. But the promise of East Africa was everything under one roof. You could wire transfer your wealthy wife's cash to one of Bachsburg's banks, hire someone to kill her from the classified section of a local newspaper and be out on the links at the famous Sin City resort—all in less than one hour.

Of course, that sort of thing was for the truly wealthy. Russell Copefeld was just a struggling New York attorney, someone who could use a couple of extra bucks now and then. That was why, when Mandobar had offered him fifty thousand U.S. dollars to start that little fight with Albondigas that afternoon…well, a fool and his money.

Copefeld didn't know for certain why Mandobar was so insistent that he disrupt today's meeting. However, he had an inkling. Doubtless it was to prove to the other crime lords that things could be worked out easily here. There were no wars here in the new East Africa. This was the demilitarized zone of crime.

As he skulked through the brush, Copefeld thought of how resistant his bosses had been to this scheme. They'd been burned on something similar once before. But that was way back in the 1970s. The world was older, wiser and far more sophisticated now. It was an idea worthy of resurrection.

Copefeld's sleeve suddenly snagged on a thorny branch. When he tugged, he heard the material tear.

"Dammit," he whispered to the empty black air.

Eyes squinting, he held up the cuff to his nose. As he rubbed the expensive silk between his fingertips in search of a hole, Copefeld heard a sound behind him.

A cracking branch.

Fearing an animal attack, he whirled.

But it was no animal.

Strong hands grabbed his arms, pinning them painfully behind his back, yanking them up until they threatened to tear from the sockets.

As Copefeld tried frantically to pull away, a figure moved in front of him. The black face was filled with menace.

"What are you doing!" Copefeld gasped.

In response, a balled fist slashed across his face. The man's ring tore an angry gash in Copefeld's cheek.

Unseen men fought with his wrists, tightening something around them.

Rope twisted and knotted. Copefeld's legs were growing weak. Wriggling, panicked, he caught a glimpse of their sweating, gleeful faces.

A smell now. Strong. Something sloshing in a tin can.

"God, please, no," Copefeld begged into the pitiless African night.

One of the men, whom he now recognized as an assistant to Mandobar, carried forward a familiar large doughnut shape. The harmless object—recognizable to even the most rural villages around the world—had a special meaning in East Africa.

A tire. The Goodyear logo was visible along the smooth black side.

Something sloshed within the hollow basin interior of the wheelless ring of rubber. Gasoline.

Copefeld wanted to vomit, but paralyzing fear locked food and bile in his knotted chest.

A necklacing. That's what they called it. Mandobar had even gone to trial for it before East Africa's laws had been subverted in favor of criminals.

As the others held him, Mandobar's man dropped the grimy tire around Copefeld's neck.

"Please," Copefeld wept. "Please, no."

As the lawyer cried hot tears, an oily rag was stuffed in his mouth. They pushed it in so hard, it triggered his gag reflex. Copefeld vomited his dinner of veal scampi and red wine. Some of it spewed from his nose, burning and mixed with bile. The rag blocked the rest. When he swallowed, the thick acid tasted of motor oil.

As his stomach clenched, gasoline from a can was splattered on his clothes. The men were shouting jubilantly.

Some of the bungalow lights came on. Sleepy delegates had come out onto porches in their nightclothes to investigate the commotion.

Floodlights flared to life, bathing the square in a sick yellow haze.

As he was shoved into the center of the broad road, Copefeld felt dozens of eyes upon him. He saw Sham Tokumo and Jamon Albondigas. On the nearest, largest porch stood Mandobar. Eyes flat, head shaking somberly. So sad.

And in that moment before his murder, Russell Copefeld had a sudden flash of realization.

It wasn't the fight in the conference room that was to be Mandobar's example. It was what would happen to anyone who decided to pick a fight in the new East Africa.

Russell Copefeld was the example.

A match was lit. Copefeld heard the stick drawn across sand and phosphorous.

He smelled the gas, the sharp odor burning with the bile in his nostrils.

Mandobar had set him up. Set him up to make a point. The hook had been baited with Copefeld's own greed.

The match danced before his eyes, the yellow flame quivering hypnotically.

Mandobar on the porch, head shaking sadly.

Copefeld wanted to scream about the treachery, but the gag prevented him from shouting.

And in another instant, it no longer mattered.

The match was tossed. Copefeld's chest ignited in a blinding, brilliant flash of yellow and orange.

The pain was horrible, the heat unimaginable. As the flames engulfed his body, the rag in his mouth ignited, burning his face, his eyes. Screaming, Copefeld spit. The rag came out in a soggy, half-flaming knot. It fell, hissing and smoking to the dusty ground.

Fully ablaze now and already blind, Copefeld mustered his last ounce of strength. Staggering, he managed only a few garbled words.

"Mandobar, you b—"

And the crackling flames consumed him.

Russell Copefeld pitched forward into the dirt. Quivering, burning. Dead.

As the sickly smell of cooked human flesh began to dissipate in the warm air, the delegates began slowly returning to their bungalows, softly shutting their doors on the horror they had just witnessed.

No one said a word. Only Sham Tokumo and Mandobar remained.

Eventually, Mandobar disappeared into the last house. The lights inside shut off moments later.

The lawyer from New York crackled gently for what seemed like an eternity. Eventually, one of the men who'd set him ablaze put a bullet into the back of his head, just to make certain. After that, Copefeld's killers threw a blanket over the smoking remains.

Sham Tokumo watched the smoldering blanket for a long time. His thoughts were far away. Some remnants of the sweet smell of cooked human flesh clung to the lazy African air. Smoke from some perverse barbecue.

Something told Tokumo this would not be the last body he would see in this venture. Eventually, he turned his back on Russell Copefeld, clicking off the porch light of his bungalow. It was after 1:00 a.m. when he returned to bed.

Though Sham Tokumo closed his eyes, sleep eluded him.

His name was Remo and what he really wanted to do was bring the baby back to life. Unable to do that, he planned to do the next best thing. He was going to kill the baby's father.

A few dozen mourners clustered together on the damp sidewalk in front of the Simeoni Funeral Home in downtown Peoria. Their eyes were as black and dreary as the upturned collars of their sopped jackets. The stink of damp cigarette smoke hung in the drizzle.

Remo ignored the thin mist that had begun to collect like a wet, gray shroud to the somber, swollen night air. As he walked up the street, he noted that the crowd was smaller than he'd seen on television the previous night.

That he had seen anything about this on TV was repellent. A family's tragedy had been broadcast coast to coast. As a result, the turnout at the funeral parlor was greater than anyone could have imagined. And so, like a popular play, the run had been extended. This was the wake's last night.

As he approached the somber two-story building, he saw that the sidewalk in front of the funeral parlor was piled high with cellophane-wrapped bundles of flowers. Mixed in with these were candles, cards and photographs of the infant victim. Soggy teddy bears drooped morosely against the curb.

It was part of a relatively new practice that clearly heralded the end of Western civilization. People starving for celebrity were no longer content to simply hear about catastrophes. They had to *participate* somehow. And so now whenever there was a cause for national sorrow, they insisted on stampeding to the florist waving their overcharged MasterCards in a frantic bid to be "involved." As a result, the lives of the deceased and the genuine sorrow of their families were reduced to things no more important than a wadded-up Big Mac wrapper.

This, among other things, did Remo think as he passed the mound of junk near the funeral parlor driveway. He steered a course toward the main entrance.

In his black T-shirt and chinos, Remo could easily be mistaken for a casually dressed mourner. He was a nondescript man of indeterminate age. The only thing outwardly unusual about him were his inordinately thick wrists. He looked to be in his thirties, had a lean build and what had been at times described as a cruel face.

Ordinarily, Remo didn't agree with that assessment. Ordinarily, he thought he had a pretty nice face—in spite of what anyone else might say. This day, however, he wouldn't be surprised if someone thought he looked cruel. This day, he *wanted* to look cruel. And in the effort, he wore an expression that was light-years beyond cruel. The violence which churned in perpetuity just beneath the surface now roiled in twin pools of menace in his dark, deep-set eyes.

A gaggle of reporters had staked out a wide area near the entrance. News crews from around Illinois and the nation had spent the past two days pouncing on everyone who came within a three-block radius of the Simeoni Funeral Home. Remo was no exception.

A reporter for one of the bigger Chicago stations spied Remo gliding like a desolate fog up the wet sidewalk. Smelling fresh meat, the man sprang into action.

"We got a live one!" the reporter barked to his cameraman. He snapped a thumb in Remo's direction. "Move in here! *Fast!*"

Fumbling with video camera and microphone, the reporter and his cameraman jumped in front of Remo, blocking his way.

"Are you a friend of the family?" the reporter demanded, thrusting his mike in Remo's hard face.

Remo stopped dead, a frozen shadow. He said not a word.

Silence was death on camera, the reporter knew. If this was going to air, he needed *talk.* "Were you saddened by the tragedy of baby Karen?" he pressed.

Remo remained silent. Immobile.

Next to the newsman, the camera operator slowly lowered his camera. He had seen something through his lens that the eager reporter had missed.

The newsman caught the camera movement out of the corner of his eye.

"What the hell are you doing?" he demanded, wheeling.

The cameraman was staring at Remo. The young man's eyes had taken on a look of quiet dread. His camera was angled toward the sidewalk. He swallowed hard.

"Get that camera up," the reporter demanded.

The cameraman shook his head. His eyes were still locked on Remo's dead, dark orbs. There was something there. Something terrifying. Something *inhuman*. The cameraman felt like a cobra's prey, afraid to move an inch.

"I think we should let this guy go," he whispered softly. His hands were locked at his sides.

"What?" the reporter snarled. "Since when do *you* get paid to think? Get that up here now!"

The reporter was grabbing for the camera when, for the first time, his would-be interview subject spoke.

"Listen to him," Remo said in a tone colder by far than the chilly rain that had begun to soak newsman and mourner to the bone. "He just saved you from getting that microphone buried in your eye socket." And to the cameraman, he said, "Destroy that tape."

The cameraman couldn't obey fast enough.

As the reporter watched in shock, the young man dropped to his knees on the wet sidewalk and began tearing streams of heavy black camcorder tape from the belly of the device. It unspooled in long curling sheets that shimmered when hit with fat droplets from the growing rainstorm.

"What do you think you're doing?" the reporter screeched, lurching for the camera.

When he yelled, a few curious faces turned his way. Those who did saw two men. One kneeling in a pile of ruined tape, the other standing above him, shrieking.

While the reporter continued to scream at his cameraman, a lone mourner slipped up the green-matted staircase and under the somber beige canopy to the Simeoni Funeral Home.

When a few of the other cameramen at the entrance tried to videotape him, they later found as they examined the footage back at their studios that the thin man in black somehow managed to be everywhere the camera wasn't. As if he were possessed with some mysterious instinct to avoid the lens.

THE COFFIN COULD HAVE BEEN a large jewelry box. It was a highly polished red, with gold handles and silver accents.

The tiny lid was closed.

Remo noted the family as he slid through the door and into the shadows at the rear of the room.

They were typically wholesome. A mother and father, both caught in the snare of middle age. Beside them, an older son in his midtwenties. And at the eye of the storm, a pretty young girl of eighteen.

Remo knew her age exactly. It had been on the news.

He had seen her high-school yearbook photo dozens of times on all the networks. Ellen Carlson had become a national celebrity in the worst way imaginable.

The previous year she had been a bright young national honors student with a promising future. Then she met Brad Miller, the ne'er-do-well son of a wealthy Peoria family.

Brad was a sullen drug addict whose résumé included a dozen run-ins with the law. When their daughter began dating the twenty-three-year-old college dropout, the Carlsons were upset. Their anger only grew when Brad got Ellen pregnant.

Pregnancy derailed Ellen's plans for college. After she had the baby, she moved out of her own family's modest home and into the Miller mansion. A summer wedding was planned. Ellen had quietly hoped that fatherhood would force Brad to grow up. When it didn't, she had suffered in silence. Until that day one week ago when he had come home at 5:00 a.m. It was her first and last complaint.

Brad had gone to the kitchen and gotten a pair of pinking shears. He brought them upstairs to the nursery that adjoined their suite. And as his infant daughter quietly sucked her hand in sleep, Brad took the scissors and jammed them into her soft, pulsing skull. He left the shears sticking out of the baby's head for Ellen to find.

The rest was national news.

After the murder, Miller had vanished. There were reports that his father had already sneaked him out of the country. Others had him hiding right in

Peoria. Everything was denied by a family spokesman. The facts, it was insisted, would prove Brad Miller innocent.

But in the entire grisly episode, there was one solid fact, unknown to the Millers or the world at large: no matter where Brad Miller was, Remo Williams would find him.

Even as he lurked at the rear of the crowded funeral home, Remo really didn't know what he was doing there. Logically, he should have started his search with the Miller family. But something had compelled him to come to this place. To see firsthand, without the dulling filter of the television screen, the result of this unspeakable act.

But the results were proving as bland as a newscast. So many days after the event—with all that had gone on between then and now—the circus had been reduced to a small circle of tired family and a line of grim-faced mourners.

Remo was turning to go when he suddenly felt a set of eyes focus on him. Years of exacting training had given him an innate sense to know when he was being watched. What he felt at this moment was more than just a casual glance. It was a knowing, penetrating look.

He quickly honed in on the source.

An old woman on a folding chair sat with the Carlson family near the tiny casket. Her long black dress was in stark contrast to the crush of flowers that threatened to engulf her frail frame. As she stared at him, her rheumy eyes didn't blink.

A young boy stood next to the woman, holding

her gnarled hand. Remo was surprised to see that he was Asian. He was only about five or six years old. His black hair was thick and tousled, framing a flat face.

If he was somehow connected to the Carlson family, he didn't seem dressed for a wake. The boy wore what looked like black pajamas. Remo knew it was actually a two-piece *gi,* the uniform of the martial arts.

The boy's hooded eyes were downcast. The sadness that clung to him was far older than he.

In a moment, the young Asian child became irrelevant.

The instant Remo's gaze met the old woman's, she released the boy's hand. Pushing herself to her feet, she began walking toward Remo. Although age had slowed her pace, her stride was confident.

Remo didn't know who she thought he was, nor did he care. An undertaker wearing a black suit and professional look of sympathy stood at a nearby archway door. When Remo turned to him, the man reached a helpful hand for the handle.

"Wait, *please,*" an elderly voice stressed from behind.

At the door, the undertaker pointed over Remo's shoulder. "Sir?" he offered politely.

Remo's first instinct was to bolt, but he didn't want to create a scene. Reluctantly, he turned. The old woman stood before him. No one had paid her any attention as she threaded her way to the rear of the room.

A pair of powder-blue eyes, the whites of which

had been washed pink from days of crying, stared up at him. A blue-veined hand gripped his forearm.

"I *knew* you'd come," the old woman insisted. Her pale brow was furrowed. Dry patches on her face indicated where she'd had recent minor skin surgeries.

Remo offered a tight smile. "I'm sorry, but I think you have me confused with someone else," he said.

"No," she insisted, shaking her head firmly, "it's you. I *saw* you. They all think I'm crazy. They almost wouldn't take me from the home for this." She waved her free hand up to the line of mourners. "But I *knew* you'd be here. I told them I *had* to come. To see you."

Remo wasn't certain what to do. The woman was obviously out of her mind.

"I see things," the old lady continued. "I know things. Ever since I was a little girl and knew my daddy shouldn't go to the docks the day of that terrible, terrible fire. My mother cried for weeks afterward. But I *told* them. They just wouldn't listen...." Her eyes took on a faraway look.

"Excuse me, ma'am," Remo said, gently trying to coax the crazy old woman's hand from his arm.

Her grip tightened. Eyes red from weeping stared deeply into his own. "There are decisions you must soon make," the old woman said, her voice becoming strangely distant. "Difficult decisions. Your life is going to be hard these next few years... *Remo*." And she smiled.

In spite of himself, Remo felt a chill tighten around his spine.

As a secret assassin in the employ of the United States government, there were only a handful of people who knew his name. And a demented old inmate of a Peoria nursing home was definitely not part of the inner circle.

He shot a glance at the undertaker. The man was engaged in conversation with another mourner.

Remo turned back to the woman.

He studied her face, trying to find something that might trigger a memory. But there was nothing. As far as he knew, he'd never met her before in his life.

"Do I know you?" he asked quietly.

She gave him the sweet smile of a grandmother he had never known—of the great-grandmother baby Karen would never meet. "You want this," she insisted.

She pressed her hand into his. There was something in it. Remo opened his hand on a small scrap of torn notebook paper. When he unfolded it, he found an address.

He looked up, puzzled.

"The bad boy is there," she said with simple innocence. "They told me. Just like they told me you'd come for him." She finally released the grip on his arm. He hadn't even realized she was still holding him. "Oh, and there's one more thing." A small black purse hung from her elbow. The old woman clicked it open and rummaged inside. She pulled out a small silver crucifix. "It was little Karen's. I got it for her at the religious store the day she was born.'' She forced the cross into Remo's palm.

''I don't underst—'' Remo began, shaking his head.

Before he could finish, a voice cut in.

''Ma, what are you doing back here?''

Remo glanced up dully.

Mr. Carlson had left the rest of his family near the coffin. He stood before Remo, a look of deep apology on his sad face. ''I'm sorry, sir,'' he said softly to Remo. ''She's in and out lately. Ma, you really should be with us.''

Taking his elderly mother gently by the elbow, he led her back up to the front of the room. When she retook her place in her folding chair, she didn't even look Remo's way. Her eyes were glazed, distant.

She took firm hold of the young boy's tiny hand. Remo could see now that he was Korean.

Fighting his confusion, Remo looked from the old woman to the crucifix in his hand. It was cool against his flesh.

He thought of baby Karen, her flesh made as cold by her own father. His face growing resolved, he closed his hand tightly on the cross.

Slipping the crucifix into his pocket, Remo walked down the short staircase and out the side door. In another moment, he melted away into the shroud of the swelling storm.

LIGHTNING CRACKLED in jagged lines across the swollen sky above the tenement, ripping through black clouds. Two seconds later, thunder roared from the nearby darkness. It was quickly followed by another burst of lightning.

Through the dirt-streaked pane of the fourth-floor bedroom window, Brad Miller watched the raging storm.

He had been cooped up in this apartment for six days. Almost a week of doing nothing at all.

His father owned the building. The elder Miller had promised his son that he'd have to stay there only until the lawyers figured something out. The fact that Brad was still stuck in this dump was proof enough that the army of Miller attorneys was having a rough go of it.

Behind Brad, the television played softly, the flickering images keeping pace with the lightning.

It was the news. He caught some of what was going on in the screen's reflection on the pane.

He had stopped watching for himself. At first it was a kick seeing his face on the news day and night. Cabin fever had long wiped that thrill away. Now it was just boring.

He had no idea what could possibly be taking so long. That baby of Ellen's was only a month old. Barely human. More like an animal.

Brad hoped fervently that the days he'd wasted in this slum would count toward his probation. The lawyers should get on that, too. He'd be sure to mention it to his mother the next time she called.

Brad watched a lazy droplet of water roll along the uppermost windowpane. It intersected with the blurry reflected image of the television screen.

For a moment, he thought his eyes were not in proper focus. The TV screen seemed to be obscured by something.

Bored, Brad turned away from the storm...and blinked.

There was a man in the room with him. Even standing perfectly still, the intruder exuded menace. His face was a death mask.

"Who are you?" Brad demanded as he took an involuntary step back.

The intruder didn't move. He just stood in front of the flickering TV, his gaze directed beyond Brad.

"You're a bad father," Remo Williams intoned. The scrap of paper with the tenement's address given to him by baby Karen's great-grandmother lay crumpled at his feet.

A crackle of lightning split the night sky.

Brad swallowed. In that moment, a lifetime's worth of arrogance derived from privilege drained away.

"I got lawyers," Brad Miller gulped. "*Tons* of them."

If Remo heard him, he didn't acknowledge it.

"My father wasn't around when I was growing up. He left me on the steps of an orphanage when I was a baby. I finally met him just a couple of years ago. He's a good guy."

Brad didn't like the sound of this. His ears thrummed as he watched the strange intruder across the room.

"I didn't meet my adoptive father until I was full grown," Remo continued. "I didn't know it at the time, but I was just an infant in a man's body. He's been a real pain in the ass almost the whole time I've known him, but..."

As his voice trailed off, Remo closed his eyes. He thought of that tiny coffin. Of the Carlson family—robbed of daughter and granddaughter.

Brad didn't know what this guy's story was, but he was getting an inkling. The moment Remo's eyes were closed, he saw an opportunity. He lunged for the door.

He barely took two steps before he felt a strong hand grab him by the shoulder. He was ripped from the floor in midstride and thrown back across the room. He landed on the unmade bed, his head smashing against the peeling varnish of the headboard. The cheap wood cracked in two.

When his groggy eyes opened, he saw Remo seated in a chair next to him, his own eyes still closed.

"I have a daughter," Remo said with eerie stillness. "Because of my line of work, her mother took her from me. My father has her now—my *biological* father. Even though I hardly ever see her, she matters more to me than I ever could have imagined."

In the bed, Brad pulled himself to a sitting position. A section of broken headboard thudded to the floor. When he pressed fingers to the back of his head, they came back smeared with blood.

"Dammit, man, I'm *bleeding,*" he panted. When Remo said nothing, Brad shifted awkwardly. The bed squeaked.

At long last, Remo opened his eyes. "I've

failed,'' he said simply. Face hard, he stared out into the bleak night.

For the first time, Brad noticed something in the intruder's hand. It was a tiny cross. In fact, it looked just like the one Ellen's crazy grandmother had given the baby just before they put the old woman in the home.

An image of the demented old hag suddenly sprang into Brad's mind. Her dust-gray face grinned teeth of brown.

She was forever claiming to have visions of this and that. ''Talking to the angels'' was what she called it. The first time Brad had met her, he vowed it would be the absolute last time, as well. The wrinkled old biddy creeped him out.

For an instant, Brad felt as if he were trapped in one of Grandma Carlson's visions. She sat before him in her nursing-home chair, shawl draped over her knees, cackling and cackling a row of dingy teeth. And then she was gone.

The image receded and Brad was back in his hideout.

Remo still sat before him. Baby Karen's crucifix jutted from the hooked knuckle of his index finger. He absently stroked the medal with his thumb.

''My family's got dough,'' Brad offered weakly. He tried to blink away the aftereffects of his weird vision. He could still hear the old woman's fading laughter.

Remo seemed in his own world.

''For more years than I care to remember, it's been my job to protect America from creeps like you. I was supposed to make a difference. But I haven't. You're proof. You grew up rich and spoiled in the wealthiest nation on Earth. You had everything, except a soul. That's the country I kill to preserve. A country with a dead national soul.''

On the bed, Brad gulped. ''Uh, kill?''

''In a minute,'' Remo promised. ''And even if by some miracle you got caught,'' he continued, ''the best you'd get'd be a slap on the wrist. And there are more like you. A *lot* more than when I started. Back then I thought I could make a difference. I was wrong. You grew up in the new improved Great Remo Williams Society. The America where the killers got killed, justice was served and in the end everyone was safe to walk the streets. But that's a crock. You're a direct product of the country I was supposed to be pulling back from the brink. And you put more value in a crumpled Kleenex than in your own daughter's life.''

His bitterness was as thick as the clumps of moist dust that skulked in the corners of the dingy bedroom.

This was all too unbelievable to Brad. With an entire town—an entire *country*—looking for him, this nutcase somehow managed to track him down. He had gotten inside silently, had prevented Brad from escaping and was now talking some psycho talk about killing to save America.

But, for a spoiled rich kid like Brad Miller, this lunatic's last words were a godsend. Brad had lived a life of blaming others for everything bad he'd ever done, and he'd just been served a way out of this mess on a silver platter.

"Yeah, this is *your* fault," Miller agreed, his eyes flashing cunning. He sat up in the bed, swinging his legs over the side. "*You're* the reason I did what I did. You didn't fix stuff like you were supposed to."

It was crazy talk, of course. But this guy had some kind of delusions about personally righting the world's wrongs.

"Maybe." Remo nodded thoughtfully. His deep-set eyes—now grown sad—glanced down at the crucifix in his open palm.

"You bet your ass," Brad enthused, standing. His legs wobbled. "It's *your* fault my baby's dead. You didn't do enough. Maybe if you'd tried a little harder, things would have even worked out between Ellen and me."

Carefully, cautious not to make any sudden moves, Brad inched his way past Remo. For his part, Remo remained seated. Almost as if he were pondering Miller's words.

"I *had* to do it," Brad offered over his shoulder. "Society made me. *You* were supposed to fix society. Somebody really dropped the ball here, and I think we all know who that somebody is."

Brad was halfway to the door by now. It was clear sailing. He took off like a rabbit. Running full-out, he ate up the remaining distance between himself and the bowed old door. When he fumbled for the knob, however, Brad felt a brush of warm air against his ear.

Remo's voice was frighteningly close.

"Just because I've failed, it doesn't mean you're my fault," Remo said coldly.

With that, Brad felt himself being lifted off the floor. As before, he rocketed back across the room. But this time, he did not land on his lumpy bed.

The window through which he had viewed much of the past six days flew up fast. It cracked into a thousand sparkling shards as Brad Miller soared through it into empty space. For one brief instant, his horrified face was illuminated by a streak of yellow lightning. As the light vanished, so did Brad. He plummeted four stories to the street.

The driving rain obscured the wet splat of Brad Miller on the pavement.

The storm was loud through the open window, the rain close. Thunder and lightning trailed off across the city toward Peoria Lake. Droplets struck the sill, splattering the grimy floor.

Near the window, Remo slipped the small crucifix back into his pocket.

He felt dirty. As if Miller were a communicable disease that could be caught through touch. No rainwater was enough to clean the grime from his soul this night.

Remo left the rain to wash away Brad Miller's sins. Feeling deeply troubled, he left the empty apartment.

3

Fourteen lacquered steamer trunks had been carefully arranged around the tidy bedroom. The wizened figure in the red silk kimono clucked and chirped as he fussed between them.

Chiun, Master of the House of Sinanju, the most awesome and feared assassins in all of recorded time, was packing. It was an awe-inspiring task.

Hurrying around the small back room in the Massachusetts condominium complex, the old Korean carried to the trunks the ornately decorated kimonos he had retrieved from his closets. Still more robes were lying folded on his unused dresser and on a low taboret.

Many of the kimonos were older than he was, having been handed down from previous Masters of Sinanju. Yet despite their age, they seemed like new. The same could not be said for their owner.

Chiun was old. His almond-hued skin was the thinnest vellum. Above each shell-like ear, a wisp of white hair protruded, each as insubstantial as a cough of fine dust. A thin thread of fine hair extended from his bony chin.

He was five feet tall and had never weighed over

one hundred pounds. His diminutive stature and advanced years combined to create an outward image of a creature of infinite frailty. Graveyards the world over were filled with those who had leaped to that unwise conclusion.

The tiny Korean with the youthful hazel eyes was one of the two most dangerous beings on the face of the planet. The only other man who could match his awesome skills had just entered the building.

Chiun had heard Remo's car park in the lot next to Castle Sinanju, the converted church that was their shared home. A few seconds later, the front door clicked shut.

As he worked in his room, Chiun cocked an absent ear. Yet, though he listened, he heard not another sound.

It was unusual for Remo not to bray his arrival whenever he returned home. Briefly, Chiun thought that his pupil might have forgotten something in his vehicle and gone back outside. He realized this wasn't the case when he heard Remo's voice at his open doorway.

''What are you doing?''

Though he did not show it, Chiun was surprised that he had heard neither Remo's rhythmic heartbeat nor a single sound from his pupil as he climbed the stairs. When he looked up, the old Korean's parchment face was bland.

''Packing,'' he replied simply. He collected a fiery orange kimono from atop the dresser and placed it in the azure trunk.

Framed in the doorway, his hands jammed in his

pockets, Remo frowned. "I can *see* that," he replied.

"Then why did you ask?"

The green silk kimono with the red-and-gold piping went on top of the orange one.

"Did Smitty give us an assignment while I was gone?" Remo asked as the Master of Sinanju shut the blue trunk.

"The emperor telephoned," Chiun admitted. "He wishes for you to call. Beyond that I do not know." With a flourish, he latched the lid of the steamer trunk.

"Then why are you packing?"

"Why does one generally pack?" the old man countered. He stooped to collect his sleeping mat.

"I don't know," Remo said wearily, his shoulders sinking. "You're going somewhere, I take it?"

"Yes," Chiun replied as he rolled the reed mat tight.

"Does Smith know?"

"I *do* have a life separate from our current employer." Turning from his pupil, he brought the bedroll to an open trunk.

"I already don't like the sound of this," Remo grumbled.

There was a yellow trunk just inside the door. On its closed lid sat a gleaming dagger. Beneath the knife sat a sheet of parchment.

The knife was about five inches long, with a pure white handle and a blade that appeared to be fashioned from solid gold. The cutting edge was dull, indicating a ceremonial purpose. When Remo picked up the dagger, he found that a familiar symbol had been etched into it.

"What's the sign of Sinanju doing on this?" Remo asked as he inspected the bisected trapezoid.

When Chiun looked up from the trunk at which he was working, his wrinkled face grew horrified. He flounced across the room like a petulant bird.

"Keep your nosy hands to yourself," the old man snapped. He snatched the knife away from Remo.

In a flash, the yellow trunk lid sprang open and both knife and parchment disappeared inside.

The lid slammed shut.

"Okay, okay," Remo groused. "I just figured I should know if you cut a deal with Ginsu." His furrowing brow clouding his dark eyes, he sank to a lotus position on the floor.

For a time, Chiun tried to ignore him, but Remo's silent attention finally got to the old Asian. The younger Sinanju Master had dragged into the room a palpable sense of gloom. To Chiun, it was a feeling both familiar and disturbing.

"What troubles you, my son?" the old man asked, his voice softening.

"You don't wanna know," Remo replied with a sad sigh.

"Do not try to maneuver me into begging for a response," Chiun warned. "I can see that something bothers you, but I am very busy." He waved one hand at the organized mess of his room. "Speak."

Remo wrestled with a reply, finally exhaling. "It's just that I don't feel good about the hit I just made," he said.

Chiun lowered the purple kimono he'd been folding. "Of course you do not," he said. "You debase our art by calling a flawless Sinanju assassination a 'hit.'" A horrible thought suddenly occurred to him. "It *was* flawless?"

Remo rolled his eyes. "No," he replied. "My elbow was bent, I used ten machine guns and I was dancing the hoochie-coo. Of course it was flawless. I'm *always* flawless."

At this Chiun cackled.

"With your hits and poochie-poos, the best you can hope for is mediocre." He placed the carefully folded purple robe into the chrysoprase-green trunk from the Chou Dynasty.

"Mediocre or not, Brad Miller's dead and I still feel like crap," Remo said bitterly. He stared at the floor.

Across the room, Chiun paused in his work. They had been watching a news story on Miller the previous night when Remo up and left the room without so much as a single word. Chiun now knew where he had gone.

The old Korean quietly left his packing. On silent sandals, he padded over to Remo, sinking to the floor before his somber pupil.

"You have done the world a service, my son," Chiun said, the wrinkles of his face drawn into a tight frown. "For a man who would murder a child robs the world of a life that will never be realized."

"So you've said," Remo replied. "But that doesn't make any of this any better." His wrists rested on his folded knees. He clenched and unclenched his hands in frustration. "I met an old woman in Peoria," he announced. "I think she might have been senile or something. She knew where Miller was when everybody else on the planet couldn't find him."

At Remo's words, Chiun's frown only deepened.

"She also said the next few years were gonna be hard for me," Remo continued. He laughed sadly. "Can't say I like the sounds of that."

The Master of Sinanju's eyes narrowed. "This crone," the older man asked, "was she a soothsayer?"

"A what?" Remo asked, glancing up. He shook his head. "No. No, she was just some crazy old lady who knew where Miller was. Probably overheard someone mention it at the wake." He deliberately left out the most important detail of the story—the fact that Grandma Carlson had known his name.

Chiun's face was troubled. He tipped his head, considering. "Do you remember, Remo, how I once told you that you suffered from Master's disease?"

That got Remo's attention. The illness to which Chiun referred occurred in every fifteenth generation. It was an old Hindu curse imposed by one of their gods on Sinanju. Chiun had claimed years ago that this was the reason why Remo felt that he alone was charged with righting the world's wrongs.

"Yeah, I remember." Remo nodded. "It was when I met the Great Wang. You dumped that on me at what was supposed to be my final step to full Masterhood. Of course, you neglected to mention the Sinanju Rite of Attainment," he added with creeping annoyance.

With a flurry of long fingernails, the tiny Asian erased Remo's last words from the air. "How else could I keep your wandering mind alert?" he said dismissively. "The important thing here is the Master's disease. It has nearly run its course."

Remo's face took on shades of dark confusion. "What do you mean?" he asked.

"I told Smith then that it would take fifteen years for you to get well. It has been that. The disquiet you now feel is from the final phase of the disease."

Remo bit the inside of his cheek in contemplation. "Okay," he said. "So what now?"

The old man's face grew suspicious. "Your prophetess did not tell you?" he asked.

"No," Remo said, shaking his head.

Chiun breathed deeply. "In that case, I do not know," he exhaled. But the depths of his hazel eyes were troubled.

"Chiun—" Remo began.

He was interrupted by a silencing hand.

"I have told you of the legend of my village?" the Master of Sinanju asked abruptly. "How in dark times, when the fishing was poor and there was nothing to eat, the villagers sent their babies home to the sea?"

Remo was confused by this sudden shift in the conversation. "About a billion times," he said cautiously.

"There is wisdom in the retelling." Chiun nodded. He forged ahead, his singsong voice taking on the cadence of instruction. "Sinanju was and is a poor village on the West Korean Bay. The harsh winters and bleak summers punish the land. The soil yields meager harvests, and the frigid waters of the bay surrender few fish. At those times when food was most scarce, the people of my village would gather at the shores of the bay and hold their infants beneath the icy water, robbing them of life."

"And they called it 'sending them home to the sea' even though they knew that it was nothing but mass infanticide," Remo added. "I *know* the story, Little Father."

"Then you know, as well, O Wise One, how only with the discovery of the Sun Source did this barbaric practice end. For countless years has the Master of Sinanju left our village to ply the assassin's art to courts of kings and caliphs. We are but the latest in an unbroken line extending back into the mists of time."

"So what?" Remo asked. "What's that got to do with me?"

A thundercloud passed over Chiun's features.

"You are ill, so I will let that lie," the Master of Sinanju said. "My ancestors toiled so that the children of our village could live. No longer must we resort to the dire practice of drowning our young. The Master's duty to the village has carried down through the ages. I bear that responsibility with pride. One day, you will do so, too."

"I don't know where you're going with this, Chiun," Remo said, "but I'm sorry. I'm not sure it's enough to say I kill to feed the kids of Sinanju anymore.''

"And if I reminded you that *I* was a child of Sinanju once?'' Chiun offered. ''What if my father was possessed with your attitude?''

"He wasn't,'' Remo said. ''And anyway, he wasn't afflicted with this dumbass Master's disease—which I'm not sure I believe in, either. Sinanju is just a dump infested by fat-faced ingrates who'd bash you over the head with a rock and steal your frigging eyeballs if they thought they could get away with it. You just *happen* to come from there and you just *happened* to stumble on me when you hired out to train some faceless American hit man for a couple of sacks of rice and a hunk of gold. We were lumped together by chance, not destiny, I kill people for a living, I hate what I do but I'm really good at it, and I just don't think I'm making a difference anymore. That's it. Case closed.'' Remo clenched his hands in impotent frustration.

By the end of Remo's tirade, Chiun's papery eyelids had closed to slits so tight a laser could not have penetrated the space between them. ''Do you truly mean that?'' he asked.

"Which part?''

"That idiocy about hating what you do?''

Remo shook his head. ''Yes. No. I don't know. It used to make me feel good sometimes to ice a creep like Miller. Today...'' His voice trailed off.

"That is part of your destiny,'' Chiun said. ''A larger part than you know. You still see yourself as the savior of all mankind. It will pass.''

And with that, Chiun rose to his feet like a puff of steam. He padded thoughtfully back to his luggage.

Remo remained seated on the bedroom floor. For a long time, he said nothing. When he finally looked up, his eyes were moist.

"*When* will it pass, Little Father?" he asked quietly.

Chiun glanced to his pupil. He was shocked to see that he held a small shiny silver object in his hand. Remo was staring at it with lost, sad eyes.

The Master of Sinanju buried his surprise. "Call Smith," he instructed. "He is waiting for you."

Remo only nodded. Slipping baby Karen's crucifix back into his pocket, he rose to his feet and left the room.

Behind him, the Master of Sinanju was deeply disturbed. There were eventful signs on the horizon for the two living Masters of Sinanju. All the omens pointed that way. Remo's circumstances made things all the more problematic.

Remo had been raised in an orphanage by nuns. There was no telling what pagan sorcery those vestal virgins had used on him. Chiun prayed to a thousand gods at once that some latent Catholicism was not manifesting itself in his pupil. Not now of all times.

He reached to collect another kimono. The weight of five thousand years of tradition heavy on his frail shoulders, the Master of Sinanju returned to his packing.

4

The dark cloud of Remo's mood hadn't improved on his way downstairs to the phone. In fact, if anything the parched nasal tone of his employer only put him in a lousier humor.

"The situation is grave," announced Dr. Harold W. Smith, head of the supersecret organization known only as CURE.

"It's *always* grave, Smitty," Remo replied morosely. "Everything around me is grave. Or *graves.*"

He was sitting on the kitchen counter. A bird had just landed on the windowsill over the sink. Its tiny head darted left and right. As they spoke, Remo watched the bird.

Smith let the remark pass. "As I was saying, it was pure serendipity that this even came to light. One of our old CURE contacts in another government agency reported it through the old network. The CURE mainframes had nothing to track, since at the time there was little electronic information. That has changed dramatically of late."

"I thought you cut all those people loose years ago."

"Most, not all. As you know, in the early days CURE relied largely on scraps of information relayed from a network of thousands of individuals. People who, although strategically important, did not know for whom they worked. The computer age eliminated the need for most of them. Fortunately, I retained a few."

"Yeah, good thing," Remo said absently. "Smitty, what kind of bird has a brown body and a red head?"

The bird hopped along the sill. It didn't even seem aware of Remo's presence on the other side of the screen.

"I don't know. Remo, please pay attention. It's still incredible to me that a scheme so massive in scope could have gone this far undetected."

"I don't know why," Remo said. "East Africa's been a mess for years. I don't think it's a cardinal. Cardinals are all red."

Smith exhaled exasperation. "Only the male. The female is a drab, grayish brown. Remo, please—"

"Really?" Remo asked. "I thought they were all red. Anyway, they're big with orange beaks, right?"

"Correct," Smith agreed. And before Remo could expand on his ornithological theme, he quickly forged ahead. "Political and social upheaval have little in common with criminal activity. East Africa was on the right track when it ended its policy of institutionalized racism, but this has the potential to be as evil. I have tracked billions of dollars from other nations that have found their way into

East African banks. Representatives of different crime interests have been shuttling back and forth for several weeks. In some cases, the leaders of criminal fraternities themselves have begun to make the journey. There is every indication that the East African government has decided to look the other way as far as crime is concerned.''

"Wait a minute," Remo interjected. "Isn't this like what happened in Scambia years ago? These guys are just ripping off someone else's idea."

"In crime there are no new ideas," Smith said somberly. "Merely new opportunities and variations on old themes."

"Okay, but does Willie Mandobar know about this?"

Smith's reply stunned him.

"Three confirmed sources point to former President Mandobar as the architect of this scheme."

Willie Mandobar was one of the most famous men on the face of the planet. A political prisoner in the old racist system, he had risen to the position of president of East Africa once that system was abolished. He had recently retired from office, turning over the reins of power to a handpicked successor in a free election. Mandobar was a smiling, grandfatherly figure. Remo couldn't believe he'd be behind something like this.

"Mandobar is pretty old," Remo offered cautiously. "Maybe someone else is pulling his strings on this."

"I would like to believe that, as well," Smith

replied crisply. "But according to a private E-mail sent to the La Cosina drug cartel, Mandobar is clearly behind this. Two other sources confirm the fact that Willie Mandobar, in retirement, has opened the doors of his nation to criminals."

"Couldn't he just gripe about social security from his winter home in Florida like every other old codger?" Remo grumbled. Scowling, he turned his attention back to his bird. Maybe it was some kind of finch.

At that moment, the Master of Sinanju breezed into the kitchen. He immediately spied the bird on the windowsill.

"Scat!" the old man snapped, slapping his hands sharply near the screen. The bird fluttered off in a panic.

Wheeling, Chiun marched to the nearest cupboards. Flinging the doors wide, he began rummaging inside.

"This is a matter that needs our attention," Smith said as Chiun banged pots. "The world cannot allow what would amount to a wholesale terrorist state to emerge from the old East African system."

"Just a sec, Smitty," Remo said.

He cupped his hand over the phone. "Chiun, wanna keep it down?"

Inside a cupboard, backside sticking out into the kitchen, the Master of Sinanju continued clanging metal pots and pans. The racket was deafening.

"I cannot hear you," Chiun sang from the depths of the cupboard.

Remo jammed a finger in his free ear to block out the noise. "Speak up, Smitty." He frowned.

"This is an extremely delicate situation," the CURE director warned. "Willie Mandobar is a hero to many. His death could have international ramifications. Neutralize him only as a last resort."

"So what do you want me to do?"

The banging stopped. A harrumph of deep consideration emanated from the black depths of the cupboard.

"Obviously, there are co-conspirators involved. Mandobar could not manage such an elaborate scheme alone. Find out who these people are and remove them. With them gone, the foundation will collapse beneath their leader."

"You hope," Remo suggested.

"Yes, I do," Smith agreed without irony.

Remo closed his eyes. "Want an alternative suggestion?"

The tone of CURE's enforcement arm made Smith instantly wary. "What?" he asked guardedly.

"A lot of these kingpins are there now?"

"Yes. It is already the largest number of criminal leaders ever collected in any one place."

Remo opened his eyes. They were cold steel. "Bomb the whole damn country," he said, his voice perfectly level.

As the CURE director absorbed Remo's dispassionate, almost *clinical* suggestion, Chiun emerged from the cupboard, a fat pot clutched in one bony hand.

Although the words were strong, the delivery was not. It was as if Remo's idealism had fought a battle with his practical side and realism had won. Yet his old longing for a perfect world still remained.

So distracted was Remo by his own thoughts, he did not even notice that Chiun had begun to test the strength of the cast iron pot by banging it mercilessly on the countertop.

"You are serious," Smith said after a brief pause.

"One hundred percent," Remo replied in a tone icy enough to chill the phone in his hand. "We've been kidding ourselves that we've been making a difference, Smitty. Ever since you bamboozled me into this rinky-dink organization, you've had me running my ass off all over the world supposedly safeguarding American values. Well, rah-rah for the flag and apple pie. I'm telling you those values are shot to hell. If you nuked that whole damn country now, in one fell swoop you'd be taking out an entire generation of predators. You want something that'll make a difference, Smitty? *That* would make a difference."

"That is not an option," Smith said stiffly.

"It ought to be," Remo replied.

"No, it should not. You and I are of a different opinion," Smith said. "I think we have made a difference. Right now crime is fragmented. But if it is allowed to consolidate under one roof, as it were, there is no telling how much more powerful it could get."

"Don't worry," Remo muttered. "Wait a few

years and you'll see." He sighed deeply. "I'll go, Smitty. Because that's what I do. But I'm not happy about the world right now or my place in it, so don't come bitching to me when I rack up a body count on this one."

"Yes," Smith said cautiously.

Periodically during his tenure with the agency, CURE's enforcement arm had lapsed into melancholia. The last time had been about a year ago. But Smith could not remember Remo ever sounding this bad.

"Er," Smith ventured carefully, "perhaps it would be wise if you brought Chiun with you on this assignment."

Across the room, the Master of Sinanju was examining the bottom of his pot in the sunlight that poured in through their kitchen window. At Smith's suggestion, the old Korean scowled. He shook his head violently. The wisps of hair above his ears were cotton blurs.

"He can't," Remo said. "He's already packing for some other trip he won't tell me anything about."

The pot went flying at Remo's head. Remo snagged it before it cracked his skull.

"What?" he asked as the old man bounded across the room.

"I will *what* you," Chiun whispered, yanking the receiver from Remo's hand. "Remo is in error, Emperor Smith, whose every word is a pearl that enriches my unworthy ears," he announced in dulcet tones. "I am merely in the process of reorganizing my meager possessions. A task suited to one as old and frail as I."

"Frail?" Remo whispered. A sharp elbow caught him in the belly.

"Yes, frail, Emperor," Chiun said, suddenly weary. "I have toiled happily in your employ lo these many years, yet lately a fatigue has set in. Not uncommon for one of my advanced years." He forced a pathetic cough.

"Oh, brother," Remo muttered.

"I hope it is only temporary," Smith said seriously.

"At my age, who knows?" Chiun said. The words were an effort to get out. "My Masterhood has gone on much longer than the norm. Perhaps it is the start of the end for me. We will not know if this is merely a passing debility until I have taken to bed for a week or two. Make it two. And please do not come to visit during that time, for I fear I will be too weak to answer the door. *Or* the telephone," he added quickly.

"I am sorry to hear that," Smith said. "Remo doubtless could have made use of your expertise as a cultural guide while in East Africa."

Chiun had been handing the phone back to Remo. But at the mention of the country's name, the receiver flew back to one shell-like ear.

"You are sending Remo to East Africa?" he asked, his brow furrowing.

"Yes," Smith said. "But I understand if you cannot—"

"Wait!" Chiun interrupted, breathless. "Is it possible? *Yes*. My lassitude of body and spirit has vanished. I do not know how you accomplished this miracle, but simply by conversing with you, O Emperor, has my robust health been restored. Your lilting voice alone must act as remedy."

"So you will be able to accompany Remo after all?" Smith asked, confused.

"On wings of doves I do your bidding, Smith, Son of Hippocrates," Chiun proclaimed.

He threw the phone back at Remo.

"Make the arrangements, Smitty," Remo said blandly. "In the meantime, I'll see if his transmission held together with that sudden shift into reverse." He hung up the phone.

Chiun had gathered up his cast iron pot and was on his way out the door.

"What was that all about?" Remo called after him.

"It is called conversation," Chiun replied. "It is a bit more advanced than the grunts and rude hand gestures you are used to."

"Ha-ha. You know what I mean. What was with that line of pap you were feeding Smith? You haven't been tired since I've known you."

"That is not true. I cannot begin to count the times you have exhausted my patience." He slipped from the room.

Hopping down from the counter, Remo dogged him to the bottom of the main staircase.

"I know you," he accused as Chiun mounted the stairs. "You're up to something."

"Yes," Chiun agreed without turning. "I am up to packing my eighth trunk. Summon a carriage to take us to the airport, and you may load the first seven for our trip. I must make haste!"

With that, the old Korean vanished into his room, slamming the door behind him.

5

Fortunately for Remo, Chiun packed light, taking only nine of his usual complement of fourteen steamer trunks.

The Master of Sinanju made it Remo's responsibility to see to it that the trunks were undamaged on their transfer flight to New York from Boston's Logan International Airport. After much arguing and a few well-placed bribes, he was allowed to retrieve the cases from the belly of the 747.

"I'm not used to being a luggage monkey anymore," Remo complained as he hauled the trunks through the terminal at JFK International Airport.

The Master of Sinanju marched at his side.

"The monkey part should be second nature," Chiun said. "As for the other, bend at the knees, not the waist."

"Har-de-har-har," Remo replied. "What are you taking all this garbage for, anyway? You've been leaving these stupid trunks home the past couple of years."

"You have admitted yourself that you have allowed your baggage transporting skills to deteriorate. What kind of teacher would I be if I let your slide into indolence continue without addressing it?''

"A merciful one?" Remo suggested, annoyed.

The dolly on which the trunks were balanced hit an uneven spot on the broad floor. Remo had to hold the yellow trunk steady to keep it from falling.

"Be careful of that one," Chiun cautioned.

It was the trunk he'd dropped the parchment and dagger into. His voice betrayed more than normal concern.

"You didn't answer me back home," Remo ventured.

"Sometimes I ignore you in the hope that you will go away," Chiun replied blandly.

"About the *knife*," Remo pressed. "That was the symbol of Sinanju carved in the handle. And it was done by a Master other than you. The fingernail downstroke was sloppier than your work. And that ivory was stained from age."

As they walked, Chiun appraised the proud expression on his pupil's face. "Who died and appointed you Sherlock Holmes?" the Master of Sinanju said flatly.

"I'm right, aren't I?" Remo challenged.

Chiun looked away. "I will tell you what I told you last night," the old Korean said. "Mind your own business."

"Sinanju *is* my business, Little Father," Remo insisted.

With that, the old Korean fell silent. Remo attributed it to his general moodiness. He didn't notice the contemplative look on his teacher's weathered face.

As he pulled the dolly across the terminal floor, Remo was suddenly distracted.

There was a line of seats across from a ticket counter. Seated in one of them was a small boy. He was so little, his feet didn't touch the floor. The toes of his sandals hung to a V in the air.

"What's *he* doing here?" Remo puzzled, recognizing the little Korean boy from the Carlson wake.

The boy still wore the same black clothes and the same sad expression. Far too reflective for a child his age.

"Who?" the Master of Sinanju asked, uninterested.

"That kid," Remo said. "I saw him with that weird old lady at the wake in Peoria last night. What do you suppose he's doing here? And all alone, by the looks of it."

Chiun followed his pupil's gaze. His bright eyes narrowed as he scanned the plastic chairs.

"I see no child," he said.

"Of course you do," Remo insisted. "A little Korean kid. He's right—"

But when he went to point him out, the boy was gone. The seat he had been sitting in was empty. As Remo watched, a middle-aged man sat in it.

"Well, he *was* there," he said. "I wonder where he went?"

As they walked, he scanned the area. He didn't know why, but the air of the terminal seemed suddenly very cold. And despite his Sinanju training, Remo felt an involuntary shudder.

SMITH HAD RESERVED them two first-class seats on a direct flight to Africa. After hours in the air, a long nap and a short conversation during which the Master of Sinanju warned Remo to keep his musings about the strange dagger to himself, the plane touched down on the simmering black tarmac of the main airport in Bachsburg, the capital of East Africa.

As Chiun's luggage was being unloaded by careless, unseen hands, the two men deplaned. Side by side, they walked amid the other passengers to the main customs area. When they got there, a quartet of bizarrely dressed women was already screeching at a uniformed East African agent.

"I don't need my bloody passport!" yelled one. "I'm a bleedin' star!"

"Yeah!" shrieked two of the others in unison.

"Girl domination!" screamed the fourth.

It was the trademark line uttered by the fourth woman that caught Remo's attention. Only when he looked closer did he realize he knew who they were.

The Seasonings had been a red-hot all-girl group for about eight minutes two years before.

Assembled after a wily record promoter ran an ad in a small English porn magazine devoted to anal fetishes and bed-wetting, Tramp, Trollop, Ho and Slut Seasoning were still trying to recapture their glory days.

The girls had been livid when their bandmate

Strumpet Seasoning had quit the group. After a failed solo act, a failed tell-all biography and six failed marriages, Strumpet was still the only member of the group anyone talked about. The other Seasonings had, thankfully, vanished from the world stage after their one and only hit. But for a terrible time two summers before, no one could get away from their signature song. Indeed, Smith had been repeatedly forced to pay to replace the radios Remo regularly smashed in his various rental cars whenever he found "I Know What You Need (Really, Really I Do)" blaring from his speakers.

"Girl domination!" shrieked Ho Seasoning at the East African agent. Ho, like the rest of the group, hadn't technically been a "girl" since the Truman administration.

"We're here for a bleedin' important gig!" screeched Trollop Seasoning.

"And if I lose my baby 'cause of you, I'll rip your fuckin' balls off and feed 'em to me cat!" screamed Slut Seasoning. She pointed to her very pregnant belly.

That was another thing about the Seasonings. In addition to their bimonthly tabloid-inspiring weddings, they all seemed to be perpetually pregnant without ever actually giving birth to anything. The four women each had a huge belly that hung out in colossal gestational fashion from beneath revealing halter tops and above skin-tight rubber capri pants of various bright rainbow colors.

After a few hushed words from the agent, the stewing Seasonings seemed to strike up some sort of bargain. When the customs official ushered the four women through a small door behind his counter, he was already unbuckling his belt.

Fortunately, there was another agent on duty. When they stepped up to the second uniformed clerk with his white shirt, black tie and wide-brimmed blue hat, Chiun pushed his way in front of Remo.

"Business or pleasure?" the customs man crisply asked the Master of Sinanju. His accented English sounded Australian, but with harsher emphasis on the consonants.

"Pleasure," Remo said.

"Business," the Master of Sinanju corrected.

"Nature of business?"

Chiun spoke before Remo could answer for them.

"I am an assassin on an important mission for the ruler of this land," the old Korean announced ominously.

Remo tried to mask his annoyance. Two minutes in East Africa and Chiun had already blown their cover.

"He's joking," Remo assured the agent. In Korean he whispered, "Quit screwing around, Chiun."

At the customs checkpoint, the uniformed man had slowly raised his eyes beneath the brim of his cap. He ignored Remo. "You work for President Kmpali?" he asked seriously.

This was the man who had succeeded Willie Mandobar as East Africa's ruler.

"Pah!" Chiun spit, waving an impatient hand. "I have had my fill of presidents as secret assassin for

America. My business is with the *true* ruler of this land.''

"Oh, great," Remo grumbled. He was already thinking about how mad Smith would be after they busted out of some dingy African jail.

But the customs official only frowned at Chiun. ''President Kmpali or not, you must register with the Finance Ministry if you intend to advertise your services in the Republic of East Africa.'' He clicked his tongue against his teeth. ''Next!'' he called, waving Chiun and Remo through.

They passed through the metal detector and into the air-conditioned terminal's main concourse. As they walked along, Remo glanced back in bewilderment.

''What the hell just happened?'' he asked.

Chiun didn't reply. As they strolled across the tile floor, the old Asian avoided the baggage carousel where his luggage had just begun to slide into view. He steered a beeline to the terminal's main entrance.

''This is amazing,'' Remo continued, shaking his head. ''You told him you were an assassin, and he didn't bat an eye. And what was that about registering with the Finance Ministry? What kind of country registers its assassins?''

''A *civilized* one,'' Chiun replied tightly.

They were through the doors and outside.

The oppressively hot East African air assaulted them immediately. The body temperature of both men instantly regulated to compensate for the change.

"We can debate that later," Remo droned. "And why aren't we getting your luggage?"

The Master of Sinanju was too distracted to reply.

A glistening black limousine was parked by the curb at the far end of a broad carport. Standing beside the car was a somber young man with skin as dark as the limo's paint.

Although his blue suit was impeccably tailored, he fidgeted uncomfortably, as if unused to his garments. At Chiun's appearance, a curious frown crossed the man's face. Pushing away from the car, he took a tentative step forward.

"Master of Sinanju?" he asked, with the same British-influenced harshness of the customs agent.

Suspicion creased Chiun's aged face as he stopped before the young man. "I am he," the wizened Korean replied, with a bow that was more perfunctory than ceremonial.

"What's going on?" Remo asked. "Who the hell is this?"

"Hush, Remo," Chiun hissed. Back straight, he addressed the native. "You were sent by Batubizee, son of Kwaanga?"

"I was, Master of Sinanju." He spoke Chiun's title hesitantly, as if uncertain he had truly found the right man.

"Then why are you dressed in that Western garb and not in the raiments of the glorious Luzu warrior empire?" Chiun asked, his face puckering in displeasure.

"The Luzu are greeted with disdain in the cities

of East Africa. My clothing makes it easier for me to blend in.''

His words did nothing to dispel Chiun's sour expression. Exhaling disapproval, the old man reached into the folds of his kimono. In a rustle of fabric, he produced the dagger embossed with the Sinanju symbol.

When he saw the knife, any doubts the black man had entertained fled. His features bloomed in pleasure, his smile revealing a row of perfect white teeth. He bowed formally at the waist.

"I bring you greetings from the son of the sons of Kwaanga, Chief Batubizee, of the line of the first great Luzu warrior chief. Hail to you, O awesome and powerful Master of Sinanju, he who graciously throttles the universe.''

Chiun handed over the knife, hilt first.

"What's this all about?'' Remo demanded, his face registering growing confusion. "And when the hell did you unpack that?''

"You ask too many questions,'' Chiun said from the corner of his mouth.

"And you haven't answered one yet. What the Belgium is going on here?''

This time, it wasn't Chiun who ignored him.

"Come,'' the young man said. "The chief waits for you in the heart of the Luzu empire.'' He clapped his hands loudly.

There was a truck parked before the limo. Men spilled out, racing back to their small group.

"My luggage is inside,'' the Master of Sinanju said.

The men dutifully ran inside the terminal. Through the tinted windows they could be seen swarming for the luggage carousel.

"Please wait with me in my vehicle," the native offered, opening the door to the limousine.

Chiun took a step toward the car.

"Everybody freeze for one goddamn minute!" Remo snapped. "Chiun, you are not getting in that car."

"If the Master so wishes, you may accompany us in the limousine," the young native offered helpfully. "Where do you wish your servant to ride, Master?"

"That other vehicle is good enough for him," Chiun said, waving toward the parked truck. "But I would be certain to keep the windows down," he added in a low voice.

The men appeared through the terminal doors, bearing Chiun's trunks. They loaded the baggage into limo and truck.

"*This* is why you were so quick to change your mind," Remo snapped as the men worked. "You were coming here already."

"For a mere servant, your deductive skills are impressive," Chiun droned near the open car door.

"Servant my ass," Remo growled. "This is incredible, even by *your* standards. You bilked Smith for the airfare. You were coming to freaking East Africa anyway, so you just hitched a ride at his expense."

Chiun's face was stone. "Mad Harold's coffers are deep," he said dismissively.

"He even sent us first class," Remo muttered to himself. "Smith *never* sends us first class."

Chiun had been scrutinizing the men as they loaded his luggage. The trunk and front seat of the limo were crammed full. There was only a little space left in the ATV as the men climbed inside. Hiking up his kimono skirts, Chiun started to get into the rear of the limousine.

"You can't just leave, Chiun," Remo said, exasperated.

"I must," the Master of Sinanju said seriously. "For I have an appointment in Luzuland. You may come if you wish. But this one is correct." He nodded to his driver, who was even now getting behind the wheel. "It would not be seemly for a servant to accompany me in my vehicle. You may follow with my luggage." He slammed the door.

"Smitty sent you here to *help* me," Remo insisted through the open window.

"You are a full Master of Sinanju," Chiun said impatiently.

"And you're a thief. Don't think you're gonna get away with this. I'm telling Smith."

"Tattletale."

"Fraud."

"I do not have time for this," Chiun hissed. "You will be fine without me. There are only two things one needs to know to survive in East Africa."

"Yeah," Remo snapped, "what's that?"

"Do not trust anyone. White or black."

"And the other?"

Chiun considered. "Perhaps there is only one thing."

He powered up the window, and the limousine drew away from the curb. The truck waited for it to pass, then fell in behind. The miniconvoy headed away from the Bachsburg airport terminal and out into the sweltering street.

Remo Williams could only stand helplessly on the sidewalk and watch them go.

Angry. And alone.

6

Nunzio Spumoni was melting in the heat.

It was East Africa. The heat and humidity were infernal. Oppressive. Relentless.

Although he kept the air conditioner cranked up to its maximum, the air in his hotel room was still wet enough to wring out by hand. Outside, it was like trying to breathe underwater. And more aggravating than the heat itself was the fact that it didn't seem to bother anyone as much as him.

"Try wearing a lighter suit, Nunzio," his cousin Piceno Spumoni suggested.

"This one is one hundred percent cotton," Nunzio snapped in reply. He mopped his forehead with a paper napkin.

The two men were sitting in a busy Bachsburg restaurant. The dining room was filled with the worst humanity had to offer. Nunzio recognized a few of the criminals from some of the many meetings he had recently attended. They were much seedier than the men he ordinarily associated with.

The air in the cramped restaurant was thick. So many people in such a confined space. So, so hot. Nunzio wanted to scream. Either that or strip off his clothes and run outside. He'd seen a fountain down the street.

He tried concentrating. Maybe if he thought hard enough, he could *feel* what it might be like to stand naked in the ankle-deep pool, cooling water dripping down his bony shoulders and running down his scrawny legs.

But though he taxed his imagination to the limit, it was no good. The heat was just too great. He flung the sopped napkin to the checkered tablecloth, wrenching a fresh one from the stainless-steel dispenser.

"Maybe it's the color," Piceno ventured as Nunzio ran the napkin around neck and chin.

"*White!* I'm wearing *white,* for God's sake! I have it dry-cleaned every day and it's still knotted in the ass and stuck to my back. Any color suit is a damnable sponge in this humidity, so please keep your ridiculous suggestions to yourself and kindly *shut up.*"

Piceno ordinarily wouldn't be put off so easily by one of Nunzio's trademark outbursts. But today was different. Piceno dutifully fell mute.

Nunzio flung another soaked napkin to the growing pile. The rattle of silver and china in the overcrowded restaurant assaulted his ears.

"Damn climate," he muttered, tugging out the collar of his shirt. With a flapping menu, he tried to force some air down onto his sweaty chest.

Nunzio had been plagued by perspiration since childhood. It was ironic, considering the fact that all the other men in the Spumoni family weighed over three hundred pounds and rarely broke a sweat. At six foot two, 140 pounds, Nunzio was the skinniest Spumoni in Napoli, yet he perspired like a man three times his size.

At least back home in Italy he knew how to control his environment. From homes to cars to offices, he carefully mapped out his schedule to spend as much time as possible in the relative comfort afforded by air-conditioning. But since arriving in East Africa two weeks ago, he had been forced to spend more time in the natural air than he could bear. He'd lost ten pounds of sweat in the past fourteen days.

"I cannot take much more of this," Nunzio breathed, flinging the menu to the table.

The napkin dispenser was empty. Fishing a sopping wet handkerchief from his pocket, he began sponging the back of his pencil-thin neck.

Piceno had been watching the front door. As his cousin smeared sweat with his hankie, the younger Spumoni sat at attention. "He is here," Piceno whispered gruffly.

Limp rag hanging from his long fingers, Nunzio glanced at the door.

The man who had just entered the restaurant was handsome enough to be called beautiful. Blond hair, grown long and greased back, framed a cover model's face. In spite of the years spent in the hot East African sun, his skin was pale and perfect. With eyes of rich green he searched the crowded room. When he spotted Nunzio, rosebud lips pouted a perfect smile. The man wended his way through the crowd to the back table where Nunzio and Piceno sat.

Although the man was maddeningly handsome, Nunzio did not envy him his looks. The thing that bothered the Italian most was the fact that this man stubbornly refused to perspire. The white cotton suit he wore as he slipped in across the table from Nunzio was a perfect match to Nunzio's in every respect, save one. The infuriating man's suit was not tinged gray with sweat.

"Nunzio, how good to see you." L. Vas Deferens smiled.

Dentists had been known to weep openly at the sight of the man's naturally perfect white teeth.

Nunzio waved a sweaty hand. "Vas," he said, nodding.

Despite the fact that a handshake had not been offered him, Deferens extended a soft, manicured hand to Nunzio.

Nunzio detested shaking hands. Especially with someone who did not sweat. Reluctantly wiping as much perspiration from his palm as his sopped handkerchief would accept, he took the offered hand.

"Piceno, you are well?" Deferens smiled. He didn't wipe Nunzio's perspiration from his palm as he shook hands with the other man.

Nunzio's cousin nodded.

"Good, good. Would you mind excusing us?" Deferens suggested, his smile never wavering. "Your cousin and I have some important matters to discuss. You understand."

Half out of his seat, Deferens extended an arm, ushering Piceno Spumoni from the napkin-covered table. At a nod from Nunzio, Piceno excused himself.

Deferens waited until the big man was out of earshot before speaking. Once Nunzio's cousin was gone, the East African placed his dust-dry hands on the table, his fingers comfortably interlocked.

Nunzio only wished his cool demeanor were contagious. The Italian continued swiping at pooling pockets of salty perspiration.

"Don Vincenzo is pleased, I trust?" Deferens said in a cold voice. His eyes were cold, as well. Deep pools of green confidence.

"He's *satisfied*. For now," Nunzio stressed. "He'll be happier when this dark business is over. As will I."

Deferens tipped his head. "Nunzio, my old friend, is it possible after all this time that Camorra still does not trust me?"

"Trust is not easy in our business," Nunzio admitted. He waved to a nearby waiter, pointing to the empty water pitcher nested among the discarded napkins. The waiter nodded and scurried off.

Deferens was nodding. "I can't blame you." He sighed. "Camorra certainly has not had an easy time of it. Survival sometimes precludes trust."

Of that, Nunzio couldn't disagree. The secret criminal organization for which he worked had spent much of the past century lurking in shadows. Once powerful, Mussolini's fascists had done their best to eradicate the syndicate after the First World

War. Entire families had been dragged into the streets and slaughtered. Betrayed by their countrymen and attacked on every level by the Mafia, the survivors of the Camorra purges remained in hiding for eight decades. Licking wounds and plotting revenge.

"Let's just say we do not do leaps of faith very well," Nunzio grunted.

The waiter arrived with a fresh pitcher of ice water. Nunzio poured a glass and drank greedily.

"That will end," L. Vas Deferens promised with icy assurance. "Camorra's future as the premier crime organization in the world is secure." His voice became a conspiratorial whisper. "By week's end, you will eclipse even the Mafia."

Nunzio snorted through his water. Coming up out of his narrow throat, his laugh sounded like a donkey's bray. "We've nearly done that without your assistance."

"Yakuza, then. Or the cartels. The Vietnamese or Chinese crime syndicates. The chorus will fall silent. All the voices that overpowered your own for so many years—all gone. Camorra will seize power like none has before."

"We had better hope so," Nunzio warned. "For *both* our sakes. Don Vincenzo will not be pleased if we fail."

Deferens waved a dismissive hand. He didn't deign to respond to such a ludicrous suggestion.

Nunzio only wished he could share this ice man's utter confidence. Sweaty rivulets rolled from his underarms. Maybe if it wasn't so hot…

"I have advised Don Vincenzo that you wish to do this thing at the end of the week," he said, careful to keep his voice low. "He agrees."

Deferens nodded. "All of the delegations will have arrived by then."

"The invitations are all out?"

"The last were sent yesterday."

"Any refusals?"

Deferens grinned. "None. The celebrity stature of our leader has given us great credibility. No one wishes to be left out. There will be a weekend of grand meetings throughout the city, presided over by Mandobar. At least, that is the plan. Of course, *we* have a different plan."

Sitting in his rumpled, sweat-stained white suit, Nunzio Spumoni pictured the familiar smiling face of Mandobar. That the former East Africa president was involved in something as nefarious as this was still almost too incredible to believe.

"When will I finally get to meet him?" Nunzio asked.

A thin smile. "If all goes well, never."

Deferens's smile was oddly disconcerting; it gave the impression of a man with a secret. But then, he had conveyed that image since the first time they'd met. The pale man in the white suit seemed always to be guarding some precious, private thoughts. Thoughts he dared not speak aloud.

As he was talking, Deferens had turned a curious, distracted eye across the restaurant.

The main wall opened on a sidewalk café. A commotion seemed to be breaking out beneath the green-and-white-striped canopy. Three men in ill-fitting suits sitting at a wrought-iron table were exchanging hot words with the lone man at the adjoining table. For his part, the stranger they were speaking to seemed unnaturally calm.

Even across the crowded restaurant, Deferens could see that the man's wrists were exceptionally thick.

Nunzio Spumoni wasn't at all interested in the dispute. His thoughts had turned to his hotel air-conditioning.

"I should get back," he said, standing. "I must call Naples."

Deferens only nodded. He was still watching the activity across the room. The thick-wristed man had just said something that seemed to upset the other men.

"Oh, please say goodbye to Piceno for me," Deferens called absently to Nunzio's retreating back.

He didn't hear Nunzio's reply. There was something coldly fascinating about the thin young man across the room. His presence alone seemed to chill the humid African air.

Deferens crossed his legs neatly and leaned one elbow on the table. His instincts told him that something profoundly interesting was about to happen. And the instincts of L. Vas Deferens were *never* wrong.

REMO HAD TRIED HIS BEST. No one could fault him. Not Smith, certainly not Chiun. Not anyone.

He'd found the crowded restaurant after an intensely unpleasant cab ride from the airport. The cabbie had spent the bulk of the trip trying to interest him in the local narcotics and prostitution trades. Remo eventually had the driver drop him off in downtown Bachsburg.

On the street, everyone seemed tied in with some kind of vice. Remo counted six of the seven deadly sins on the way to the restaurant. The last holdout was gluttony, which reared its ugly face the instant he was seated next to a trio of thugs in the outdoor café. They were all over six feet tall, weighed well over two hundred pounds and looked as if they could punch their way through a prison wall.

The men had been loud already. It only got worse when Remo's meal arrived.

"Hey, get a load a dat," one of them said to his companions as the waiter set a plate before Remo. His New Jersey accent was thick. "What kinda faggy shit is dat?" He turned his attention to Remo. "Hey, what kinda faggy shit is dat?"

Remo did his best to ignore the question.

The brown rice was clumpy. That was fine. But the steamed fish had a thin aroma of garlic. Remo had specifically requested no seasonings.

"Hey, I'm talkin' to you," called the gangster at the next table.

"And I'm ignoring you," Remo said absently as he frowned at his fish. He didn't look at the man. "And everything you say doesn't have to be prefaced with 'hey,'" he added.

"Hey, what did he say?" the man asked his companions.

"Says he's ignoring you," one of the others said.

The first man's face grew at first shocked, then angry.

"Do you know who I am?" he growled at Remo.

Remo finally turned a bland eye to the man, looking him up, then down. *"Homo erectus?"* he said, uninterested.

The man's face turned purple. "What the fuck did you call me?" Veins bulged on his broad forehead.

The others had at last taken note. Their rat eyes trained fury at Remo.

"He called you a queer hard-on, Johnny," one snarled.

The face of Johnny "Books" Fungillo, of New Jersey's Renaldi crime family, went from fluorescent purple to rage-drained white. He clambered to his feet, flinging his table away. Chairs and pasta-filled plates crashed to the floor. People in the immediate area scattered.

Fat fingers ripped a heavy automatic pistol from beneath his jacket. Johnny aimed the gun at Remo, his hairy knuckle tickling the trigger.

"Whaddaya gonna call me now?" he snapped. "Huh?" His eyes were wild.

Now that he was standing—flanked on both sides by his Renaldi Family companions—Remo was far better able to get the full view of Johnny Fungillo.

"I'm not sure now," Remo mused, thoughtful. "You *are* standing upright. But you look more like one of the great apes. Maybe you're Australopithecus."

Johnny had no idea what that last word meant. But it didn't matter. The skinny little rice-eating fag had just gone from calling him a homo to an ape. It was more than Johnny Books could stand. Face contorting with raw fury, he pulled the trigger of his automatic.

The explosion brought shrieks from the main restaurant area. Some people fled into the street, though many remained where they were.

In the middle of the sidewalk café, Johnny Books was panting, sweating. He'd fired point-blank into the rat bastard's face. That'd teach him to call somebody a homo hard-on ape. He peered through the thin cloud of gunpowder smoke, looking for the body that would be sprawled on the ground.

When the adrenaline haze cleared, however, he was shocked to find his target still seated in his chair, a contemplative expression on his face.

"And yet you use tools," Remo commented. "Do true apes use tools? Maybe we could get Jane Goodall to classify you. You could be a whole new subspecies."

Johnny Fungillo didn't know what was going on. He stood there in shock, staring at the distant smoking barrel of his gun. In all his professional life as a Renaldi Family enforcer, he'd never once had an instance where he used his weapon and the target he was pointing at didn't wind up dead. Yet there was the insulting little creep sitting before him, breathing and talking as if he hadn't a care in the world.

He wouldn't miss a second time. Johnny took aim

again—more carefully this time than before. He fired. This time when the explosion came, Johnny Books swore he saw movement, a blurry image of the skinny guy sliding to one side.

It was impossible. Men just couldn't move fast enough to avoid a bullet fired point-blank.

But to his shock, his target was still sitting calmly in his chair.

"And now it's time for Lancelot Link to surrender his opposable thumbs," Remo Williams said coldly.

He knew he shouldn't make a scene. Not in a crowded restaurant. Smith would go ballistic. On the other hand, the world sucked, Chiun had abandoned him and he was alone in a country that seemed to welcome depravity with open arms.

As Johnny Books squeezed his trigger a third time, he thought he saw another blur. Then the world seemed to spin wildly and he was suddenly sighting down on Jimmy "Mooch" Muchelli, his tablemate and fellow Renaldi foot soldier.

Jimmy's face grew shocked, there was a loud explosion and Jimmy's face turned very red.

Mooch Muchelli's features were little more than a crimson smear as he toppled back onto their overturned table.

"Bad pre-hominid," Remo chastised, very close to Johnny's ear.

Johnny Books wheeled to the voice.

Remo wasn't there. But Johnny's other companion was.

Bobby DiGardino had apparently drawn his own

gun at some point during the commotion. But the Browning was now planted smack-dab in the middle of Bobby's forehead, barrel shoved deep in the gangster's nonfunctioning brain. As Johnny watched—now with more horror than rage—Bobby dropped to his knees and plopped face first into a plate of scungilli.

"Until you chimps can prove you've mastered fire and the wheel, no guns," Remo lectured them.

Panicked now, Johnny whirled once more, his hand shaking as he met Remo's dark eyes.

There were only two options open for Johnny "Books" Fungillo, as far as he could ascertain. He could try once more to shoot the skinny guy with those deep menacing eyes. But so far that hadn't exactly been a rousing success. The other option was the better bet. Made all the more so after he'd given the body of Bobby DiGardino a quick glance.

Turning from Remo, Johnny hauled back and heaved his automatic as far into the depths of the restaurant as he possibly could. Waiters covered their heads with trays to deflect the ricochet when the gun discharged on impact. Throwing up his hands in surrender, Johnny smiled sheepishly at Remo, a sheen of prickly sweat darkening his perpetual five-o'clock shadow.

"Hey, you know somethin'?" Johnny Fungillo ventured. "You're right. I'm a monkey-fag-hard-on-ape-astroturfpitcherpuss. You got anythin' else you wanna call me, you go right ahead, mister." Hairy knees knocked inside baggy pants legs.

Standing before the trembling gangster, Remo

was already regretting his actions. The three mobsters hadn't given him much of a choice, but that didn't matter. Killing in broad daylight in a crowded restaurant was a stupid thing to do.

That was it. The mission was over. He had been depressed coming into it and had allowed his own problems to cloud his judgement.

After this, Smith would probably make him slip quietly out of the country. If the CURE director wanted something done in East Africa, he would have to rely on Chiun to do it. Assuming he could find the Master of Sinanju. All of this passed through Remo's mind in one angry moment.

But as he stood there, wishing he could melt into the background, a startling thing happened. Something he had never experienced in all his time as a professional assassin.

A tiny trickle of applause rose softly from one corner of the restaurant. Someone else quickly joined in. And in a shocking instant, the entire restaurant erupted in thunderous applause.

At the eye of the outburst of approval, Remo didn't know what to do.

Johnny Books glanced to the main restaurant, a dumb expression on his sweating face. Hands still raised, he offered the crowd a shrug that turned into a confused bow. When he turned nervously to his assailant, he was surprised to find that Remo had disappeared.

Johnny spun left, then right.

No sign of the skinny name-caller anywhere.

Great relief drained the blood from Johnny Fungillo's underused brain. Eyes rolling back in their sockets, the New Jersey mobster fainted face first onto his spilled plate of fettuccine. He fell so hard, he broke one of his opposable thumbs.

"Excuse me, sir!"

Remo heard the smooth, efficient voice a minute after he'd slipped out of the sidewalk café.

He scowled as he looked over his shoulder.

The coldly handsome man had trailed him from the restaurant. Jogging, he caught up to Remo, a perfect smile on his chiseled model's face.

"We should talk," the man said, puffing to keep up. Though he had run half a city block in the sun and heat, he'd failed completely to break a sweat.

"I'm kind of busy," Remo said, still walking.

"Not for me," the man insisted. For an instant, the too genial smile vanished. "Allow me to introduce myself. I am L. Vas Deferens, defense minister and head of internal security for East Africa."

"Whoop-de-do for you," Remo replied.

The sidewalk was alive with foot traffic. A steady hum of street-clogging cars rolled by to their left. Remo noted a single limousine had pulled to the shoulder of the road and was now trailing him. He felt the mistrustful glare of Deferens's bodyguard driver through the tinted windshield.

"Yes," Deferens said flatly. The smile returned, though it seemed more forced than ever. "And your name is…? I make it a point to learn the identities of the men who impress me. It happens so rarely."

"Try a different bathhouse," Remo suggested.

Deferens's rosebud lips pulled to a faint frown. "I cannot legally compel you to tell me your name now. But it will be necessary eventually. Are you registered?"

"Not even engaged," Remo said.

A hint of confusion. "This would be what? American banter? I'm afraid it impresses me far less than your work back there." Deferens nodded back beyond his trailing limo, toward the restaurant. "I was the one who started the applause, by the way."

Still walking, Remo glanced at the pale blond man in the spotless white suit.

The East African was somewhere in his early to late forties. His cool outer demeanor wrapped a cold angry core. His grin was flash-frozen conceit.

Remo had a sudden desire to plant his hand, wrist deep, into that pale, smug face.

Instead, he screwed his mouth shut and kept walking.

"You must register properly if you are going to advertise your services in East Africa," Deferens insisted.

"Advertising's for amateurs without reputations," Remo muttered, paraphrasing an old Sinanju tenet. "The truly great don't have to hawk themselves in the classifieds."

At this, Deferens shook his head. "You don't strike me as a fool. If you are here now, you are serious about your business. Given your performance in the restaurant, I don't think there's any question what that business is. Of course, we take a relaxed attitude toward that sort of thing here. But not commerce. You must register within the twenty-four-hour required period or face the consequences.''

"I won't be here that long," Remo promised.

Deferens tipped his head thoughtfully. "Pity," he said.

A business card appeared in one soft hand. If he'd been carrying it since he'd left the restaurant, it didn't show. Despite the intense heat, there wasn't a sign of perspiration on the cardboard. He slipped the card into Remo's hand.

"If you decide to stay and need work, contact me," Deferens said seriously. "If we do not see each other again, it has been a distinct pleasure to meet you."

Braking behind Remo, Deferens stepped briskly to the curb. His car stopped obediently. The door sprang open as if from its own volition and Deferens climbed inside. With a thrum of its powerful engine, the car was absorbed into traffic and slipped off down the busy street.

Alone on the sidewalk, Remo looked down at the card in his hand. Deferens's name, title and Bachsburg number were printed in black, raised letters.

A manipulation of fingers brought the card from thumb to pinkie. By the time it had gone from one side of his hand to the other, the card had been slit into five neat strips.

He let the sections flutter to the concrete.

"Dipshit country," Remo muttered to himself.

For a brief instant, he was angry at Chiun once more for abandoning him. But almost as soon he realized that the East Africa the Master of Sinanju knew would almost certainly not have anything in common with this one. Chiun would have as difficult a time interpreting the customs of this modern Sodom as he was having.

The revelation brought little comfort.

Stuffing his hands deep into his pockets, Remo wandered off down the busy Bachsburg street.

7

And thus it was that a Master of Sinanju did return to the land of Kwaanga Luzu, discovered by Master Nuk in the year of the Dead Milk Sky. But, lo, the nation to which this current Master did come was not the rich and prosperous land described by Nuk in the Master's Scrolls...

AS THE TRUCK bounced along the rutted path, a cloud of thick dust rose in its wake. The Luzu tribesmen accompanying Chiun jounced on their threadbare seats. Beside his Luzu driver in the front seat, the Master of Sinanju could have been frozen in amber. Though the rest were thrown from side to side, the old Korean remained suspended in space, as if beyond the vicissitudes of tire ruts and bad driving.

Although his face was an inscrutable mask, his thoughts were deeply troubled.

Nuk had painted an image in the Sinanju histories of a Luzuland blessed with rich soil and full crops, with a people strong and proud. But where Chiun expected to see fields of gently waving grain, he saw mile after mile of barren wasteland. Where he thought he would see powerful men and robust maidens, he found emaciated husks of human beings.

They had left the rented limousine in Bachsburg. Chiun had been transferred to a battered GMC Suburban at the edge of the East African capital. He was glad Remo hadn't been around for that disgrace. The big truck bounced and creaked its way along the winding, rutted road in the desert wilds north of the country's urban center.

"Who are these pitiful creatures?" the Master of Sinanju queried as they passed a miserable collection of people squatting forlornly in the dust at the side of the road. He assumed they were vagabonds from some other tribe who had found their way to Luzuland.

His driver had stripped off his jacket and tie. Most of his dress shirt buttons were open.

"They are Luzu," his young driver said, shame in his voice. His name was Bubu.

"How is this possible?" Chiun said, a hint of bewilderment in his squeaky tone. He shook his aged head. "These dirt eaters cannot be the children of Kwaanga."

"They are, Master Chiun," Bubu insisted. His jaw quivered in impotent fury at the admission.

There was much strength in the young man, although his well of disgrace ran deep. They passed many more pitiful Luzus on their way to the main village, yet Chiun said not another word. But when they reached the main settlement, it was all the old man could do not to cry out in shock.

Houses of peeling clapboard and pitifully thatched roofs lined the dirt streets of the poverty-stricken shantytown that was the heart of the Luzu civilization. The Suburban and the other truck containing Chiun's steamer trunks slowed to a stop in the broad cul-de-sac that was the town's dead center.

Chiun was stunned at the appearance of his welcoming committee. He had hoped that the people they had passed along the long road to the Luzu city had somehow found themselves in disfavor with the current chief. To his horror, he found that he couldn't have been more wrong.

The people who waited to greet him looked as if mere existence were an effort. Their secondhand clothing was threadbare and drained of color. Their eyes were sunken and bereft of hope. Skin was pulled taut and dry around fat, protruding bones. Teeth jutted forward in large and yellowed overbites of malnutrition.

Chiun hid his stunned disgust behind a look of imperious indifference as the Suburban rolled to a stop in front of the largest of the ramshackle buildings. Behind the first truck, the other vehicle squeaked to a groaning, dusty standstill.

A faded purple carpet, gilded along the edge with gold embroidery, extended from the open black mouth of the huge shack in front of which Chiun's truck had stopped. The moment his sandals touched the threadbare rug, a large figure emerged from the shadowy doorway.

The man's fat face glistened brightly. As he

strode forward, his voice boomed out over the sullen crowd in the square. "Greetings, O great son of Nuk!"

"Greetings, Batubizee, son of Kwaanga, king of the Luzu," the Master of Sinanju replied when the two men met in the center of the rotted carpet.

Each bowed deeply and formally.

Batubizee wore a purple ankle-length burnoose. Although the carpet and robe had once been the same color, the chief's raiments had better withstood the assault of time. The ceremonial purple was rich and vibrant. On Batubizee's head sat a squat golden crown, the front of which held three fused circles. Tiny diamonds were embedded in the front of the headpiece.

Bubu had followed Chiun up the carpet.

"He was possessed of the sign," the young native announced quietly, passing the chief the ceremonial dagger.

Batubizee took the knife, nodding as he did so.

"I do not need some trinket to tell me who this is," Chief Batubizee proclaimed. "His bearing alone tells me that this is the true son of Nuk." But though his words were strong, there was an undertone of uncertainty.

Chiun noted the hesitation in the Luzu leader's voice.

"Many generations have passed since the time of Nuk, ruler of the Luzu," the Master of Sinanju intoned. "Nuk has long since sought the repose of the Void. I am son of Chiun, pupil of H'si T'ang."

"Of course." The Luzu chief nodded. "Great warriors, all, I am sure."

Standing in the squalor of his village, dressed in the finery of days long past, Batubizee couldn't help but give the impression of someone embarrassed by the pitiful state he found himself in. He was like a once rich man, now destitute, in a losing battle to maintain as much of his former air as possible.

"We must confer," the chief said softly.

Chiun nodded silent agreement.

Batubizee turned to his people, raising his flabby arms high in the air. "My people, this is truly a glorious day! One that will be spoken of for generations to come! Today is the beginning of the new Luzu Empire!"

The cheers that had trailed Master Nuk as he sailed away centuries before had long before faded to morose silence. The men and women gathered in the dust of this day remained sullen and quiet as the Master of Sinanju and Chief Batubizee ducked inside the big house.

Afterward the crowd silently dispersed.

THE ENGINE HUM of Defense Minister Deferens's limousine had faded in with the other background traffic. Remo drifted down the sidewalk, lost in private thoughts.

The businesses in this part of town seemed devoted to all things pornographic. He therefore wasn't surprised when Trollop Seasoning bounded out onto the sidewalk from one of the small shops, her arms loaded with packages. Her thick purple heels clattered loudly as she hustled to a waiting car.

"Girl domination!" she shrieked over her shoulder at the store's closing door.

The other Seasonings screeched the same words from somewhere in the dark recesses of the sex shop.

Trollop dumped her booty in the car. As he passed by, Remo noted that the vehicle had government plates.

He had gone only a few feet more when a grating voice chimed in from behind him.

"Well, hello, sailor!" cried Trollop. Balancing on five-inch heels, she hurried up beside him. "You look like a guy who likes a good time!"

"I like my eardrums more," Remo replied.

"Huh?" Trollop asked. She didn't wait for a response. "What say we find someplace quiet and make it loud!"

Remo stopped so abruptly, Trollop plowed into him.

There was something distinctly odd about her exposed belly. It felt too soft and cold.

"Are you talking sex, Austin Powers?" he asked.

Her crow's-feet wrinkled appreciatively. "The best you ever had, baby," Trollop vowed.

"Will you talk while we're doing it?"

"Talk?" Trollop scoffed. "Baby, I'll *scream.*"

Remo mused for but a second. "Pass."

He continued on.

Trollop obviously was not used to rejection.

"I can rock ya till your fillings pop out," she promised, hurrying after him.

"Don't have fillings," Remo said. "I lost a couple of teeth playing high-school football, but they grew back."

"You still had baby teeth in high school?" she asked.

"Nope," Remo replied simply.

She didn't even hear. As she clip-clopped beside him, Trollop rubbed the sides of her strangely elastic protruding belly in what was supposed to be a seductive manner.

As her tongue lapped her glossy lips and her eyelids batted ropy lashes, Remo briefly wondered what kind of parent in their right mind would have allowed their teenaged daughter to buy into the whole "Seasonings" concept.

"Next alley we pass, I'm yours," she breathed. "I know what you need, what you really, *really* need."

That did it. It was the quoting of her band's most famous song that finished Remo. He stopped dead.

"Condoms," he announced.

Her smile broke full on bleached teeth. "Got 'em," she replied excitedly. She began fishing in her purple purse.

Remo shook his head. "Not enough. I know where you've been. I'll need seventy or eighty. Enough that I won't even have to be in the same room while we're doing it. And you're going to need some kind of gag. Preferably one with some kind of locking mechanism and a key that can be easily lost.''

"I'm on it!" Trollop promised. "Wait right here!"

Turning on one huge heel, she thundered down the street.

The rest of the Seasonings were just walking out of the sex shop, their arms loaded with overstuffed bags when Trollop plowed into them. The big boxes that were balanced on their massively pregnant stomachs went flying in every direction.

Remo wasn't around to witness the fallout. When the screaming started, he was already ducking around the corner of the busy four-lane street.

He didn't have time to revel in the little bit of unhappiness he'd delivered into the lives of the four women who had irritated him so much. The instant he turned the corner, he became aware of someone watching him.

It wasn't one of the Seasonings, or even one of the many prostitutes who trolled the streets of Bachsburg. With a shudder, he realized that it was the same strange sensation he'd felt at the Carlson wake.

Without breaking stride, he casually sought out the source.

Years of exacting training designed for the express purpose of not telegraphing moves to an opponent couldn't prepare him for the shock of what he found. Any pleasure he'd gotten from tormenting Trollop Seasoning bled away.

Standing on the sidewalk on the opposite side of

the busy street was the child from baby Karen's wake. The same Korean boy he'd seen at the airport in New York.

Remo stopped dead. Someone bumped into him from behind, cursing him for stopping so abruptly. Remo didn't even hear.

It was impossible. First in Peoria, then the disappearing act at JFK and now here.

There was something very odd going on.

As the cars continued to rush past, Remo caught only glimpses of the boy between them. At one moment he was staring at Remo, his big brown eyes filled with a world of sadness; the next he had turned away. With small, mournful steps, he began walking slowly down the adjacent street.

On the other side of the road, Remo shook his head. "Not this time," he muttered firmly.

There wasn't time to wait for a break in traffic. From a standing position, Remo vaulted into the street.

His toe caught the hood of a speeding Jaguar. It made neither dent nor scratch as he pushed off. Brushing the roof of a Volvo, he skipped over the two racing Saabs that were heading in the two opposite lanes before landing at a full sprint on the far sidewalk.

But when he reached the spot where he'd last seen the boy, he was no longer there.

Remo scanned the sidewalk, spinning a complete circle.

The foot traffic was not so great that the boy could be swallowed up by it. Yet he was nowhere to be seen. As he had at the airport, the young Korean child had vanished.

Remo didn't know what to make of it. But one thing was certain. The depression he had been feeling was beginning to be eclipsed by a growing sense of apprehension.

Keeping his eyes peeled for the strange apparition, he began walking down the suddenly eerie East African sidewalk.

8

Tea and fruit had been laid out on a long low table in the center of the small dining area. There were also strips of fish that had been cured in salt, making them inedible to the Master of Sinanju.

Choosing a small sliver of citrus fruit, Chiun settled amid the rugs and pillows arranged on the dirt floor of the oversize hut. On one knee, the Master of Sinanju balanced a china teacup and saucer; on the other knee was a matching plate with his meager slice of fruit.

"Your journey was a pleasant one, I hope," Chief Batubizee said. The big man had settled into a comfortable pile of cushions across from the old Asian. Bubu stood behind him, off to one side.

"As pleasant as travel through the air can be," Chiun replied, lifting his china cup.

Batubizee nodded. "I have never been in an airplane. They are frightful contrivances. I fear the wings will drop off and they will plummet to the ground."

"A wise concern." Chiun nodded. "Yet to avoid all progress is to be mired hopelessly in the past."

Letting his words hang in the air between them,

the old man bit into the wedge of fruit. It was sweet and pulpy. Frowning, he ate only one-quarter, leaving the rest on the expensive china plate.

Batubizee fidgeted on his pillows. He shot a quick glance at Bubu before looking back at the Master of Sinanju.

"Do you not wish to know why I summoned you?" the chief asked.

"I assumed you had not brought me all this way to eat what little food is left in this barren land," Chiun replied.

As the old man sipped carefully at his green tea, a dark cloud passed over the Luzu chief's brow.

Batubizee took a deep breath, drawing the musty smell of the big room deep into his lungs.

"Mine is not the tribe your histories describe," he admitted. A proud man, he fought hard to hide his shame. "We are not as the Great Nuk left us, all those years ago."

"Nuk the *Unwise*," Chiun corrected.

The chief's brow furrowed once more. "I beg your pardon?" he said, confused.

Chiun set his teacup to the floor. "In the annals of my House, the honorific 'great' is not bestowed lightly. All Masters aspire to it, but only one has yet achieved it. And Nuk is not that man."

Batubizee shook his head. "Forgive me, Master of Sinanju, but this cannot be. Nuk was a man like no other. So it has been told from the time of Kwaanga, passed down from one generation to the next. Your ancestor was a warrior of great strength and skill."

"As are *all* Masters of Sinanju," Chiun said simply. "And if a man gives all of his sons the same name, how will any of them know when he is being called? Imagine the confusion in our histories if everyone was described as the 'great this' and the 'great that.' Hence Nuk the Unwise."

"But he *was* wise," Batubizee insisted. "He shepherded the Luzu Empire to greatness. If not for him, we would be but poor vagabonds, dwelling forgotten in the wilderness."

At this, Chiun fell silent.

The stinging silence wasn't necessary. Batubizee realized the irony of his own words the instant he had uttered them. Still seated, he pushed his shoulders high in a sorry attempt to recapture his dignity.

"It was not always so," the Luzu chief said bitterly.

"No," Chiun agreed. "Nuk the Unwise set sail from a thriving civilization. For centuries after his departure, when word of the Luzu reached the shores of my village, it told of the strong and prosperous empire Nuk had established in the wilds of Africa."

"For many years it was true," Batubizee admitted. "Until the Europeans." The last word was spoken like a curse. "Our wars with the English went poorly. The whites established settlements that grew into cities. They took our land and called it East Africa. Because of them, we die." His strong voice quavered with passion.

Chiun considered the chief's words for a long moment. When he finally spoke, his voice was soft.

"What the whites have done to you with their so-called civilization is not unique. My own land has been visited many times by the armies of emperors, khans and presidents. The Luzu I have seen seem infected in their souls. You cannot blame the government in Bachsburg for what I have witnessed here."

Batubizee's nostrils flared with thin impatience. "The whites showed my people a new way of life. They had power and wealth that dwarfed our own. Over the past century, many of our young fled to the cities. Poverty flooded the void they left. Now even the slums of Bachsburg are richer than the land of my fathers."

"I have traveled much in my long life, O Luzu chief." Chiun nodded wisely. "The West's influence is inescapable, though one flee to the most distant corner of the world."

Nodding at Chiun's words, Batubizee willed himself calm. "There was a time that I thought I could affect the white system from within. When free elections were established, I campaigned for president of East Africa."

Chiun raised a thin eyebrow. "A Luzu chief run for president?" he clucked in disapproval. "Surely things are not so bad. If you want for anything, rally your people and take by force from the whites in Bachsburg."

Batubizee shook his head. "The whites are no longer the problem—though the system they created has outlived them. As for my taking anything by force, the government in Bachsburg with its tanks and guns does not fear the spears of a few starving tribesmen.''

Chiun had been growing quietly annoyed by the Luzu chief's defeated air. But at this he shook his head firmly, gossamer tufts of hair quivering with the first blush of real anger. ''That cannot be,'' he insisted. ''Or has the gift of Nuk been lost with your ability to plant and hunt?''

Batubizee stiffened. ''No,'' he said thinly, ''it has not. But though it has been passed from one generation to the next—even to this day—we are not Masters of Sinanju. While we faced men who were our equal, we were strong, but those days were gone long before my time. East Africa is proud that it is the only nation on Earth to have dismantled its nuclear stockpile, but it still has many guns. And while Sinanju might not fear these weapons, my people do. I need your help, descendant of Nuk, to help them overcome their fear.'' He leaned forward. ''I would remind you that this was part of Kwaanga's original agreement with Master Nuk.''

The chief's defeated tone had only fed the Korean's frown. But now it was clear the Luzu leader also felt that Chiun was a doddering old man who needed to be refreshed on the details of Nuk's contract. Chiun hid his offense behind a veneer of irritation.

''This is why you summoned me from the side of the emperor I now serve?'' he asked, his irritation clear.

Batubizee shook his head. ''It is but part of the reason. Do you know of Willie Mandobar?''

Chiun exhaled impatience. "Of course. He is the convict president who is a hero to the idiots of the West."

"He is president no more," Chief Batubizee said ominously. "His lackey, Kmpali, rules from the white palace. But the evil Mandobar yet lingers like a disease. He is using his influence to turn the nation he ruled into a haven for wickedness."

At this Chiun's brow furrowed. "Is not his wife the evil one?"

The chief shook his head. "It was thought by many that she was the evil behind the good. But they were divorced many years ago, and she was driven from power. While he ruled, she was even punished in the courts. It is Mandobar himself who is the wicked one. If he is successful in his scheme, East Africa will become the focus of corruption for all the world. And that poison will flood into Luzuland."

Try as he might, Chiun couldn't imagine a Luzuland any worse than the one he had already seen.

"What is it you wish from Sinanju?" the old Asian asked.

Shifting his broad bottom on his mound of pillows, Batubizee clapped his hands.

Bubu stepped quickly forward, a sheet of wrinkled yellow parchment in his dark hand.

"I invoke Kwaanga's contract with Nuk," Batubizee announced imperiously. Pulling the paper from Bubu, he presented it to Chiun. "This wicked shadow from the south threatens to destroy the whole of the Luzu Empire. To ensure the safety of my people and honor the bond of your House, Sinanju must slay the evil Willie Mandobar.''

Chiun took the paper in his long, tapered fingers, giving it hardly a glance. He already knew it was a standard agreement for the era. Nuk's mark appeared at the bottom alongside the symbol of Sinanju.

''You have read your contract well,'' Chiun said, even of voice. The parchment quivered at the end of his long talons.

Batubizee nodded gravely. ''You are bound to obey.''

Chiun nodded agreement. ''That is true,'' he said. ''My House is obligated by the terms of this agreement to assist you at any future time if ever there is a threat great enough to topple the Luzu Empire. If what you say is true, clearly that threat now exists.''

A smile of cunning split the Luzu chief's face. ''Excellent,'' he enthused. ''I will have you taken—''

Chiun raised a wickedly sharp nail.

''Except,'' he interrupted.

The contract still remained in his other hand. But it no longer quivered. In fact, Batubizee noted, not even the normal currents of air passing through the squalid hut seemed to disturb the delicate sheet.

The chief's smile settled into sagging jowls of suspicion. ''Except what?'' Batubizee asked.

An index fingernail sought a spot on the parchment. ''You have forgotten this mark.'' When the old man saw the look of confusion on the Luzu chief's face, he tipped his aged head. "Surely Kwaanga passed down its significance?"

Batubizee squinted at the proffered contract. Chiun's long nail tapped at a single squiggle, faded from age but still visible, above the Sinanju symbol.

Batubizee glanced up, his puzzlement only deeper. "Is that not an error?" he asked of the small mark.

Chiun sat back to the floor, finally examining the contract for himself.

"Sinanju does not make errors," he sniffed as he studied the ancient paper. "That is the symbol for payment. Yes, my House is obliged to take on any task that meets the terms of this agreement, *provided* the Luzu compensate us for the service." When he looked back up, his eyes were steady.

Batubizee was clearly stunned. He looked helplessly at Bubu. An angry frown had sprouted on the young man's face. When the chief looked once more at Chiun, all vestiges of his regal attitude had fled. An expression bordering on frightened despair clutched his broad features.

Chiun was nodding gently, his tufts of trailing hair a thoughtful echo to the slow movement.

"Nuk might have been unwise. But he was not a fool."

And the Master of Sinanju offered a faint smile.

9

Remo wandered morosely through the streets of Bachsburg for nearly three hours. In all that time, he didn't see his little Korean shadow again. He was assaulted twice by muggers and was propositioned countless times by prostitutes who seemed to sprout like weeds from the cracks in the sidewalk. Upon eyeing his lean frame and pensive, cruel eyes, most of the ladies of the evening broke with tradition, offering to pay him. Each time, he declined.

Smith had wanted him to knock out the underpinnings of Willie Mandobar's corrupt scheme, but Remo found that since the latest disappearance of the mysterious Korean boy, his depression had worsened. Whether it was caused by Chiun's Master's disease or the boy didn't really matter. Whatever the reason, at the moment he didn't feel much like killing his way up the chain of command in the African nation.

At a busy intersection, Remo found a bank of gaily colored public telephones. He stopped near them for a while to watch the traffic. After counting 106 blue cars and 61 red ones, he finally grew bored enough to make the call he didn't really feel like making.

Reluctantly, he snagged up a phone. Dropping in a fistful of change, he began depressing the 1 button repeatedly, activating the special rerouters that would transfer the call to Upstairs.

As he waited for the static clicks to finish, Remo tried to spark some enthusiasm in *something*. To this end, he made a private bet with himself that it would take the CURE director two rings instead of the usual one to answer.

DR. HAROLD W. SMITH was amazed.

These days, it was not often the taciturn New Englander with the perpetually dyspeptic expression and enveloping gray demeanor experienced any kind of emotion at all, let alone something as strong as utter amazement. Yet there was no other way to describe what he was feeling.

The scant reports from East Africa had come to his attention barely a handful of days ago. But ever since he had dispatched Remo and Chiun to that nation, information had been increasing every hour—almost exponentially. What began as a trickle rapidly became a flood.

Weary eyes of flinty gray scanned the raw data as it was collected by the CURE mainframes, which were hidden behind a secret basement wall far below.

The wall that hid the Folcroft Four from prying eyes was representative of everything around Smith. Nothing was as it appeared. The building in which he worked was an elaborate disguise. To the world, Folcroft Sanitarium in Rye, New York, was an exclusive institution for the chronically ill and mentally deranged. Its public face masked the work of CURE, the most damning secret in the history of America.

Even Smith himself was a lie. His post as director of Folcroft occupied almost none of the time he spent locked away in his Spartan administrator's office. As the efficient head of CURE, Smith had spent nearly forty years safeguarding America from threats both domestic and foreign. East Africa certainly fell into the latter category.

Over his shoulder, a pane of one-way glass overlooked the sanitarium's private back lawn, which stretched down to the gently lapping waters of Long Island Sound.

Smith didn't have time to even glance at the serene beauty of the yellow sunlight as it sparkled off the rolling black waves. His spotless glasses were trained with laserlike focus on the computer screen buried beneath the surface of his gleaming onyx desk.

When the blue contact phone jangled to life at his elbow, Smith barely reacted to the sound. The rest of his body continued to study the information on his monitor as a single arthritis-gnarled hand snaked out to pick up the old-fashioned receiver.

"Smith," he said crisply.

"Dammit, why do you always have to pick up on the first ring?" Remo said in an irritated voice.

"Remo," Smith said. He blinked away fatigue, turning his attention away from his computer.

"Yeah, it's me," Remo said. "And just so you know, I'm in East Africa, I'm alone and I'm irritable. So don't piss me off."

"Alone?" Smith asked, surprised. "Didn't Chiun accompany you?"

"He sure did," Remo said aridly. "And then bagged out on me the minute we got here. Don't start on that, Smitty. I've already explored that particular canker sore one time too many."

Remo's tone was such that Smith decided not to press further. Changing topics, he forged on.

"What do you have to report?"

"Well, Chiun ditched me at the airport, they put garlic on your fish here even when you ask them not to, I kacked two guys at lunch and the country's defense minister is heavy into plantation suits and hiring hit men."

Smith sat back in his chair. "Are you saying East Africa's defense minister is in on Mandobar's scheme?"

"It sure looked that way," Remo said. "He isn't fazed by dead bodies, anyway. Guy's name is Elvis something."

"His name is L. Vas Deferens," Smith corrected. "That is Vas, as in *pause*."

"However it's pronounced, he's one cool customer," Remo said. "I've gotta admit, I'm thinking of taking him up on his offer. He's way better looking than you. I could clean up on his sloppy seconds."

Smith refused to become distracted. "And you are saying Deferens saw you—" he searched for the right euphemism "—at *work?*"

"Him and a restaurant full of people," Remo said. "And before you start on me, it was not my fault."

Pushing up his rimless glasses, Smith pinched the bridge of his nose. "Were *you* seen with him?" he asked wearily.

"Beats me," Remo said. "I skedaddled from the restaurant, but he caught up with me outside. His driver saw us for sure. Plus there were about a billion cars going by."

"Remo, given the delicate nature of this assignment, it should have been a priority with you to avoid public exposure—more so than usual." Smith's hours at his computer had made him bone tired. Exhaling the acid stench of bile, he readjusted his glasses. "As defense minister of East Africa, Deferens is known. By allowing yourself to be linked publicly to him, you automatically remove him from the list of those you can eliminate."

"What kind of dopey reasoning is that?" Remo said sourly. "No one's gonna make any connection."

"Perhaps. However, we cannot take that chance," Smith said. "Given the circumstances, it might be wise if you kept a low profile for now. Where is Chiun?"

Smith could almost see Remo's foul expression.

"I told you, I don't want to talk about it."

"Remo, be reasonable," Smith said. "It's possible you cannot follow through on the mission as outlined. Perhaps Chiun can. I need to speak with him."

"Good luck," Remo snorted. "The last I saw him, he and the rest of the Royal Explorers Club were schlepping off into the wilds of Luzuland."

A knot of concern. "Luzuland?" Smith asked, puzzled. "Why was he going there?"

The answer was the one he hoped he wouldn't get.

"Who knows?" Remo groused. "Another million-year-old Sinanju contract, by the sounds of it. But if he expects me to get tangled up in some ancient House obligation where I've got to wrestle a hippo or marry the chief's spinster sister, no way. Remo don't play that anymore."

Smith's thin lips had tightened. As Remo spoke, he tapped an angry finger on the smooth surface of his desk.

"You have succeeded, Remo, in making this situation more problematic for us than it already was," he said, his voice tart with accusation.

"Don't blame me for Chiun going AWOL," Remo warned.

"I am referring to *both* of you," Smith retorted.

"You're the one making this harder than it has to be," Remo accused. "Why don't we just do what we should have done in the first place? Let me go zap Mandobar. He's the chief crook and bottle washer here. With him gone, the rest of them will just fade into the woodwork."

"Mandobar is *already* gone," Smith said tersely.

Remo paused. "What do you mean?"

"He left the country during the night. It was only announced an hour ago. President Kmpali was on a goodwill tour of the Far East that was not going well. According to reports, Mandobar was recruited because of his stature to aid the current president in his mission to bring investment to East Africa."

"Then let me go after him."

"No," Smith insisted. "That is not an option." The CURE director sighed. "We can assume Mandobar has left the country to maintain some of his integrity should word of what is happening in East Africa leak out. Perhaps we can still follow through on our original plan. Give me a little time to see if another option presents itself." Smith checked his Timex. "Call me—"

He was interrupted by a new voice on the line.

"Hands up!" the muffled voice barked.

Seated in his cracked leather chair, Smith's spine stiffened. "What was that?" he demanded worriedly.

He held his breath, awaiting Remo's response. When Remo spoke, he was more irritated than concerned.

"Just a sec, Smitty," he said, aggravated.

STANDING AT THE East African phone booth, Remo had sensed his assailant's furtive approach. When the stiletto jabbed into the small of his back, his body had already willed blood to flow into the dense muscles.

Given the surprisingly unyielding nature of its

target, the knife skipped out of his attacker's hand, clattering to the sidewalk.

"Don't move," warned his as-yet unseen assailant as he pounced on his lost weapon.

The East African voice had the usual harsh consonants of the former British colony.

Remo turned, already knowing what he'd find.

The kid was no more than nine years old, with features a mix of white and black. He had retrieved his small knife and was brandishing it menacingly.

"Gimme your wallet," the kid scowled.

"Isn't this a school night?" Remo replied tersely.

The youth didn't appreciate the unexpected response. To prove he meant business, he jabbed his knife at Remo's belly.

With his free hand, Remo snagged the blade. When his two extended fingers closed around the sharp metal, the knife blade snapped in two. A long silver section clicked to the sidewalk.

"Scissors break knife," he said.

The kid wasn't listening. He was staring in wonder at the broken remains of his weapon.

Before the shock of what had happened could trigger the kid's impulse to flee, Remo reached out and grabbed him by the scruff of the neck. Twirling him in place, he gave the youth a good solid kick in his hindquarters.

The broadside of Remo's loafer propelled the would-be mugger five yards down the busy street. He landed in a painful protracted slide on his bottom that lasted another five yards. When he scampered to his feet, most of the seat of his trousers was missing. Thin smoke rose from the tattered edges. Visible flesh had been scraped raw.

Howling in pain, the boy scurried away, fanning his smarting derriere.

"Unbelievable." Remo scowled, returning to the phone.

"What was that?" Smith's worried voice asked.

"Freaking Sodom and Gomorrah," Remo snapped. "I'll call you in a while, Smitty, assuming I haven't turned into a salt lick first."

And when he slammed the phone into the cradle he did so with such ferocity the concrete around the steel pedestal cracked.

10

The mountain route to the Luzu treasure storehouse had been carefully recorded in the histories of Sinanju by Nuk. Chiun made no note of this as the rotted old Suburban steered the familiar path into the hinterlands of KwaLuzu.

Bubu drove Chief Batubizee's truck along the old trail across a vast arid plain and up into a jagged collection of low-lying rock hills. When they were halfway up the mountain road, Chiun spied what appeared to be a new development at the distant fringes of the Luzu territory.

"What is that place?" the old Korean asked, his eyes narrow.

Batubizee shared the back seat with Chiun.

"It was built in haste by former government workers," the Luzu chief replied. "It is said to be a place of evil."

Chiun eyed the distant bungalows with suspicion until the Suburban crested the mountain. The dollhouses disappeared behind an outcropping and were gone.

The path took them down the other side of the mountain and into a barren valley. Scars in the rock denoted many an abandoned diamond mine. They drove beyond these decaying ruins of the ancient Luzu empire until they reached a secluded part of the valley.

Chiun recognized the huge stones that served as markers to the Luzu treasure house. They looked like two giant's feet that had been petrified in rock. Turning, Bubu backed the Suburban into the shade between the rocks.

"I did not know we would have to pay," the Luzu chief said, creeping anxiety in his voice.

"Failure to accept prompt payment for a service is unforgivable in Sinanju," Chiun announced. "Worse is to extend credit. That was Nuk's error, and his lesson. No Master before or since has ever engaged in his folly."

Batubizee and Bubu shared a glance in the rearview mirror. Unlike his nervous chief, the young man's expression was unreadable.

When the three of them got out of the truck, Batubizee took the lead. He brought them up an ancient path that—although seeming to be a natural formation—had been chiseled into the rock with great care.

The path led up the side of the mountain and to an angled plateau. At the rear of the ridge, the rising wall indented deeply. Batubizee walked into the wide declivity.

The rock at the rear of the passage was sheered in such a way that it made the face of the mountain appear unbroken. At the far end of the hollow, Batubizee stepped close to a tall chunk of fingered rock. He turned back one time to Chiun, anxiety brushing his big eyes. All at once, he vanished, swallowed up by the stone face of the cliff.

Chiun had sensed the hollowness beyond the stone wall. When he got close, he found that the rock behind which the chief had gone was a few feet from the wall of the cliff. The gap between offered a narrow opening to a black cave.

The Master of Sinanju slipped around the rock and entered the cavern. Bubu followed on silent feet.

The treasure cave was nearly bare. The Luzu Wars and subsequent poverty had siphoned almost everything away.

Empty coffers had been piled against a hand-carved wall. On the floor were rolled a few dusty and rotted tapestries—the tattered remnants of a once great empire.

In this empty cave of the Luzu, the Master of Sinanju saw a lesson. Even though the Sinanju treasure house was full, there could very well come a time when the tiny Korean village found itself in this same dire situation. He only wished Remo were there so that he could impress on him the importance of what this represented.

"We are not as rich as we were in the time of Nuk," the Luzu chief apologized, interrupting Chiun's thoughts. He stood across the cave near a small linen-covered chest. The only one of its kind in the large, empty room.

"You were not rich when Nuk discovered you,"

Chiun replied, his singsong voice echoing against the bare cavern walls.

Batubizee nodded stiffly.

With Bubu's help, the chief hefted the chest from the dirt floor. Carrying it over, the two men placed it at Chiun's sandaled feet. After a second's hesitation, the chief sprang the lid.

Although the chest was large, it was only half-full. Chiun saw at once that the greenish-tinged gold coins contained within it were of the kind minted for Nuk centuries before. In spite of the many abandoned mines they had passed on their way there, not even a single diamond was in the ratty old box.

Crouching next to the case, Batubizee looked up at the Master of Sinanju, a hopeful expression on his broad face.

"Is it enough?" he asked sadly.

Chiun looked from the chief to the gold. Bending, he removed one of the rotting coins from atop the pile. He held up the gold piece, inspecting it in the stream of wan light that slipped into the cave between the fissure in the rock.

The old man's silence spoke volumes.

Batubizee suspected what the answer to his question would be. Bitter disappointment flooded the chief's soul as he looked despairingly on what little remained of the glory days of his once mighty empire. He did not have the right to expect anything anymore.

Above him, Chiun harrumphed abruptly. When the chief looked up he was just in time to see the coin vanish within the folds of the old Korean's brocade kimono.

"This will do as a down payment," Chiun intoned, his face dull. He folded his arms inside his voluminous sleeves.

Batubizee was beside himself with joy. He clambered to his feet. "Thank you, Master of Sinanju!" he exclaimed.

"Do not thank me," Chiun sniffed. "I will need a dozen of your most fierce warriors. If you cannot pay for our services in full, do not expect Sinanju to do all the work."

He started for the door of the cave.

Batubizee nodded as he followed, his chins bobbing excitedly. "It will be as you say, son of Nuk."

"And stop saying I am that fool's offspring," Chiun grumbled, annoyance creasing his wrinkled face as he stepped back into the sunlight. "I am not some three-hundred-year-old son of a dimwit."

Batubizee didn't argue.

Perhaps the legends were true. Maybe this was the one man who could lead his people from despair.

Feeling the hope rising within him for the first time in a long, long time, the Luzu chief hurried out of the murky treasure cave.

11

The first thing Remo did after he'd checked into the most expensive hotel in Bachsburg was to order thirty thousand dollars' worth of Iranian caviar. When it arrived, he promptly flushed the black sturgeon eggs down the toilet.

He was surprised that so little caviar cost so much, but was pleased when such a small amount still had the effect he'd been looking for. Blue-tinged toilet water overflowed onto the bathroom's tile floor and spilled out onto the plush carpeting of his expensive hotel suite.

When angry workers arrived with buckets and boots, Remo claimed he was only returning the caviar to its natural habitat. Their intense displeasure was precisely what he was shooting for. That coupled with the fact that he knew Smith's grayish face would turn purple when he got the room-service-and-repair bill bolstered Remo's mood.

Stepping more lightly than he had the past few days, he left the hotel and wandered down the main streets of Bachsburg. He didn't know it at the time, but he was heading in the direction of the presidential palace.

Two BLOCKS AWAY, Private V. D. Pecher of the Citizen Force of the Republic of East Africa was completing the last of his late-afternoon rounds. He marched crisply around the exterior of the huge presidential palace, the barrel of his semiautomatic rifle braced smartly against his shoulder.

President Kmpali was away. A missing president always meant a peaceful shift at the ornate building of French and Portuguese design. Such had been the case for several days.

Private Pecher liked it when it was quiet. Truth be told, he didn't know what exactly he might do if it ever got noisy when the president was there.

Pecher—like many of the guards—was white. And in his most private thoughts he still didn't like the idea of having to guard a *mooka* president. Of course, Pecher kept this to himself. While most of the other white guards agreed with him, one could not say such things in this new East Africa.

And so Private V. D. Pecher did his job, always wondering what it would have been like if the last white president, O. C. Stiggs, hadn't turned the keys to the kingdom over to Willie Mandobar and his band of *mooka* rebels.

On this last afternoon of his young life, Pecher was thinking unpleasant thoughts about Mandobar as he rounded the north side of the palace complex and began marching across the broad east face of the main five-story building.

He instantly saw the commotion at the front gate. Several other guards were already gathered there.

Even as Private Pecher began stepping more lively in that direction, a voice cut in on his hip radio.

"Code 3 disturbance, main gate. North and east security personnel close it up, double time."

As soon as the command was issued, Pecher broke into a sprint. On his race to the gate, he was joined by other guards. Although his training was supposed to have prepared him for anything, what Pecher found when they arrived at the gate startled him.

An ancient Asian in a sea-green kimono stood before the small guard shack. Fanned into a semicircle behind him were another dozen men attired only in the traditional yellow loincloths of the Luzu Empire. Purple paint streaked their ebony faces. Braced beside the right leg of each Luzu was a long, curving machete. Daggers jutted from loincloth straps. An angry Citizen Force lieutenant stood at the mouth of the open gate, barring the old Asian's way.

"I would see the fiend Mandobar," the visitor announced imperiously.

Panting and confused, Private Pecher and the other new arrivals looked to their commanding officer.

"I *told* you already," Lieutenant I. P. Freeley replied with thin impatience. "Former President Mandobar has gone to China with President Kmpali."

Hazel eyes narrowed craftily. "Ah, but is he away for the Master of Sinanju?" Chiun asked.

Lieutenant Freeley assumed that the man to which he was speaking was this Master of Sinanju—whatever that was. The old man alone would have been little more than a comical nuisance. It was the presence of his silent entourage of armed Luzu warriors that made the Citizen Force man nervous.

"He is away for *everyone*," Freeley insisted. "You will have to leave here now." Taking a step back, he nodded to a guard in the shack. "Close the gate."

With an electronic whine, the tall barred gates began sliding slowly in from either side. They hadn't gone more than five feet before they stopped dead.

When the lieutenant searched for the reason the gates had stopped closing, he found that the little Asian had placed a sharp fingernail against one thick metal bar. A painful groan of metal issued from the straining track.

"Remove your hand," the astonished lieutenant commanded.

Chiun remained where he stood, one arm extended.

"I will check myself," the Master of Sinanju said. Turning, he confided to Bubu, who led his Luzu companions, "Politicians are notorious liars, presidents doubly so."

The motor began to shriek and smoke.

"Remove your hand *now*," Lieutenant Freeley repeated.

He reached for his sidearm. Following the lead of their commander, Private Pecher and the other Citizen Force soldiers aimed their weapons at the wizened figure.

Near the shack, the smoking motor screamed loudly. Something snapped, and it stopped making any noise at all.

Chiun finally removed his fingernail from the gate.

"This man is under arrest!" snarled Freeley. "Take him!"

Hands tucked inside the sleeves of his kimono, Chiun seemed ready to offer no resistance. But when Pecher and another private came forward, there was the tiniest flicker of a smile at the papery edges of the old man's thin lips. And, unnoticed by the guards, he gave the subtlest of nods from his ancient, speckled-egg head.

The instant Pecher reached for Chiun's silk sleeve, Bubu's machete sought air, flashing up and around. Catching a glint of brilliant East African sunlight at the apex of its curving arc, it soared down, thunking solidly into the nearest extended rifle barrel.

Private Pecher *felt* the hollow clang of metal upon metal. Reflexively, he tugged the trigger of his rifle. Unfortunately, the young private didn't have time to realize that Bubu's machete was buried halfway through the barrel.

There was a blinding flash as the bullet struck the lodged blade of the machete. When the gun exploded, shards of twisted metal blew back into Pecher's face. He flipped to his back, his face a pulpy ball of flesh and fused rifle.

Even as the private fell, the rifles of the remaining guards flashed alert, sighting down on the machete-wielding Luzu warriors.

"Drop your weapons!" screamed Lieutenant Freeley at the motionless natives. As he yelled, he noticed that the old Asian who had started the confrontation was gone.

At the gate, the Luzus held their ground. They offered the soldier no choice. "Fire!" he shouted to his men.

To his left, a green blur. The same color as the old man's kimono.

Rifles suddenly flipped this way and that. The lieutenant tracked the flash of movement through the line of soldiers. When Chiun appeared at the far end of the line, not one weapon was aimed at the Luzu warriors.

"Get the Luzus!" Freeley commanded, wrenching his side arm from its holster. "*I* will take care of the old man!"

But before he took a single step, he realized the horrible truth. The natives were no longer outside the gate. His stomach froze to ice when he heard the first warrior cry.

A flashing machete. The head of a man rolling onto the nearby lawn.

Lieutenant Freeley wheeled around.

One of his men ran toward him, his face split open in a sideways smile. Gripping the front of the lieutenant's uniform, the man slid to the ground.

The Luzus were everywhere. Machetes attacked necks and arms. Gun barrel struck gun barrel as panicked soldiers ducked and swirled. Horribly sharp blades found chests and bellies. Glistening entrails slopped onto burning asphalt.

The guard from the shack raced into the fray. A hurled machete thudded between his shocked eyes.

His men dying all around him, Lieutenant Freeley sought out the man who had brought these maniac Luzus to this place. At the edge of the lawn, Chiun was watching the massacre, his face puckered in displeasure. The lieutenant aimed his automatic at the delicate, bald head.

Freeley felt the whir of air before he even had time to pull the trigger.

The machete struck his forearm on the downstroke. With a fat thump, both hand and gun plopped to the driveway. The automatic clattered away.

Grabbing his pumping arm stump in horror, the lieutenant stumbled away from the growing pile of East African corpses. As he fell, dazed and bloodied, inside the guard shack, the final standing guard surrendered his last breath.

THE LUZU WARRIORS stood proudly in the baking sunlight, ankle deep in bodies. Faces beamed beneath purple war paint. Panting, Bubu sought the Master of Sinanju's approval. But, still standing to one side, Chiun was anything but satisfied.

"I have never beheld a more pitiful display," the tiny Asian clucked unhappily. "It is no wonder you people have found yourself in such a pathetic state."

"But Master Chiun, we have won," Bubu insisted.

"Win, lose," Chiun said dismissively. "Words created for foolish games of chance." Bending at the waist, he picked up Bubu's machete. It was still jammed through the barrel of Private Pecher's rifle. "Such sloppiness," the old Korean complained. "If you lost your weapon in a true battle, how would you defend yourself?"

Bubu could feel the eyes of his fellow natives on his flushed skin. "I still have my knife," he offered, embarrassed. The bloody dagger he had used to defend himself during the battle was back in his waistband.

With an impatient snort, Chiun tugged at the machete's handle. The hopelessly wedged metal came free in his hands like Excalibur from the stone.

The Master of Sinanju didn't give the natives time to be awed. "This is not the blow Nuk taught you," he frowned, throwing the V-chopped rifle away in disgust.

As he spoke, there was a sudden scuffling noise behind Bubu. The Luzu warriors spun to find Lieutenant Freeley stumbling from the guard booth. He braced a rifle in his one good hand.

"Observe and learn," the Master of Sinanju told them.

Before Bubu or the others could react, a whirl of green flew past the assembled Luzus.

Face ashen from shock and loss of blood, Freeley tried to draw a bead on the advancing terror in green. He was still trying when Chiun descended on him.

In a blur, the machete flew up, then down.

There was a gentle sound, like soft church bells on a snowy winter's midnight.

The first stroke severed half the barrel. The second invisible chop cleaved the stock in two. The third downstroke removed the screaming guard's other hand.

With a side-to-side chop, Chiun sliced the scream in the man's throat. Eyes open wide in shock, Lieutenant Freeley's head tumbled onto the hot East African pavement.

Chiun spun from the falling body.

"*That* is how it is done," he announced unhappily. He slapped the machete into the amazed Luzu's hand.

Bubu nodded dumbly.

"Gather your other weapons," Chiun commanded.

The Luzus had left spears beyond the fence. Quickly collecting them, they hurried onto the rolling lawn of the presidential palace. With a pensive frown, Chiun stooped and snagged the hair of the dead lieutenant, hefting the head in the air. Grisly bundle in hand, he joined the natives in their determined race across the lush green lawn.

THE LATE-DAY SUN WAS HOT on Remo's back as he wandered up the broad sidewalk.

This section of town was far better than the part he'd been in earlier that day. It seemed that the criminal activity of the rest of Bachsburg wasn't tolerated near the main government buildings.

His stroll along the tidy, well-swept sidewalks was a balm to his troubled soul. He had almost begun to feel better when he stumbled on the first body.

The man was some kind of soldier. A long blade had slit his abdomen from sternum to pelvis. Dead organs yawned from the wide gash.

Blood ran like a sticky red river away from the palace gates. There it collected in dry pores in the concrete, soaking into the arid sidewalk.

Remo stepped around the still damp stain, peeking around the high brick column to which the open gate was attached.

More bodies were spread all around the mouth of the drive. The blade strokes employed against all these men were surprisingly clean. Almost as if…

A troublesome thought suddenly occurred to him. Frowning, he crouched beside the nearest body. There were deep lacerations in the man's neck but very little blood on the face of the wound. The blade had gone in and out fast. Blood loss had occurred after the body had fallen.

The cuts were clean. Too clean.

Standing, Remo's eyes darted left, then right.

"What are you up to?" he muttered as he searched the immediate grounds. No one was around.

Stepping farther up the drive, he found the final proof he needed.

The headless body of a Citizen Force lieutenant

lay near the empty guard booth. A rifle sat in three neat sections near the man's severed hand. His head was nowhere to be found.

"Dammit, Chiun, can't you ever give me a minute's peace?" Remo growled.

Bloodstained footprints led to the lawn. Twelve barefoot men. Even though he didn't see a trail, Remo knew with certainty that a thirteenth set of feet had followed that same bloody path.

"Smith is gonna go apeshit over this one."

Scowling with his entire spirit, Remo stole across the lawn, following the path made by the skulking Luzu warriors.

ASSISTANT CHIEF OF STAFF O. U. Queene was preparing to leave his small office in the East African presidential palace when the door burst open.

Looking up from his desk, he was startled to see a group of armed natives swarming into the room.

Queene fell back in his chair.

"What is the meaning of this?" he gasped. He eyed their spears and machetes with dread.

The natives failed to answer. As Queene blinked in abject terror, the two men standing directly before his cluttered desk silently parted. Between them stepped a tiny figure in a green robe. The wizened Asian carried something in his long, tapered fingers. When Queene saw what that something was, he clapped a horrified hand over his mouth.

Chiun plopped Lieutenant I. P. Freeley's severed head onto a pile of paperwork. Dead eyes stared vacantly forward, a hint of last-minute terror etched forever in their darkest recesses. From within the black orifice of a mouth, a fat white tongue jutted out at O. U. Queene.

"Where is the evil one?" Chiun intoned.

"Oh, my...oh my..." Queene blinked. He was staring into the hypnotic orbs of the dead lieutenant.

"Answer me!" Chiun snapped, slapping a palm to the desk. The severed head bounced.

"Oh, um, who?"

"Mandobar," Chiun said.

"Oh." Queene nodded. "He's, oh... He's not here. Election. New president. Um, Kmpali. Maintains a small office. But not here now. They're both gone."

Chiun whirled to the Luzus. "This one spoke the truth," he said, waving to the lieutenant's head.

"I can pencil you in for an appointment," Queene offered numbly, gathering up his black-bound scheduling book. When he reached for a pen, he found a lolling tongue. He recoiled. "Tell you what, I'll *remember,*" he promised.

When the assistant chief of staff looked up hopefully, the old man and the Luzu warriors were gone. Unfortunately, they'd forgotten to take their decapitated head with them.

The political aide rose stiffly from his chair. He found a small towel and tossed it gingerly over the head.

On deliberate, plodding feet, he made his way to the bathroom where he proceeded to vomit up a year's worth of stomach acids into the gleaming white bowl.

THE TRAIL OF CITIZEN FORCE bodies led to a side door of the palace. Slipping through the massive door, Remo found three more bodies on the polished floor of the ornate foyer.

Again, he noticed the cleanness of the blade strokes. They were too precise for normal men. To Remo Williams, Apprentice Reigning Master of Sinanju, the incisions were disturbing on a level far beyond mere murder.

There was a time when Masters of Sinanju used weapons. But after the Great Wang—the first Master of the modern Sinanju age—weapons became obsolete. Never ones to throw away a potential moneymaker, however, some of the earliest Masters of the post-Wang age had sometimes sold some of the outdated weapons techniques to wealthy clients—this so that the buyer could feel as if he were getting some kind of lasting legacy from Sinanju. As far as Remo knew, this practice and the skills of those thus trained hadn't survived much beyond Sinanju's earliest contracts with Egypt and Phoenicia. Yet here it surfaced, a full continent away.

Another body steered Remo up the grand marble staircase. Aside from the ghosts of those slain, the palace seemed deserted. Remo followed the grisly trail up to the third floor. A few droplets of blood led him to an open office door. He found the missing guard's head peeking out from under a towel on a desk. Somewhere distant came the sound of violent retching.

"Okay, I give up," Remo grumbled from the doorway. "Where are you?"

As if in response, an angry shout issued from beyond the closed office window. Hurrying across the room, Remo found that the window overlooked a broad rear parking area.

He spotted Chiun instantly.

The Master of Sinanju and a dozen loincloth-wearing natives were running alongside an L-shaped addition that stabbed out behind the palace. The group had fled the main wing of the building in which Remo now stood. The old Korean was obviously taking a slower pace so as not to outdistance his companions.

From his vantage point, Remo was able to see something Chiun and the natives couldn't. A phalanx of armed soldiers was sweeping across the lot from the other direction.

Alone in his upper-story office, the sound of desperate dry-heaving issuing from an adjacent bathroom, Remo had a moment's hesitation.

Chiun had abandoned him at the airport without so much as a backward glance. It'd be just deserts to leave him here. Let him and his pack of Johnny Weissmuller wanna-bes figure out a way out of this mess.

But though the impulse to abandon his mentor was strong, conscience got the better of him.

"Ungrateful old geezer," Remo snarled as he snapped the seal on the bulletproof window.

The window rocketed up into the frame, embedding itself deep in the thick wood casing. Glass panes rattled as Remo scampered out onto the inch-wide ledge beneath the window. He took off along it at a sprint.

Far below, the two converging groups had just encountered each other. Across the parking lot, the pop-pop-pop of automatic rifle fire rose into the humid air.

At the corner of the main palace wing, Remo's hands and feet snagged the inlaid white bricks. Using toes and fingertips, he descended rapidly to the ground. He was off in a flash the instant his feet touched the earth. The soles of his Italian loafers failed to disturb a single blade of grass as he flew after the Master of Sinanju. Gliding from grass to asphalt, he was halfway to Chiun before he was finally spotted by the approaching Citizen Force guards.

Bullets began whizzing in his direction.

Though the president was away, there were still many state vehicles parked in the lot. As Remo raced past a big sedan, trailing bullet holes peppered its side in his wake. Still more bullets shattered car windows, spraying glass onto empty seats.

Dodging flying lead with every step, Remo caught up with the Master of Sinanju in a small garden at the far edge of the parking lot.

Luzu warriors crouched in a defensive line. Rows of parked cars separated them from the approaching soldiers. When Remo ducked from sight, the gunfire stopped abruptly. His sensitive ears heard the hushed exchanges as the Citizen Force soldiers continued to press their cautious advance.

Chiun stood unconcerned in the shadow of a bush

trimmed by palace groundskeepers into the shape of a leaping tiger.

When Remo appeared in their midst, the Luzus reacted with raised spears and machetes. At a harsh word from Bubu, however, they let him pass. They returned to their crouches as Remo stormed up to the Master of Sinanju.

"Have you gone nuts?" Remo snapped at the maddeningly serene old man. "This is the goddamn presidential palace of East Africa you just sliced and diced your way through." He jerked an angry thumb at the natives. "Who the hell *are* these clowns?"

"They are friends of the House of Sinanju," Chiun replied blandly.

"Oh, yeah? Since when do we make friends?"

He was interrupted by two Citizen Force soldiers who picked that moment to leap out from behind the last row of cars. The Luzus moved so fast, the soldiers' rifles proved irrelevant. Hurled spears pierced chests. Flashing machetes removed arms and heads. As the soldiers fell, the Luzus screamed a triumphant battle cry.

"And another thing," Remo asked, turning from the mauled bodies. "What's with these moves of theirs? That's pre-Wang if I've ever seen it, and according to the history you drilled into me, Pharaoh Ikhnaton's the last guy we sold the old techniques to. So unless these jokers are some wandering lost tribe of ancient Egyptians, I smell another Masters' Scrolls cover-up."

The blossoming look of anger on his teacher's

face was all the proof Remo needed to know he'd struck paydirt.

"I *knew* it!" he exclaimed.

Chiun scowled. "Take your fanciful deductions elsewhere," he spit.

"You're not dodging this one that easily," Remo warned. "I assume they paid on time?"

"Always," Chiun retorted. But though the word was spoken sharply, there was just a hint of hesitation in his voice.

"And paid *well,* too, I bet," Remo accused.

Chiun refused to be drawn in. "Can I assume that since you have found the time to bother me that you are over your silly self-absorption?" he asked.

"Don't change the subject," Remo said. "Chiun, Smith is gonna go berserk over this. He's already ticked at me just for talking to one measly stranger."

Chiun's face was bland. "Why?" he asked. "Did you purchase more magic beans?"

"Very funny," Remo said.

More soldiers swarmed the area. Only one managed to get off a shot before the Luzus cut them to ribbons.

"It was some high muckity-muck in what's *left* of the government," Remo said, waving a hand at the mounting stack of bodies. "Smith was going to bench me and send you in, but now you've flown off on some crazy Edgar Rice Burroughs safari."

By this point, the number of Citizen Force soldiers had been greatly reduced. The Luzu warriors swept around the parked government cars, finishing off the cowering remnants of the presidential guard with quick machete strokes. A few distant soldiers fled on foot. The Luzus didn't give chase.

When the victorious warriors raced back to the Master of Sinanju, Bubu led the pack.

"Not you again," Remo groused.

The native ignored him. "The battle is ours, Master of Sinanju," Bubu panted.

Chiun nodded. "Let us hasten back to Luzuland," he intoned seriously. "We must inform your chief not only that his enemy has fled in fear, but that he must prepare his people for government retribution for our actions."

The barefoot Luzus took off like a shot, jumping the curb and flying back across the lawn. Before Chiun could sprint off with them, Remo snagged him by one flapping kimono sleeve.

"Wait a damn minute," he snapped. "You can't run off after all this. We'll probably have to get out of the country. Smith's gonna be shitting bricks when news of this massacre gets out."

Chiun's eyes were shards of hazel ice. "I am honoring a contract far older than Smith," he said hotly. "Sinanju worked for the Luzu Empire long before there even was an America."

"I'm sure that'll be a real comfort to him," Remo replied angrily. He threw up his hands in disgust. "Fine," he snarled. "Go traipsing into the jungle and reenact more scenes from *Luzu Dawn* for all I care. But I am *not* covering for you on this one."

Chiun's wrinkled face grew dark. "That is because you are a good son, Remo," he said with bitter sarcasm. "And good sons always turn like hissing vipers on their fathers in times of need. Tell your precious Smith whatever you want. And when you are through punishing me for your unjust world, perhaps you will find one minute to consider who you owe more to, Smith or me."

With that final biting accusation, he was gone. The old Korean became a flouncing green blur as he raced around the side of the building in the wake of the fleeing Luzus.

This wasn't how he'd wanted to leave it. Remo hadn't even had a chance to ask his teacher about the little Korean boy who seemed to be haunting his every step. Scowling from the sting of Chiun's words, Remo turned to go, as well.

Something caught his attention.

Standing among the corpses, he heard the sound of a lone car engine. It was coming up the long stone driveway behind a high hedge. Remo was ready to bolt when through a break in the shrubs he saw the shadowy image of a familiar face behind a tinted windshield.

He hesitated.

There might yet be a way to salvage this. Of course, he'd have to do it without Smith's approval. And in that moment, Remo came to what he decided was the most well-thought-out decision of his life.

"Ah, screw it," he snarled.

Folding his arms over his chest, he waited for the approaching government car to find him ankle deep in bodies.

12

The nervous chauffeur of East African Defense Minister L. Vas Deferens wanted to turn the government car around as soon as he spotted the first decapitated body sprawled across the great gravel drive at the rear of the palace.

"Sir?" the man asked anxiously, looking over his shoulder at his cold-as-ice employer.

"Drive!" Deferens barked.

Nodding, the driver skirted the body and continued along past the row of high shrubs that ran parallel to the road. Worried eyes scanned for machete-wielding Luzus.

Reports of the attack on the palace had been issued over the car radio. According to the internal defense ministry broadcast, the Luzu nation had taken up arms against the ruling government for the first time in more than one hundred years.

Until Minister Deferens had ordered complete radio silence, the news had been horrifying. Decapitations, eviscerations—it was an East Africa that hadn't existed since before the time of their great-grandparents.

At this time of evening and with the president out

of the country, there hadn't been many people inside the palace. A few terrified government workers had fled into the street. Deferens's driver wanted more than anything to join them.

Up ahead, two more bodies lay on the road next to the thick hedge. The driver stopped before the headless corpses.

"What are you doing?" Deferens demanded.

"More bodies, sir," the driver said tightly, struggling to keep down his lunch.

Two white hands gripped the back of the driver's seat. Deferens leaned far over to the windshield, his handsome face pinched. The chauffeur hoped the sight of the bodies would force his employer to come to his senses. He was ready to put the car in reverse and back the hell out of there when the defense minister glanced at him, his eyes flat.

"Drive over them," Deferens ordered coldly.

The chauffeur looked at the mangled corpses.

"Um, but sir..."

Deferens leaned very close to the man, bringing his perfect pale face an inch from the driver's ear. The defense minister's breath was sweet.

"Or get out and *I* will drive," he said menacingly.

The tires smoked as the car lurched forward. Two body-flattening bumps and the road leveled off.

L. Vas Deferens settled, annoyed, back into the seat. He didn't appear at all concerned that he was driving toward a mob of rampaging Luzus.

In the rear of the car, Deferens drummed his pale

fingers impatiently on the door's dark molded handle.

The limo crunched up the gravel road, finally breaking around the high hedge and into a circular lot lined with huge pots filled with topiary animals.

There were mutilated corpses scattered in a wide area around the parked cars of the adjacent lot. And standing amid the dead was a lone figure.

The chauffeur had been at the door of the restaurant when Remo eliminated Johnny Fungillo's lunch companions. Seeing the same man calmly standing amid these bodies, the driver felt a hard knot of fear tighten in his belly.

As the car headed for him, Remo neither flinched nor budged. In the back seat, Deferens leaned forward, his eyes narrowing in suspicion at the sight of Remo.

"What is *he* doing here?" he said to himself.

"Shall I drive over him?" the chauffeur asked hopefully.

Deferens didn't hear him. "Stop the car," he demanded.

"Um, right here, or on him?" the driver asked.

"Now!"

The chauffeur slammed on the brakes. Spitting stones, the long car screeched to a stop five feet from Remo. Deferens didn't wait for his driver to open his door. Popping it open, he jumped out into a pool of coagulating blood. He stormed around the front of the car to Remo.

"What is the meaning of this outrage?" the defense minister snapped at Remo.

"That's a relief," Remo exhaled. "So you're saying this isn't a typical day around here?"

More cars raced up the drive. Soldiers spilled from them and from around the side of the building.

"Stay here," Deferens barked at Remo. He hurried to the guards, pointing them in various directions. A few stayed with him when he came back to Remo's side. "Why are you here?" he demanded, his face stern.

"You know, this looks like kind of a bad time," Remo said. "I can come back later."

"*Why?*" Deferens snarled. "Tell me now or, by God, I will have you shot where you stand."

Remo glanced to the guards. "Just stopped by to see you," he said, keeping his voice low. "But if this is hell week, I think I'll pledge another frat."

Deferens seem only to be half listening. With the immaculate toe of an expensive hand-sewn shoe, he flipped over a corpse. Deep gashes slit face and throat.

"This is obscene," Deferens grumbled. He found a clean spot on the dead man's uniform and used it to wipe the blood from his soles. "These men were killed with weapons," he announced as he rubbed every last trace of sticky blood away.

"I noticed that, too." Remo nodded. "Unarmed," he offered, raising his hands helpfully. "Looks like some kind of knife."

Deferens's chiseled face was suspicious. "*Machetes,*" he supplied tightly. He turned to his remaining men. "Search the grounds," he ordered. "Shoot to kill. And be more careful than these *id-*

iots.'' He kicked the man on whose uniform he had cleaned his shoes.

Wheeling to Remo, he barked, "You are with me."

Remo fell in beside Deferens as the minister stormed toward the palace.

"You picked a bad time to visit," Deferens growled as they walked.

"It was either this or the local Global Movieland, but my tour guide said that got blown up by terrorists."

Deferens whipped open the door. A quartet of Citizen Force guards nearly tripped over them on their way out.

"This wing is secure, sir!" one exclaimed.

"Join the others searching the grounds," Deferens commanded. As he and Remo entered the palace, the running guards spilled outside.

The interior was cool.

"Have you registered yet?" Deferens demanded as they mounted the marble stairs.

"That's what I wanted to talk to you about," Remo said. "Like I said before, I really don't like to advertise."

"I'm not interested in your likes or dislikes. In East Africa you register with the government. The penalty issued by the finance ministry for failure to comply is far greater than *any* your IRS could imagine."

"You haven't been to America lately," Remo said. "And anyway, this isn't a tax dodge. I like to keep a low profile. If I register with you and my name gets out to the wrong people, it could prove hazardous to my health.''

"Your health is already in jeopardy," Deferens warned.

Remo's smile was coolly confident. "I feel fine.''

On the second-floor landing, Deferens led Remo to a polished mahogany door. The defense minister noted as they walked that Remo's shoes made not a sound. Deferens's own footfalls echoed like rifle cracks off the fresco ceiling.

At the door, he paused. "You were good with those men at the restaurant," he said, crossing his arms. The movement did nothing to wrinkle his white suit. "*Very* good. Of course, you realize I could have you shot right now.''

"If you shoot me, I won't be able to work for you.''

The defense minister's lips tightened. Wordlessly, he slapped the door open and marched inside.

The office suite was large and tidy. A few empty desks and a row of comfortable chairs filled the waiting area.

"Wait here," Deferens commanded.

He marched ahead, down a long hallway to a distant office.

"I'm bad at judging interviews," Remo called after him. "Does this mean I got the job?"

In response, he heard what sounded like an old-fashioned rotary phone. The dialing was cut off by the sound of L. Vas Deferens's office door slamming shut with a palace-rattling crack.

13

The intrusion of the ringing phone into Mandobar's afternoon came at a time when no servants were present to answer it. It rang and rang and rang in the small house, the last in the isolated village of bungalows that had been constructed for the Great Day.

Looking absently out the window, Mandobar ignored the telephone.

Thoughts drifted to this week's work.

Mandobar was in China. Yet Mandobar was *here*.

It was all so delightful. Gooseflesh appeared on the dark neck of the Great Day's architect just thinking about the timing of the week's events.

A broad smile stretched across the wide, famous face.

It was a face that had gone all around the world. Lauded by presidents and kings, kissed at Hollywood parties, beloved by those who didn't know or refused to see what was truly going on behind those smiling eyes.

Out the window, the East African sun beat harshly on the dusty strip of arid land where the drug cartel lawyer had been necklaced. What was his name? Russell something.

There had been a minor backlash from that. The Cali cartel had been upset that their man had been singled out. Of course, they didn't know he had been working under the table for Mandobar. In the end, they had been mollified by a few extra tax breaks. Plums granted only the best clients of East Africa, Mandobar had promised.

A black smear indicated the spot where Russell Copefeld had been burned alive. The day after the necklacing, someone had suggested raking the dirt over to cover it up. Mandobar had gone wild. It was to stay until the sun bleached it away—a sign to the rest. And when it finally faded...well, there were always more lawyers.

Copefeld's mortal mark baked in the afternoon sunlight. A washed-out streak of black fading to gray was all that remained to mark the passing of a life. For Mandobar, not the first such marker. *Definitely* not the last.

The smile broadened, threatening to spill off the sides of the world-famous face.

Ring, ring! Ring, ring!

The phone finally became an annoyance that demanded attention. A weary fat hand dropped down to the telephone, lifting the offending lump of plastic to an ebony ear.

"What is it?"

The voice of L. Vas Deferens was tight.

"There has been an incident at the presidential palace. An attack on the grounds. Many are dead."

Mandobar sat up straight. The wicker chair in the sitting room of the bungalow creaked in gentle protest.

"Do *I* need to be concerned?"

"I am afraid containment will be difficult," Deferens continued. "I *had* kept the spillover from our enterprise away from this part of Bachsburg. The international press isn't interested in anything that happens beyond these gates."

"Yes, yes," Mandobar said, already impatient. "Who was it?"

"Luzu, according to initial reports," Deferens replied. "Or at the very least, men in native garb. Somehow they penetrated our security using only spears and machetes. We suffered heavy casualties, but the attackers managed to escape unharmed—at least that is what I was told."

Mandobar leaned back in the chair. The wicker groaned.

"This is not good, Vas."

"No," the minister agreed. "And beyond what I have told you, there is no more information. I have men scouring the grounds as we speak. However, I thought you should know as soon as possible."

"Yes." Mandobar hummed pensively. "Spears and machetes? You are certain of this, Vas?"

"I saw the bodies myself," he insisted. "Assuming it isn't an enemy unknown to us attempting to distract us at this crucial time, there is only one real suspect."

Mandobar sighed deeply. A big, wheezing exhalation of air. "I have too much at stake to risk having this plan ruined by a backward fool." The well-known cheerful voice grew cold. "Go to Luzuland, Deferens, and *kill* Chief Batubizee." White teeth bit gleefully at the order.

The receiver fell back in the cradle, severing the connection. Mandobar pushed the offending phone far to the back of the table beside the big wicker chair.

Struggling to find a comfortable position in the chair, Mandobar's eyes once more found the window. This time there was a wistful glint in their dark depths.

Beyond the dusty pane, far down the scorched road and its cluster of bungalows, yellow sunlight gleamed brightly on the high mirrored walls of Mandobar's great meeting hall. The dawning sun two days hence would wash its warming rays across the ruins of that same magnificent auditorium. The birthplace of the *new* East Africa.

A ridge of low mountains—pocked with the shafts of played-out diamond mines—rose above the hall. And out beyond was Luzuland. Where that perpetual thorn in the side of East Africa, Chief Batubizee, ruled like a pathetic throwback over his dead empire.

And alone in the air-conditioned bungalow, the famous Mandobar eyes sagged into gloomy lines, sad that they would not be present to witness the murder of the last Luzu warrior chief.

14

The closed door to the heavily soundproofed room cut off all sound from the office of L. Vas Deferens to the rest of the suite. Even Remo's supersensitive ears could only detect a low murmur of one voice. The person to whom the defense minister spoke proved impossible to hear.

The call didn't take long. In less than five minutes, the door swung open and Deferens came down the hall.

Remo was sitting in one of the waiting-room chairs.

"My office, please," Deferens said. It was clearly an order, not a request. He spun without another word.

Remo followed him to the open door.

Deferens's office was large and tastefully furnished. Wainscotting rimmed the white walls. A big desk commanded a broad section of floor. Behind it, a massive curving window bracketed by tidy bookshelves looked out across the front entrance to the presidential palace.

Remo noted as he entered the room that the remains of the slain Citizen Force soldiers had already been removed from around the main gate.

"You people work fast," he commented as he took a seat before the desk.

As he was sitting down behind his desk, Deferens glanced out the window. "You would be wise to not mention to anyone what happened here today," he suggested, settling into his chair. "Now, what is your name?"

There was no sense in lying.

"Remo. I'd have to check my wallet to see what last name I'm using this week," he answered truthfully.

Deferens leaned back, steepling his slender fingers to his chin. "You know, Remo, I could still have you executed at any time." He studied his visitor's face for a reaction.

Remo shrugged. "We've all gotta go sometime."

Deferens lowered his hands. "You are either very confident or very, very stupid."

"Confident, not stupid," Remo assured him. "But for the record, some of the most confident people I've ever met were also the dumbest. You ever hear of Kim Basinger?"

Deferens wasn't really listening. He was studying Remo's face. He seemed particularly interested in his eyes. All at once, he dropped a hand to his desk.

"You're hired," the minister announced.

Remo was surprised. "Just like that?"

Deferens nodded sharply. "In spite of all evidence to the contrary, you have come here at a fortunate time. I am in need of good men. Now, either you are boastful, in which case you will wind up very dead very soon, or you are as good as you think you are. If this is the case, I will consider myself lucky to have found you. Are you working for anyone right now?''

"No," Remo lied. He tried to exude the confidence of a suave hired gun. "But I like to keep my options open. In my line of work, you sometimes have to go with the flow, what with all the killing and guns and stuff." He looped a confident arm around the back of his chair.

For his part, Deferens was hoping he wasn't making a big mistake. This man sitting before him struck the minister to his core as someone who was exceedingly dangerous. Yet he acted like a complete ignoramus.

"Good," the defense minister ventured slowly.

Tugging open a drawer, he took out a ledger. He flipped it open and, after Remo had supplied him with his cover surname, began writing on a yellow check.

"We will waive the regular government fees for you. You will be paid directly from this office, tax free, in the form of East African government checks. They can be cashed at any bank in Bachsburg."

Remo instantly thought of Chiun. Although this wasn't a real job, the Master of Sinanju would go ballistic if he ever found out Remo accepted anything less than cold hard cash.

"I get paid in gold," Remo insisted.

Deferens gave him a baleful look. He tore a check loose, sliding it across the desk to Remo.

"This is a retainer of five hundred thousand dollars. You will get a similar check every year you work for me, with bonuses based on a formula of my design."

Remo looked at the check lying on the desk. He'd never been good at negotiating. Deferens hadn't even entertained the notion of paying in gold. Maybe Chiun wouldn't be as upset if he got the price up.

"One million," he pressed.

The defense minister continued talking as if Remo hadn't even spoken. "You may continue to work for other clients. But by accepting this retainer, you agree to drop whatever it is you are doing at any given time if I need you. I mean this, Remo. *Any* time."

"That part sounds okay," Remo said hesitantly. "But the money's not enough. How about 750 grand?"

"The money is not negotiable," Deferens said coldly.

Remo studied the check. Chiun would *kill* him if he found out he'd accepted someone's first offer.

Across the desk, L. Vas Deferens studied Remo's deeply thoughtful face. He resisted the urge to frown.

"Of course, if it's not to your satisfaction, I can still have you shot," Deferens warned. "When word of what has happened here today gets out, I will say you were part of the assault team responsible for the massacre. If your reputation is as you claim, it will be easily believed. Either way, you will be working for me.''

Remo considered not Deferens's words but the situation he found himself in. He could kill the minister right now and doubtless sever one of Mandobar's major links. But Smith didn't want him killing Deferens at the moment.

Weighing more heavily on his mind was Chiun. With all the weirdness of the past two days, he shouldn't give a damn what the Master of Sinanju might say about his accepting a check, but that was just like Chiun. Always piling on. Even when he wasn't around.

''Ah, the hell with it,'' Remo growled, snatching up the check. ''I'll take the job.''

When he stuffed the check into his pocket, his fingers brushed the hard edges of the small crucifix. Thoughts of baby Karen's wake and the apparition that had been following him ever since flooded Remo's mind.

Across the desk, Deferens didn't see the dark expression that settled on Remo's brow.

''Excellent,'' the minister said efficiently. ''You'll be happy to know I already have a job for you.'' He steepled his fingers. ''It is far more important 'than removing a few common drunks in a restaurant.''

Remo noted a flickering smile of satisfaction on the defense minister's bloodred lips. With his pasty skin and dark mouth, he gave the impression of a sated vampire.

"Remo," Deferens announced simply, "I want you to go to Luzuland and kill Chief Batubizee."

And this time when the sad-faced Korean boy apopeared before Remo, his cherub's face was filled with fear.

15

Chief Batubizee saw the clouds of dust rising high into the clear African sky in the wake of the speeding trucks. They could be seen for miles around as the vehicles drove across KwaLuzu, the "land of the Luzu." The fire of the setting sun burned the sky above the spreading clouds.

After the old Master of Sinanju had left with his small band of warriors earlier that day, the chief had changed back into his everyday clothes, which consisted of faded blue polyester slacks and an old red shirt.

His flowing purple robe was for ceremony only, and since he had only the one, he did not wish for it to become as worn and tattered as all his other clothes.

With the appearance of the dust clouds, Batubizee ducked back inside his large hovel. He emerged in his traditional robe and Luzu crown. Symbols of a bygone age.

It took another twenty minutes for the trucks to reach the village. A handful of pitiful natives was sprinkled about the square.

Batubizee was standing before his home when the

Suburban finally appeared at the far end of the main road, leading two more trucks. All three vehicles rolled to a stop before the chief. Luzu warriors sprang to the road.

As Bubu jumped out from behind the wheel of the lead vehicle, the Master of Sinanju appeared like a wisp of wrinkled smoke from the passenger's side.

Batubizee was again struck by the age of the wizened Asian. His impression had been the same when first he laid eyes on the Sinanju Master. He was old. Frail. *Weak.*

The oral history of his people spoke of Master Nuk as a powerful figure, strong limbed and tall, with piercing eyes that could cut more sharply and precisely than any of the diamonds from the nearby barren mines. This was Batubizee's image of a Master of Sinanju—not the old man who had just emerged from his Suburban.

Batubizee again struggled with disappointment as the Korean hurried over to him.

"Welcome back, Master of Sinanju," the chief intoned. "You have brought me the head of the evil one?"

He was looking beyond the old Korean. From what he could see, none of his warriors carried the head of Willie Mandobar to present to their ruler.

As Bubu took up his silent post behind the chief, his young face was grim.

"All is not well," the Master of Sinanju said gravely.

At his tone, Batubizee felt the first stirrings of concern. "What has happened?" the chief demanded, turning from Bubu. "Where is the head of the fiend Mandobar?"

"Still attached to his shoulders," Chiun replied. "According to his lackeys, he has fled East Africa."

Batubizee's big eyes grew wider.

"And you took them at their word?" he snapped. The truth of the feeling he'd been having since first he laid eyes on the little man began to creep into his booming voice.

"They spoke truth," the Master of Sinanju responded, silently noting the chief's change in tone. "He is not here."

"They *lie!*" Batubizee insisted. "He would not leave at such an important time! They have deceived you, old one."

Chiun could not keep the ice from his voice. "Sinanju has methods of detecting deceit in a man's words," he explained evenly. "I saw only truth."

"Can you even see at *all?*" Batubizee snapped, throwing up his hands in disgust. "Exactly how many of his minions did you have my men slay to find this *truthful* information?"

Chiun bore both insult and tone with a stoic face.

"Many of the palace guard are dead," he responded, his eyes level. As he regarded the angry tribal chief, his hands locked with chilly calm onto opposite wrists within the sleeves of his kimono.

"And my warriors were seen?"

"Since we did not slay everyone from here to Bachsburg, yes," Chiun said.

Batubizee shook his massive head. "You old fool!" he spit. "You have led them to me!"

Bubu stepped forward, casting a glance at Chiun.

"The old Master could not—" he began, his voice pitched low.

"*Old,*" Batubizee interrupted. "You are correct. This old fool is not the Master of Sinanju of our histories. Nuk was a vital and powerful man. The lions would not even eat this thing of bone and gristle." He stabbed a finger at Chiun. "Mandobar has destroyed the nation to which Luzuland is an arm. You promised his head!"

"Even Sinanju cannot kill a man who isn't there," Chiun said simply.

The Luzus in the square were attracted to the raised voice of the chief. Even as they came forward, more appeared from dilapidated huts.

Batubizee towered over the tiny Asian, his anger growing. "Could you even see him if he *was* there?" the Luzu chief demanded hotly.

"Please," Bubu stressed. "Let Master Chiun—"

"*Silence,*" Batubizee snarled. He waved a disdainful hand at Chiun. "This feeble thing is not even to blame for this disaster. *I* am. It is *my* fault for trusting the legends. The Luzu Empire was already dying. Now, on its deathbed, I have strangled it."

A proud man, Batubizee knew he had already let the common villagers see too much. Shoulders sagging, he shook his head at Chiun.

"Go, old one," the chief said, defeated. The effort to speak seemed draining. "Return to your American emperor. I should not have summoned you in the first place."

Turning wearily, he began trudging morosely to his hut.

He had taken barely two steps before there came a commotion from behind. When Batubizee turned, he found the Master of Sinanju standing where he'd left him. The old man had removed his hands from the sleeves of his robes. Clutched in the bony fingers of one was a long, curving machete. Batubizee saw that the blade Bubu had carried from the truck was no longer in the young native's hands.

The machete was damaged halfway up the blade where it had come in contact with the Citizen Force rifle.

As both Bubu and Batubizee watched with growing concern, the Master of Sinanju pulled a spear from the grasping fingers of a nearby warrior.

Chiun's bright hazel eyes burned deep into those of the Luzu chieftain. Peering into their frigid depths, Batubizee suddenly felt naked.

Chiun turned abruptly from the gathered throng.

All eyes tracked the wizened form of the Master of Sinanju as he strode away from the group, a weapon in each hand.

"What is he doing?" the chief asked Bubu, struggling to keep the hint of sudden fear from his voice.

The young native's expectant eyes were trained on Chiun. "Watch," he whispered.

Noting the tingle of excitement in the younger man's tone, Batubizee fell silent.

Women who sat in the dirt of the square separated as Chiun passed. Their wasted children ceased playing in his wake. Flies buzzed around malnourished heads as all eyes turned to the strange old man.

At the far end of the square, towering above a pair of tumbledown huts, a mighty baobab tree sprouted from the arid ground. Its dark and pitted trunk was nearly thirty feet in diameter. The highest of its long, gnarled branches clawed more than sixty feet into the hot East African sky.

Chiun stopped at a dried-up fountain at the center of the vast square. From where he stood, the tree was farther than any man could throw.

As natives watched in growing fascination, the tiny Korean raised the machete high in the air, curved tip of the supersharp blade just behind his shoulder. The spear he hefted in his other hand, close to his ear.

A hush fell over the crowd. Even the insects of dusk seemed to hold their breath in anticipation.

When the tension became more than any of them could bear, one bony hand shot forward.

The spear launched from Chiun's fingers with an audible crack. Almost simultaneously, the other hand whipped down. Another crack and both spear and machete were rocketing across the square toward the huge tree.

Time drew a different pace around the weapons. All eyes could see them as they sliced hot air.

At the midpoint between Chiun and the baobab, the machete sprang forward. Blade struck spear, cleaving the blunt end. With a determined whir, it split the spear up its length, building speed as it went. The machete broke through the far end, skipping ahead of the still airborne spear halves. An instant later, the blade found its mark, thwacking loudly against the trunk of the baobab.

The Luzus felt the ground beneath their bare feet shake from the vibration of the impact.

And as Chief Batubizee and the others watched in amazement, the fat trunk of the huge black tree cracked up the middle. The baobab split into two flowering halves, revealing the pulpy interior of the ancient trunk.

Before the first leaves from the deciduous tree could begin raining on the square, the twin sections of the bisected spear sank deep into the newly cleaved trunk, one to each side. They quivered in the humid African air like awkward new branches. And, with thundering slowness, the two sections of tree crashed to the ground.

When Chiun turned back to Chief Batubizee, a light gurgle of water was trickling from the exposed interior of the giant tree. Emaciated children stumbled to the water.

His face stone, the Master of Sinanju padded silently to the Luzu ruler. He looked up into the stunned face of Chief Batubizee.

"It is wise to question history, chief of the Luzu," Chiun intoned somberly. "For historians are men, and men do often lie. However, history's graveyards are heaped with dead—king and peasant alike—who have questioned the abilities of the Masters of Sinanju."

He let the words hang between them for a moment before turning on his heel. Without looking back, he padded slowly away. When the wizened figure had disappeared behind a tight knot of miserable huts, Chief Batubizee finally exhaled. He hadn't been aware that he was holding his breath.

"I attempted to warn you," Bubu whispered.

None of the others present would dare speak thusly to their chief. Not that they'd even thought to speak. All eyes were locked in awe on the last place they had seen the ancient Korean with the deadly flashing hands.

The display had been impressive. Batubizee hoped the old one's skills were as impressive with real men.

Bad luck had forewarned the government in Bachsburg of his intentions. In spite of the Master of Sinanju's powers, they would respond.

The Luzu leader said not another word. Bubu in tow, he ducked back inside his large hovel.

CHIEF BATUBIZEE'S SURMISE ultimately proved correct, although the swiftness of the incursion would surprise even him. Twenty minutes after he entered his hut, a new cloud of dust appeared on the distant darkening horizon. A small band of East African government killers led by Remo Williams had entered the homeland of the Luzu.

16

In the front seat of the Chevy Blazer, Remo saw with faraway eyes the stone marker that noted their passing into Luzuland. Where they traveled, grass and other low scrub filled the vast plain that had once been plowed farmland. Here, a sickly tree sprouted from the earth—there, a massive hive swarmed with fat, black insects. In the near distance, mountains kissed the sky.

The hired killers he was with chatted endlessly as they drove. Remo heard not a word.

The air-conditioning in the truck was on high, though for the other occupants it remained hot. For Remo, heat had become something alien. The chill he'd felt the second time he'd seen the mysterious vanishing child had now become a penetrating cold that seeped into his bones. That he was dealing with something supernatural was no longer a question.

When the little Korean boy with the sad face had appeared this time, he was standing at the elbow of L. Vas Deferens in the presidential palace of East Africa. The defense minister obviously didn't see the boy, for he had no reaction whatsoever to the apparition. He continued to give Remo instructions as if there weren't a mournful ghost standing in their midst.

Finally given the opportunity to speak to the child, Remo had no choice but to sit by and watch. The entire time he stood there, the deeply fearful expression the boy wore had not fled his flat features. His eyes never strayed from Remo's. When the meeting at last ended and Remo had his instructions, the little boy had turned and walked into the wall and was gone, leaving a chilled Remo with a creeping sense of apprehension that had yet to fully dissipate.

The speeding truck bounced along the road. Locked to the seat, Remo didn't seem to move at all.

Remo had accepted the assignment from Deferens with no complaint. Of course he didn't plan to kill the Luzu chief, but he needed to speak with the Master of Sinanju. And the defense minister's men knew their way around East Africa.

The three men he was now with had several times attempted to draw him into their conversation, but Remo had remained mute the entire trip from Bachsburg. His absent eyes were directed out the side window, staring at everything they passed yet seeing nothing.

"I still don't like that *he* gets to do Batubizee," the driver whispered to the others. His East African accent was harsh and guttural.

He was referring to Remo. It wasn't the first time they'd spoken about him as if he weren't there. After being silent so long, the men had begun to act as if Remo were surrounded by a soundproofed bubble.

"I don't care about that," one of the big men in the back seat dismissed. "One *mooka*'s the same as the next to me. Just as long as we get bloody on some Luzus."

Remo had determined that *mooka* was some sort of East African racial slur. As far as the rest, the men were exceedingly anxious to meet resistance once they reached the main Luzu village. They were certainly prepared for it. There were enough weapons piled in the back of the truck to arm a small revolution.

"They say that Luzu warriors are amazing with weapons," one of the men in the back cautioned.

"*Mookas* with pointy sticks," the driver said mockingly. "I'm really worried. Let's see 'em outrun a bullet."

"Don't be too sure," the cautious man replied. "From what I heard about their attack on the palace today, *I'm* gonna be watching my back."

"Don't worry," the driver said with cheerful sarcasm. "We got our new expert on all things Luzu here."

He slapped a broad hand to Remo's shoulder. Or at least he tried to. The hand swept through empty air.

Remo seemed not to have shifted in his seat. He continued staring out the window.

The driver grunted a frown and turned his full attention back to the rutted trail.

They drove another ten minutes in silence. The

orange of the setting sun had melted into streaks of expanding reds when Remo first caught the scent.

It was difficult to discern it in the closed cab of the truck. The air conditioner worked to recycle the already fetid air. On top of that, the men he was with smelled like cheese soaked in Brut. But it was there.

Sitting up, Remo powered down the side window. A burst of warm, clean air filled the stale truck interior.

"What are you doing?" the driver snapped. "You're letting all the cold out."

Remo didn't reply. Alert for the first time on their long drive through Luzuland, he expanded his nostrils, sampling the hot dusty breeze.

It was there, carried on the eddies that swirled around the speeding Blazer. The warm scent of rice and hyacinth.

The grass grew high on either side of the long road. As they flew toward it, Remo saw the mouth of a footpath leading through the savannah. It was angled off the main road.

"Stop the truck," Remo commanded abruptly.

The driver twisted to him, a scowl creasing his ruddy face. "We're nowhere near the village," he snapped. "Now roll up the damn window."

Remo didn't listen to him. He reached over with the toe of one loafer and tapped the brake. With a painful squeal of locked tires, the truck slammed to a dust-raking stop.

The men in the rear were flung against the back of the front seat. Only the pressure of Remo's hand against the driver's chest kept the man from crashing through the windshield. Even as the men were catching their breath, Remo was slipping the truck into park and pocketing the keys.

"Don't go anywhere," he said as he popped the door. It opened onto the foot trail.

On the seat beside him, the driver had already come through the shock of their jarring stop.

"Gimme those keys, Yank," he threatened, rage sparking his dark eyes.

Remo shook his head. "Sorry." He shrugged.

And to keep the men from following him, he fused the driver's fingers to the dashboard.

While the other two men pulled at their friend— whose hands had suddenly and inexplicably become indistinguishable from the surrounding plastic of the dash—Remo hopped from the front seat and took the path into the brush.

On either side, the swaying grass rose to his shoulders. The gray of dusk raked up from the ground like witch's claws.

He only needed to walk until the truck could no longer be seen when he came upon the little boy.

It looked as if he'd been waiting there for some time. A circle of grass around where he sat on his rump had been crushed flat. The boy had picked much of the dry grass from the area. He had woven it into the shapes of huts, which he'd arranged into a model village. Roads had been carved into the scratched-up dirt. The tiny men he had chipped from small stones stood among the huts.

The boy didn't even note Remo's approach, so

engrossed was he in play. But when Remo stopped above him, the boy looked up from the town he had built. His brown eyes caught the reflected red of the dying sun.

"I like to fish," he announced abruptly. "Do you like to fish?"

The non sequitur was certainly not what Remo had expected as the boy's first words. Remo didn't know what else to say. The kid was some kind of ghost, but he had the big inquisitive eyes of any normal fresh-faced youth. He found himself answering truthfully almost before he realized it.

"Not really," Remo admitted. "I like eating them, don't like catching them."

"I did." The boy nodded. "There was a big sea where I lived. I used to like to fish there when I was little. But the fishing was poor, and there was little fish to catch and so the men of the village hired themselves out to warlords and emperors." Sadness brushed his bright brown eyes. Looking down, he moved one of his little stone men.

The rice-and-hyacinth smell that had led him there was the scent that clung to Chiun's house back in Sinanju. But for Remo, the words he had just spoken clinched it. Just now the boy had started off talking like any normal child of six, but had taken a turn and lapsed into a rote recital of early Sinanju history.

Sitting on a cushion of grass, the boy moved another stone man next to the first. Remo noted that none of the figures he had made were smiling. All wore the same flat expression. Neither happy nor sad.

As the boy played, Remo crouched beside him.

"Who are you?" Remo asked.

At this, the boy's eyes grew infinitely sad once more. Remo instantly felt guilty for asking the question.

"I am the Master Who Never Was," the boy replied. "I have been before and if fate so chooses, I will be again."

Remo shook his head. "I don't understand."

The boy scrunched up his button nose. "You don't? Most grown-ups do. Are you dumb?"

For a moment, Remo seemed at a loss. As he searched for the right words, the boy abruptly pushed away his homemade toys. He scampered to his feet.

"Want to see what I can do?" he asked, his eyes wide with the innocence of youth. Before Remo could answer, the boy held out his two balled fists. "You do it, too," he instructed seriously.

Remo was surprised at the way the boy stood. It was the light stance used for Lodestones, a training exercise meant only for two full Masters of Sinanju. If the boy wasn't wrapped in some ghostly disguise that hid his real age, someone of his years should not have advanced so far in Sinanju training.

To mollify the youth, Remo got to his knees before him and mirrored his posture.

"Now, the object is to not touch hands." His hooded eyes widened. "Do you understand?" He nodded slowly, in an open tone that wasn't meant to insult.

Before Remo could respond, the boy struck forward.

Remo matched the blow, hands drawn back with the child's knotted fists. He tracked the tiny hands out and allowed the boy to come at him again, once more mirroring the youth's darting movements.

"No, you have to come at *me,* too," the boy insisted with a frown.

Remo didn't feel comfortable striking out at a child, even if he was a ghost. But he didn't want to disappoint the kid. Keeping his movements slow and wide, he threw two broad strokes the boy's way.

He was surprised to find his actions matched perfectly. It was as if the boy's hands were locked in orbit around his own. Always near, never touching.

They played Lodestones for a few minutes, their movements growing progressively more complex. The boy seemed lost in the game. While certainly not up to the level of a full Master, Remo was amazed at his abilities. He was far more advanced than he should have been. A child of his age would have been a prodigy in Sinanju.

After a time, the boy finally grew bored.

"I learned that when I was very little," he announced, dropping his hands. "A long, long time ago."

"Who taught you?" Remo pressed.

The boy looked him deep in the eyes, tipping his head to one side. "Do you like toys?" he asked. "I wasn't allowed to have them. But sometimes I snuck away and made some with the other children. Like this.'' He picked from his small village one of the stone men he'd made.

When he held it out, Remo was impressed by the detail. The features on the toy man were Asian.

"You can have it if you want," the boy said.

When he pressed the figure into Remo's hand, Remo felt the same unnatural cold he'd experienced at the airport in New York and again on the sidewalk in Bachsburg. There was a total lack of warmth to the boy's body.

Once he'd closed Remo's fingers around the figure, he looked up. His eyes were bright. For the first time, Remo noticed flecks of hazel at the brown edges of his irises.

"Sometimes when you look at things, you don't see them, Remo," he said, with a wisdom older than his physical age. "Sometimes you have to look from the side to know what it is you've seen. It's almost your time. Be sure when you go to look that you see what you should, not what you want to see."

He seemed to want to smile. But the ability to do so had been trained out of him long before he'd shucked his corporeal form. Once he was through speaking, the little boy merely put his hands to the sides of his black tunic and allowed the growing night to claim him.

Remo was left alone in the endless soughing plain, a look of confusion seeping across his face.

At his feet, the rocks and grass the boy had been

playing with still sat. But the woven huts of a moment before were now simple piles of grass. The stone men, once more chunks of smooth gray rock.

Remo opened his hand.

A carved Korean face looked up at him.

He slipped the figure into his pocket. Turning from the mashed-down field, he headed back down the path to the waiting Blazer, his face tight with silent reflection.

ON A HIGH BLUFF that looked out over the great, sweeping plains of the Luzu empire, a lone sentry stood.

Behind him, the dead rock mouth of a played-out diamond mine swallowed night shadows. Before him, the gods bled into the vast twilight sky.

Eyes trained keen watched the solitary truck as it traveled the off-road path from Bachsburg. When the vehicle stopped suddenly, the native grew more alert.

A dark figure emerged, vanishing into the tall grass. Dusk was nearly gone by the time he reappeared. After another minute, the truck resumed its stubborn path into the heart of Luzuland.

The sentry watched it come.

One truck. Only a handful of men.

The bright light of the rising moon found no expression on the native's features.

Spear in hand, the sentry slipped down the round rock face. On bare feet he ran back toward the main Luzu village.

NIGHT DESCENDED on Africa like a settling shroud. As the moon yawned full in the star-choked sky, bathing the rolling plains in spectral white, the Blazer headed deeper into Luzuland.

In the truck's dashboard were ten deep indentations, the shape of the driver's fingers. Behind the wheel, between hateful glances at Remo, the man flexed each hand in turn, trying to force away the residual numbness.

Unlike the first leg of their journey, Remo's thoughts had found focus. As they drove, he stared out the windshield, alert to all that was around them.

The old rutted path grew worse. Around him, Deferens's men bounced and jostled on squeaking springs.

When they had at last traversed the plain and the truck broke through the claustrophobic stretch of dry grass, a rocky expanse funneled them into a string of low hills.

The instant they entered the ravine, Remo was alert to the men crouching high up on the canyon walls. When he looked, he saw dark figures silhouetted against the white glow of the night sky.

One of the men in the back had seen the natives, as well. Eyes growing wide, he scanned the jagged rock line far above. There were dozens of silent Luzus, washed in the black of night. They traced the path of the speeding truck.

"We got company," the man in back growled, already fumbling over the seat for one of the weapons crates.

It was all he managed to say before the window

at his right shoulder shattered in around him and the business end of a hurled spear split his skull just above the ear.

The other man in back screamed.

In the front, the panicked driver spun left and right. "What happened?" he yelled, loosening his grip on the wheel.

The truck immediately pulled wildly to one side, scraping the wall of black stone in a shriek of sparks.

Remo grabbed the wheel, steering them back to the path. "Eyes on the road," he warned, annoyance in his voice as he watched the natives. "I want to get there in one piece."

As soon as he spoke, he detected multiple objects rocketing their way. Too many to avoid.

"Oh, great," Remo managed to grouse just as the windshield shattered at the impact of five hurled spears.

Remo caught the spear that was meant for him by its sharpened nose. A fingernail flick and it clattered harmlessly over into the back. Three more he harvested from the air. Unfortunately for the driver, Remo was too far away to stop the fifth.

The spear pounded the man square in the chest, prying ribs and puncturing lung. Releasing a shocked gasp of air, the driver promptly slumped over the wheel.

The truck was already losing control before yet another spear pierced a front tire. It exploded in a spray of tearing rubber and choking dust. Frayed black sheets flew away in anger as the racing truck dropped and spun.

As the truck whipped sideways, the naked wheel snagged a jagged rock. They went up and over.

In the passenger's side, Remo folded his arms in quiet irritation as the world spun upside down.

Bodies and shattered glass whipped about the cab. The big truck rolled wildly, end over end, along the ravine road, roof and doors buckling as momentum propelled it forward.

Only when they finally crashed and rolled to a creaking, grinding stop, did Remo uncross his arms.

"Chiun had better not hear about this," he muttered to himself. In response, the last survivor in the rear groaned.

Remo ignored the man.

The truck had landed at an angle on its crushed roof. Through the window slits, Remo saw dozens of bare ankles. His ears detected a chorus of thudding heartbeats. Brushing glass from his chinos, he climbed out into the cloud of softly rising dust.

About two hundred warriors encircled the wreck. At Remo's appearance, spears were raised menacingly. Remo didn't seem concerned with them in the least.

"You're all my witnesses," he said, addressing the multitude. "If anyone asks, I was *not* driving." He slapped more dust from the knees of his pants.

Behind Remo, the last of the men who had accompanied him from Bachsburg crawled out into the dirt, a British assault rifle clutched in his shaking hands.

"*Mooka* bastards!" he screamed.

His finger didn't have time to brush the trigger before a single spear struck him in the shoulder. It tore straight through flesh and bone, throwing him backward and pinning him to the crumpled hulk of the truck.

When the man opened his mouth to cry out in pain, another hurled spear flew inside it, snapping his head into the Blazer. His body slumped, held in place by the two spears. The gun slipped from his fingers.

Remo turned from the dead man. "Okay, I'm serious," he said to the Luzu army. "I don't want you telling anyone I did this, 'cause I didn't."

Chiun had been a real pain in the ass about his driving skills lately. On top of everything else, he didn't want to take the blame for this latest wreck.

In response to his words, a spear flew his way.

When it was a hair from his eyeball, Remo batted it by the shaft. It clattered harmlessly to the rocky ground.

"Cut it out," he said, peeved. "And since you just killed my guides, I'd appreciate it if you'd take me to wherever Batubizee is."

At the mention of their chief, another dozen angry spears sailed at him. With unseen swatting hands, Remo knocked them all away.

"Listen, I hate to play on my celebrity status," Remo said as the last spear fell and the first murmurs of concern began to rise from the ranks of the Luzu, "but I *am* a Master of Sinanju."

Doubtful expressions blossomed on the faces of the Luzu warriors.

"You lie," one menaced.

Remo bit the inside of his cheek, wondering how to prove his identity to them. "It'd help if I'd brought my Sinanju decoder ring." He frowned, glancing around.

When he saw the machete in the hands of a nearby native, a thought suddenly occurred to him. Reaching over, Remo snagged the weapon. To the crowd, it was as if the blade had appeared in his hand by magic. Spears rose menacingly.

"Don't get your loincloths in a bunch," Remo grumbled.

He didn't raise the weapon against any of the Luzus. Instead, he marched around the side of the overturned truck.

Suspicious eyes tracked him as he went.

A door had been ripped off the Blazer in the crash. The bent shape nestled amid a pile of rocks near the wall of the ravine. Raising the machete, Remo slashed it down against the painted panel of the door. With a few rapid strokes, he etched a trapezoid in the steel. A final, single blow brought a bisecting slash mark through the geometric shape.

"There," Remo announced, turning from the door. "Satisfied?" He tossed the machete back to its owner.

The symbol of the House of Sinanju had the desired effect. Shocked gasps rose from the ranks of the Luzu army.

"*Sinanju,*" a few men hissed, awed. With growing wonder, they looked on the stranger with the milk-white face.

"Told you," Remo said. "Now can we shake a leg?"

The Luzus weren't sure what to do. Although their first impulse was to kill Remo, the symbol of Sinanju was too great a thing to ignore. It was finally decided that they would do as he requested and bring him back to their chief. But given the abilities he displayed, they would treat the intruder with extreme caution.

Shrill whistles called the natives on the hills down into the gorge. They fell in with the rest of the crowd. The entire army began marching through the ravine on foot.

And at the front of the armed horde, prodded with the points of three hundred spears, Remo Williams trudged deeper into Luzuland, a growing scowl on his skull-like face.

17

Once fertile land had long since grown arid. In the moonlight were visible the ancient scars of collapsing canals and earthen dams. If water pooled in them at all, it was at another time of year and then purely by accident. Artificial reservoirs that had collected rainwater during the height of the Luzu Empire were now filled with dusty silt and brush.

As the Luzu army led him along a bone-dry canal, Remo took note of the scraggly brown brush growing wild all along its crumbling banks. Beyond the ancient irrigation system, a huge expanse of savannah was charred black—victim of a recent uncontrolled fire sparked by lightning.

Everywhere he looked were remnants of the civilization that had once thrived here.

Arid wells sat in the middle of nowhere. Too perfect tiers on a hillside was proof of steppe farming from another century. As they entered the shantytown that now served as the main Luzu village, Remo saw a huge pile of rocks that had been part of a large stone building. The rock had been cut from an abandoned quarry in the nearby mountains.

A sentry had spotted the war party when it was

still far off. By the time Remo and his army arrived in the village, the main square was filled with frightened Luzus.

If he hadn't been depressed already before coming to East Africa, the pathetic KwaLuzu capital would have sent him into an emotional tailspin.

The sight of so many distended bellies and malnourished faces filled Remo's heart with pity. Skeletal faces watched, eyes too big for shrinking sockets, as he was led through the crowd, past rows of crumbling huts and pathetic tin houses. They steered him to a large home near the stone remains of a dried-up well.

At the sound of his approach, a man who could only have been Chief Batubizee stepped out of the tumbledown house. A robe hung limp from his broad shoulders, and a tarnished crown of gold encircled his balding head. Remo was quick to note that the chief didn't seem to lack for food.

At Batubizee's elbow was the native who had collected Chiun at the airport. When he saw Remo, Bubu's eyes registered surprise.

"Who is this?" Batubizee boomed to the Luzu army, disapproval evident in his loud voice.

"He claims to be of Sinanju," a Luzu warrior offered.

Bubu leaned close to the chief's ear.

"He did arrive in the company of the Master," the young Luzu whispered.

It was Batubizee's turn to look surprised. "You serve the Master of Sinanju?" he demanded of Remo.

It was all Remo could do to hide his contempt. In an entire civilization of hunger and despair, it was apparent that Batubizee alone sat down at a full table every night.

"Feels like that a lot of the time," Remo replied, his eyes flat. "Right now I'm just looking for him."

A chilly voice broke in from behind.

"You have found him, ungrateful one."

When Remo turned, he saw Chiun at the edge of the crowd, his wrinkled face cold. The wasted natives shrank from him in fear. Even Batubizee seemed anxious at the sight of the wizened Asian.

"Your servant has arrived, Master of Sinanju," the Luzu chief called.

From a distance, Chiun's narrowed eyes regarded Remo. "He is no servant of mine," the old man replied in loud and ominous tones.

Remo had hoped the tiny Korean hadn't carried back to Luzuland the baggage of their confrontation at the palace. But by the sounds of it, the old man was ready to sic the entire Luzu nation on Remo just to teach his pupil a lesson.

As Chiun stepped forward, the multitude parted. Not a ruffle appeared in the multicolored peacocks that were embroidered on his saffron robe. When he stopped before Remo, his hazel eyes were chips of flinty accusation.

"Could you cut me a break, Little Father?" Remo asked in a hushed tone. "I really need to talk to you."

An eyebrow rose almost imperceptibly. Noting the troubled undertone in his pupil's voice, the Mas-

ter of Sinanju's mouth thinned. He turned to Batubizee.

"He is much more than a mere servant," Chiun
proclaimed. "I introduce to you my son, the current
Apprentice and future Reigning Master of the House
of Sinanju."

Batubizee shot a glance at Bubu. "He is white,"
he told Chiun, as if the old man could have somehow missed the fact.

"Only on the outside," Chiun assured him. "His
blood is the blood of my ancestors."

"More or less," Remo cut in, irked at the race-
baiting.

"Quiet," Chiun snapped in Korean. "Do not embarrass me in front of the Luzu." Whirling to the
crowd, he threw his arms up high. Kimono sleeves
slipped down, revealing bony arms. "Hear you now,
children of Kwaanga! My son in spirit has come to
your land to aid us in our fight against the wicked
Mandobar!"

If he expected a cheer from the crowd, he never
got one. The gathered Luzus regarded him with
sickly silence tinged with latent fear.

"That's not exactly why I'm here," Remo suggested.

Before Chiun could caution him once more to still
his tongue, Chief Batubizee raised his voice.

"Why then have you come here, son of Chiun?"
the Luzu chief asked, puzzled.

Remo regarded the bloated ruler with level eyes.
"Assuming you're Batubizee, I was sent here to kill
you," he said.

Beside him, Chiun's eyes saucered in shock. Bubu jumped protectively in front of the surprised chief. And all around the square, Luzu warriors raised their weapons menacingly.

His face bland, Remo scanned the angry crowd.

"Of course, if this is a bad time, I could come back after supper."

TEN MINUTES LATER, Chiun had somehow convinced the entire Luzu nation that Remo was joking and didn't need to be killed. The two Masters of Sinanju had joined Batubizee and Bubu inside the chief's squalid home.

Chiun was thankful that Remo didn't comment on the tattered rug or the ragged silk pillows as the three oldest men sat on the floor. Bubu continued to stand, his gaze glued on Remo. He watched with neither malice nor mistrust. The young native was merely silently alert.

Remo noted an innate stillness to the guard even as Chiun continued to apologize for Remo's words of a few moments before.

"I promise you he meant nothing by it," the Master of Sinanju insisted. "Sometimes he speaks before his thoughts are fully formed."

"I do not understand." Chief Batubizee frowned. "Why would he say such a thing? Is your son an imbecile?"

"Hello? Sitting in the same room." Remo waved, irked.

Chiun ignored him. "No, he is not an imbecile,"

he said to the chief. "Yes, you are an imbecile," he said more harshly to Remo in Korean.

"Little Father, I need to—"

Chiun cut him off with a sharply raised hand. "He is too busy attempting to solve the woes of a cruel and savage world to think clearly," he promised the chief. "But he apologizes if he has insulted you in any way. Is that not right, Remo?"

Remo's face was sour. "Yeah, that's right," he said. "*Now* can we get outta here?"

A nasty string of rapid-fire Korean and the Master of Sinanju turned once more to Batubizee. "Forgive him his rudeness, sire, for he is afflicted with a curse that forces him to see all of the injustices of the world as his personal responsibility. It has left him callous and rude."

"I'll give you rude, Chiun," Remo snarled in Korean. "You've got a whole tribe of women and children out there with xylophone rib cages and this gaspot's in here squatting on the cooler hogging all the sandwiches and Skittles."

In the center of the room, Batubizee's eyes narrowed at Remo's rough tone. "What did he say?" he asked Chiun.

"He is merely expressing anger at himself for being inadequate to the task of offering a proper apology," the Master of Sinanju insisted. "Isn't that true, Remo?" he said through clenched teeth.

Remo rolled his eyes. "Whatever," he said.

The chief let their words hang in the musty air of his hut for a pregnant moment.

"The men with whom you came here work for

Minister Deferens,'' Batubizee finally said in a cautious tone.

"I know." Remo sighed. "I do, too. Or Deferens *thinks* I do. Anyway, I only came here with them to find Chiun."

"But *they* intended to kill me."

Remo nodded. "That was his plan. Don't worry. I wouldn't have let them follow through."

"The chief does not need you to safeguard his life as long as *I* am here," Chiun sniffed. He was studying Remo's face. "You contracted with someone other than Smith?"

Remo avoided Chiun's penetrating gaze. "Not really," he hedged. "It was just a cover." He was relieved when Batubizee interrupted.

"I am not surprised that Deferens would try to have me killed," the chief intoned, his moon face pulled into a thoughtful frown. "He is an evil man."

"You got that vibe, too?" Remo said, deadpan. "By the sounds of it, he's up to his dimpled chin in this Mandobar thing."

Batubizee nodded. "It is as I feared, Master of Sinanju," he said somberly. "Our attack has brought a swift response from my enemies. When Mandobar learns these men have failed, he will have Deferens send others."

At the door, Bubu suddenly chimed in. "They will need to get past the old Master *and* me," he insisted, his eyes burning with the fire of passion.

Remo was surprised when the guard wasn't scolded for speaking out of turn.

Batubizee simply held up a silencing hand, and

the young man took an obedient step back. The flames of fierce loyalty that burned within Bubu did not ebb.

"After his presidency ended, when news of what Mandobar had in store for East Africa reached my ears, I sent men to investigate," Chief Batubizee said. "This was before I summoned you, Master of Sinanju."

Chiun nodded silent understanding.

"Now it is sad yet true that many Luzu have left their ancestral land," the chief continued. "Some found their way to Bachsburg, so when my warriors reached the city, their Luzu brothers there aided them in their quest to learn the truth of what was happening in the city built by oppressive whites that was now being corrupted by a wicked black. In their search for the source of evil, they found Deferens."

Remo hadn't been interested in Batubizee or Mandobar or what either man wanted for East Africa. He wanted only to get Chiun alone in order to discuss the strange happenings of the past two days. But Chiun clearly had no intention of moving any time soon. And, in spite of himself, he found that he was being drawn into the chief's account of what was happening in Bachsburg.

"I don't get it," he said. "Why'd they stop at Deferens? Why didn't you just send them after Mandobar?"

"By this time, Mandobar had retired from public life and was living in Kequ in the province of Pretraal," Batubizee explained. "Well guarded and far away from the minions working on his terrible plan.''

"Okay," Remo said reasonably. "Then bump off Deferens."

Batubizee shook his head. "A man can live with one hand or foot. To kill Deferens would have been meaningless. Mandobar simply would have promoted another in his place."

"But not necessarily the new defense minister," Remo argued. "I can't believe everyone in the government is in on this."

"No," Batubizee said. "But we do not know who is and who is not. The Kmpali government is as corrupt as Mandobar's was. This much is admitted to by all. There is no telling who in Bachsburg is an honest man any longer."

Remo couldn't argue there. The Luzu chief had just expressed the sentiments Remo had been feeling about the entire world before coming to East Africa.

"When I realized the extent of this poison and the threat it represented to the Luzu people, I at last summoned Master Chiun," Batubizee said. "No other chief had invoked the Sinanju contract since the time of Kwaanga, and I did not wish to be the first. But in the end, I was helpless to do anything else. When I learned that Mandobar had been given an office at the palace, I saw it as my opportunity. Perhaps the last for my people." He shook his head sadly.

To Remo, the chief's sorrow for his subjects seemed genuine, yet he could not banish the image of the starving tribesmen he had seen outside, nor of the bloated man who sat before him now.

"Well, Mandobar's out of the country for now," Remo said. "So if you want to make a dent in his plan by capping his loyal defense minister foot soldier, I won't stop you."

The chief gave a mocking laugh. "Deferens is loyal only to himself," he said. "My warriors tracked him for days. That fiend has secrets, even from his master. He and a criminal called Spumoni are even now plotting an evil unknown to Mandobar. They meet in areas of Bachsburg Deferens would ordinarily not travel to. He has been seen climbing in and out of sewers several times."

"Sewers?" Remo said, surprised. He pictured the fastidious L. Vas Deferens. "We're talking about the same guy here, right? Dresses like Mr. Roarke? Looks like he's had his hair Scotchgarded?"

"A sewer sounds an appropriate lair for one such as he," the Master of Sinanju offered.

"I'm serious, Chiun," Remo said. "The guy I met would have his neighbor's dog shot at sunrise for making on his lawn. What was he doing climbing in a sewer?"

"My men attempted to find out," Batubizee said seriously. "Two groups of Luzu warriors followed Deferens and the rest down into the Bachsburg sewer system. Only one group returned alive. The bodies of the rest were pulled from the waste at a sewage-treatment plant the next day."

Remo frowned as he considered this information.

"What do you suppose he's doing down there?" he mused aloud.

Unscissoring his folded legs, Chiun rose to his feet like a puff of fussy steam. "A mystery we must leave to another time," the old man announced. He turned to the Luzu chief. "Though this attempt on your life has failed, I fear it will not be the last," he said seriously. "While your highness prepares your warriors, I will confer with my son. Perhaps he has learned something from your enemies that could be of value to us."

Batubizee nodded grimly. With Bubu's aid, he struggled up from his mound of pillows. Gathering his robes up from around his ankles, he ducked out the hut door, guard in tow.

"It's about time," Remo said, standing to face his teacher. "It looked like you were gonna sit there all night."

"It would have served you right," Chiun replied thinly. He shook his head. "There is no reason, Remo, to behave as rudely as you did to the chief. Master's disease or not, a client should always be treated with respect."

"Some client," Remo scoffed. "This whole tribe looks like it doesn't have a pot to piss in. He probably paid you with a sockful of his own subjects' gold teeth. Which, by the way, it looks like they don't need anyway."

At the mention of payment, Remo completely missed the downward-darting eyes of the Master of Sinanju.

"And I didn't come all the way out here to kiss

up to Batubizee.'' Remo's tone grew worried. ''Something weird's going on, Little Father. Weirder than I can get a handle on. I need you with me right now, not traipsing around the outback with King Hungry-Hungry Hippo.''

The pleading in his pupil's eyes gave Chiun cause for concern. Pursing his lips, he shook his eggshell head.

''I cannot leave, my son,'' he said softly. ''Until Batubizee says otherwise, my place right now is at his side. There are obligations we of Sinanju have to these people.'' He took a deep breath, exhaling thoughtfully. ''I have not yet told you the full story of Master Nuk, he who discovered the Luzu.'' And the way he stood made it seem as if the burden of his responsibilities was almost too great for his frail form to bear.

Remo's shoulders sank. When he spoke, it was with no animosity. Merely somber acceptance.

''All right. Stay here,'' he said quietly. ''But if I have to sit through the entire story of Master Nuk and how Sinanju became tangled up with the Luzus, I vote you tell me the tale of the Master Who Never Was first.''

He watched for Chiun's reaction, assuming he'd elicit some surprise for even knowing anything at all about the young ghost boy who had been dogging him the past few days. But it was Remo who was surprised.

Chiun's papery skin failed to flinch. Only one quizzical eyebrow rose slightly.

"There is no such Master's tale, Remo," the old Korean said, shaking his head in confusion. And there was not a hint of deception in his puzzled voice.

18

Oily water dripped from mossy, slime-covered walls. Even the corroded metal rungs embedded in the ancient brick felt greasy to Nunzio Spumoni. Revulsion touched his sweaty face as he climbed the ladder to the lower platform.

Although it was cooler in the sewer tunnels that crisscrossed beneath the busy streets of Bachsburg, the Camorra representative still perspired. But with hands slick from the ladder, he dared not dig in his breast pocket for his handkerchief.

Nunzio delicately tugged the collar of his damp cotton shirt with one finger as the defense ministry men led him down the arched tunnel.

The stench was powerful, even through his surplus gas mask. The stink of tons of human waste battled past rubber and filter. He had always had a delicate stomach. Nunzio had no idea how his companions could stand coming down here with faces uncovered.

A dark river of frothy filth rolled relentlessly by the raised platform on which he walked.

The sewage was wide and deep. The last thing in the world Nunzio wanted was to fall in. He kept his eyes on the floor as he stepped with slow caution on the wet stone.

Feet clattered with the urgency of their purpose.

"This way," directed the man in the lead.

He ushered Nunzio and the rest into another subterranean corridor. This one was older than the last. Sheets of salt-white slime stained the century-old walls. Clumps of rust-colored mold chewed away at the crumbling mortar.

Nunzio stepped gingerly along the slippery walkway.

The men who led him through these catacombs were all whites. It still amazed Nunzio that somehow in the modern East Africa, a government official. as highly placed as L. Vas Deferens managed to associate with no blacks whatsoever.

In the 1980s, Hollywood stars and music industry giants in search of a cause had focused on the racial injustices of East Africa. Russia and China had racism, oppression, state-mandated feticide, imperialism, gulags, religious intolerance, expanding nuclear stockpiles and enough murdered dissidents and purged peasants to make the Altamont Rock Festival look like a half-filled phone booth. But they also had communism, which made every despicable thing done by their governments an exercise in equality. Since the East African system wasn't Communist, it was fair game to every empty-headed millionaire entertainer with a soapbox and a mouth. It was almost twenty years since the start of their crusade and, thanks to their great work, integration in East Africa had progressed to the point that criminals of all races could work together in peace and harmony. Except, it would seem, for those employed by Minister L. Vas Deferens.

As Nunzio Spumoni picked his careful way along the catwalk, his thoughts were far from the political upheaval that had transformed East Africa. His only concern right now was not falling into a river of shit.

His toe touched a slick, fat brick. When he brought his heel down, the stone popped loose. Before he knew what was happening, both feet flew out from under him. Nunzio was about to topple off the platform when strong arms grabbed hold of him, pulling him upright.

His companions seemed more disgusted by the skinny man's sweaty jacket than by the sewer.

Worried that they wouldn't bother to catch him a second time, Nunzio exercised even greater caution than before as they turned into an adjacent tunnel.

Minister Deferens was walking toward them, a gas mask obscuring his soft features. In spite of their surroundings, there was not a single smudge on his snow-white suit.

"Ah, Nunzio," Deferens said, stopping as the Camorra agent approached. The minister's voice was muffled. "I see you've survived the perils of the Bachsburg sewer system."

Nunzio's breath was hot inside his mask. He could feel the first itching of a prickly red rash beneath the rubber.

"Barely," he replied. "I don't know why we have to meet down here."

"Business, my friend," Deferens insisted. "And speaking of business, how is our last holdout?"

"I spoke to Don Vincenzo this afternoon," Nunzio replied. "He has been in contact with Don Giovani, who will *personally* represent the Sicilian Mafia. He'll be here tomorrow."

Although the defense minister's mouth was obscured, his eyes crinkled happily beyond the wide plastic goggles of his mask. "That is wonderful news," he enthused. "And Don Vincenzo will be coming, too?"

Nunzio shook his head. "No certain answer," he said. "Given what we have planned, he is still hesitant to come."

Deferens's eyes steeled. "No, no, no," he said. "If Don Vincenzo doesn't make an appearance, Don Giovani will not stay. And if Giovani leaves, others might, as well. Forgive me, Nunzio, but your people are deeply suspicious. I must insist that Don Vincenzo come to the city for an hour or two. Don Giovani need only *see* him here. He may leave then."

Nunzio Spumoni shrugged his sweaty shoulders. "I'll call him when I get back to the hotel," he said, exhaling.

Deferens nodded. "Stress that all the major syndicates around the world will have representatives here within the next twenty-four hours. Given the size of their entourages, we should be able to wipe out the upper echelon of nearly every organization in the world, save Camorra." He stepped aside, extending a pale hand. "Speaking of which, we're about finished here. If you are interested."

He ushered Nunzio farther up the tunnel.

A few dozen yards more and they came to a confluence of sewer lines. Their own tunnel split off in three directions. Near the mouth of the nearest aqueduct, a recessed well was built into the slippery wall. In the opening sat an ominous stainless-steel device.

Nunzio Spumoni gulped. Fresh trickles of sweat formed beneath his reed-thin arms, running down his torso.

"Are the others in place, as well?" he asked. He kept his muffled voice low.

Deferens nodded. "We would be ready to go now, if Don Vincenzo desired us to." The minister's eyes grew sadly pleading. "Please, Nunzio, convince him to come." Delicate hands pressed against the breast of his perfect white suit. "Promise him from me that no harm will come to him."

"I will do my best," Nunzio promised. His wide eyes behind his plastic goggles studied the casing. "Although you should know he was not pleased to learn that Mandobar has fled to China. If he is not willing to take the risk for his own plan, why should Don Vincenzo?"

"Why didn't you say, Nunzio?" Deferens said, frowning. "If this is the problem, tell Don Vincenzo there is more than one Mandobar. Ours never left East Africa."

Nunzio Spumoni raised a surprised brow. He'd heard before that some heads of state employed doubles for certain situations. The world had come to know that Saddam Hussein used many. But as far as Nunzio knew, the doubles didn't function as full replacements for high-profile events. Was it possible that the Chinese were so blind they couldn't tell a phony Willie Mandobar from a real one?

"So I may tell Don Vincenzo that Mandobar is here?"

"Absolutely," Deferens insisted. "And please tell your employer that he may leave in complete safety as soon as he is seen here. You will be joining him on the flight back to Naples, presumably?"

Nunzio glanced at the device planted in the moss-covered wall. "I have no desire to be here when it happens."

Deferens caught his troubled look.

"There is nothing to worry about," he promised. "*I* am staying here until not long before, Nunzio. It will be perfectly safe...provided, of course, the wind is blowing in the right direction afterward." His eyes smiled once more.

Another gesture from his delicate arm and the defense minister led Nunzio from the tunnel to his waiting entourage.

"I suppose I really cannot blame you for wanting to leave, Nunzio," Deferens mused as they threaded their way along the slippery path. "It will be safer for you back home. After all, as far as I know, in Italy the terrorists have not yet started using nuclear technology."

Nunzio had to be careful not to lose his footing when Deferens gave him a cheerful slap on his sweaty back.

19

Both Masters of Sinanju had decided that Chief Batubizee's hut was too depressing. Remo and Chiun were strolling amid the pitiful huts of the main Luzu village.

The night was warm. Despite the surrounding miles of drought-ravaged land, a sweet scent carried on the breeze. White moonlight bathed the shabby village.

Once Remo had told the Master of Sinanju all that had occurred to him over the past two days, a thoughtful expression found root on the old man's age-speckled brow.

"Most strange," the wizened Asian nodded. As he padded along the dusty path, slender fingers stroked his thin beard.

"You're telling me," Remo said. "So who is this kid, Little Father? And why is he following me around?"

"I do not know who he is," Chiun admitted. "The scrolls do not speak of a Master Who Never Was. But you first saw him in the company of your wisewoman. Both spoke of your destiny, so we can assume they are both merely acting as vessels of the gods, speaking to you on their behalf.''

On this subject, Remo remained mute. He had once had a healthy skepticism for Chiun's tales of gods interacting with mortal beings, but that was long ago. He had seen too much by now to continue in the role of doubter.

"If they know what the grand plan is for me, I wish they'd just spit it out," Remo muttered. "Everything doesn't have to be so damned cryptic all the time."

"It sounds clear enough to me," Chiun replied. His voice grew soft. "The boy was speaking of your pupil, Remo. The one you will take to train as Master to succeed you."

Remo stopped dead. "He didn't say that." He frowned.

Chiun's smile was sad. "Did he not say it was nearly your time? And the crone told you that the coming years will be difficult for you. Such is the case when a Master takes a pupil. Believe me, *I* know." He resumed walking.

Remo followed beside him in thoughtful silence. Luzu men and women watched them as they passed.

"I never gave any of that much thought," Remo said after a long pause.

"Perhaps that is why the gods found it necessary to dispatch an emissary," Chiun replied.

"I wouldn't even know how to find a pupil." He was speaking to himself now, trying to absorb the ramifications of all that was being said.

"It is traditional for a Master to train his own offspring," Chiun offered.

Remo's eyes widened. "No way," he insisted. "Freya's not having anything to do with any of this."

Chiun's face puckered in displeasure. "Of course not," he said, scowling. "Why would your thoughts fly immediately to your daughter? You have a son, as well."

"Oh." Remo nodded. "Winston."

Winston had been a grown man when Remo met him. Remo's daughter was still a teenager. Both were living with Remo's biological father on an Indian reservation in Arizona.

In truth he did not know why he thought of his daughter and not his son first.

"I don't know about Winston, Little Father," Remo cautioned. "He's not exactly Sinanju material."

"They are not necessarily alone," Chiun replied mysteriously. "Your bull-like rutting habits of years ago has likely given us many more male offspring to choose from. But rather than squander years scouring orphanages around the world for children who have your beady eyes and unpleasant temperament, you could sire another now. We need only return to Sinanju and find a suitable maiden to accept your seed."

Remo shook his head. "I don't like that idea, Little Father," he said. "And not just because most Sinanju maidens look like they've taken one hit too many from the shit end of the ugly stick. I just don't think it's right to breed a baby just to raise for this crazy life. A baby's supposed to be the product of two people's love for each other, not some experiment in assassin's eugenics.''

Chiun raised his bony shoulders in a tiny shrug. "Then you are left with the same choice of finding an heir I was. Go out in the world and trust that fate will supply you with what you need. With any luck, you will do better than I.''

Remo hardly heard the gentle gibe. "It's always been you and me,'' he said. "Can we handle bringing someone else on board this mess?''

"You will be doing all the handling,'' Chiun replied, in a low and even tone. "When the time comes for you to train your successor, I will return to Sinanju.''

Remo froze. "What?''

"Do not pretend you did not know this was the case, Remo,'' Chiun warned. "In all the stories of Sinanju, have you ever heard one in which two generations of Masters were still actively plying their art while one trained a successor?''

"Well, no, but—I never gave it much thought.''

Chiun resumed his slow, reflective pace. "That is because it has never happened,'' he said somberly. "It is not proper for a teacher to remain active when his student takes a pupil of his own. When you find your successor, I will retire to Sinanju, there to sit in the warming sun of the bay and mend the nets while I watch the men go out to fish. In a few years, when your pupil passes the first phase on his path to Masterhood, I will leave the shore and enter the caves near the village for the traditional period of seclusion.''

Remo couldn't believe what he was hearing. Chiun was talking about a ritualistic cleansing of the spirit taken on by all retired Masters of Sinanju. The rite could take several decades, and once he entered into this last phase of his life, Chiun would only emerge from his solitude to die.

With Chiun's words, Remo's heart hollowed.

''I don't want you to just lock yourself off from the world like that,'' he said, quiet emotion straining his voice.

''The world will get along without me,'' Chiun replied. ''Besides, it is tradition.''

''Screw that.'' Remo scowled. ''Can't you just this once break with tradition and do what *you* want? I mean, God, there can't be another Master in the history of Sinanju who's been more slavish to those stupid scrolls. I think your ancestors would forgive you one lapse.''

Chiun's face grew serious. ''While I have done my best to uphold our traditions, it would not be my first and only sin were I to avoid the period of seclusion,'' he intoned. ''When the time comes, I will do as I must.'' He shook his head, dismissing all they had said. ''This is not the time for this conversation. The gods have merely endeavored to plant this thought in your mind. We could have many more years before it becomes time for you to act on what you have learned.'' Though his words were meant to bolster Remo's spirits, his eyes told a different story.

Chiun found a nice flat rock beyond the last straggling huts of the village. Scampering up it, he settled cross-legged to the boulder, encouraging his pupil to do so, as well. They sat across from each other, father and son.

For Remo, the whole world suddenly seemed very small and very precious. Like the wizened figure that now faced him—the one person on the entire face of the benighted planet who had ever given him anything of any real meaning.

Chiun's laugh lines were deep creases in aged leather. His once white hair had, in the autumn of his life, given way to yellow. To Remo, in that moment, his teacher had never seemed quite so old or frail.

Nearby, the clawing branches of the baobab raked the dirt. The machete still protruded from its cracked trunk.

"Getting a point across?" Remo asked gently.

"Sometimes it is the only way to get fools to listen," the Master of Sinanju replied simply.

A few women scraped the shattered tree's pulp for water. Moon shadows played across the children at their ankles. As they went about their work in the dark, they didn't seem as malnourished as they had when first he arrived. A sudden peal of laughter carried back to them on the warm breeze.

Given all they had just discussed, there seemed an air of finality to the world. Remo resolved to enjoy the moment.

"This reminds me of the Loni," he commented as he watched the Luzu children.

"Why?" Chiun asked. "Because that was an African tribe and this is another? This continent is littered with the bones of former empires, Remo."

"Maybe." Remo nodded. "But I remember that time. You practically had to set yourself on fire to fulfill some crazy prophecy." He looked at his teacher, his eyes level. "I won't let you do that again."

Chiun soaked in the warmth of his pupil's tone. "Your concern is touching but unnecessary. There will be no purification by fire. In that other time you mention, there was a Sinanju contract that had not been satisfied. Our ties to the Luzu are different."

"How so?" Remo asked. "A contract's a contract."

"Ordinarily, that is true," the Master of Sinanju said. "Do you remember, Remo, the story of Master Nuk?"

"Nuk," Remo said, considering. "He succeed Koo?"

Chiun's heart swelled with pride. He had remembered. There were times when Remo's devotion to the history of the House of Sinanju nearly matched his own.

"Yes," the old man said. "Do you remember his tale?"

"Wasn't much to remember." He began repeating the story by rote. "'And, lo, Nuk the Unwise did travel to the belly of the dark beast. There he found a people in despair and did nurture them to greatness. Eventually, they paid.'" He shrugged. "That's all you ever taught me."

"That was all that was written in the *official* records of our House," Chiun replied. "However, the Master has access to other histories."

"You're always saying that," Remo chided. "When do I get a chance to look at the top-secret stuff?"

"Are you Master yet?" Chiun asked aridly.

His words brought back their earlier conversation. "No," Remo said softly.

"Then be quiet." Resettling his robes, Chiun took on the pose of teacher. "Now, the people from whom Nuk sought employment were the ancestors of the Luzu. It was a dark time for our House. During Nuk's tenure as Master, there were few emperors in need of his services. The great treasure house in the village, while full from the efforts of previous Masters, was in danger. There was talk that the babies might one day have to be sent home to the sea."

"But there's tons of dough there," Remo suggested. "It'd hold the whole village for about a billion years."

"And at the end of that time?" Chiun said, his brow arched.

Remo sighed. "I know. Always plan ahead."

"That is correct," Chiun said with a crisp nod. "And so when the normal avenues failed to yield work for him, Nuk did travel to the land of the Luzu, and made he of these impoverished nomads a powerful nation."

"How's that?" Remo asked. "If they didn't have any money, why would Nuk come within a country mile of them? I thought we only ever went where the cash was.''

The old Korean was growing uncomfortable. ''Nuk took the promise of future earnings from the Luzu. For in the hills near these simple tribesmen were diamonds more flawless than the finest in the Sinanju treasure house. These early Luzu were not advanced far enough to mine the gems, and a Master of Sinanju does not dig. Therefore, Nuk did shepherd the Luzu to greatness. Over time they did grow and prosper to the point where they were able to mine the diamonds from the rocky hills. Nuk was paid and went on his way.''

Remo had been listening to the account with interest.

''Sounds like a pretty savvy move to me,'' he commented with an appreciative nod. ''Small investment, big payoff.''

Chiun gave an annoyed cluck. ''We are not a house of financial brokers,'' he complained. ''Payment for a contract year is due in full, up front. Preferably gold. We invest not in stock markets, but in the future of Sinanju. Anything could have happened to the Luzu during the years Nuk nurtured them. Famine, war. A single plague could have wiped out all that he worked for.''

''I suppose. But it didn't. Nuk got his payday.''

''That is not the point. Nuk should have found an employer who paid immediately. His years with the Luzu created a dependency of them on us. He even resurrected the long-abandoned practice of offering weapons training to his charges due to the guilt he felt. Because of Nuk the Unwise, we are responsible for these people as we are for no other.''

"Nuk the Unwise," Remo mused. "Back when you made me learn the names of all the masters, I always thought that one sounded a little harsh."

"Harsh, perhaps. But well earned," Chiun said.

"Probably, from our mercenary standpoint. But the guy worked hard to be a Master of Sinanju. We went through it, we know what it's like. So what if he screwed up a little along the way? He got paid in the end. But that doesn't matter. The final kick in the teeth to poor Nuk is someone scribbling 'unwise' in front of his name in the scrolls."

"Pray that your pupil does not give you a worse honorific," Chiun said somberly.

While Remo didn't want to think of his future pupil right now, Chiun's last words caused his ears to prick up.

"You mean the pupil gets to pick the honorific of his Master?" he pressed.

A look of flickering horror passed swiftly across the parchment face of the Master of Sinanju. He quickly banished it far beneath a bland veneer of tan wrinkles.

"I am not certain," he said vaguely. "I have been forced to nursemaid you so far beyond the point of my own retirement that I forget that particular rule."

The prospect of Chiun's retiring forced all lightness from Remo's tone. "So what's our story here?" he asked. "Because of Nuk's empire-building, we've got to come back here at the drop of a hat whenever they ask?"

"No. The situation must be grave enough to threaten the Luzu Empire. Only then is Sinanju bound to act."

"Some empire," Remo said mockingly. "Ten thousand stick figures and one big fat chief. He's got a hell of a nerve, by the way. Looking like that when the rest of his people look like they're one empty plate away from the cemetery."

"You worry still about the injustices of the world." Chiun sighed. "I will be pleased when this sickness finally runs its course."

"If getting over Master's disease means I'll start subscribing to Batubizee's 'let 'em eat cake' philosophy, then I pray to every god you've got that I *never* get better."

A shocked intake of air. When he glanced over, Remo found a look of pure horror on his teacher's face.

"Remo, still your tongue," Chiun whispered. Troubled eyes scanned the night sky. He tracked the course of a shooting star with a deeply worried look. "You must beg forgiveness for your ill-chosen words," he warned.

"What?" Remo frowned. "Chiun, I—"

"Remo, *please,*" Chiun begged. His eyes were desperate.

Rare were such entreaties from the Master of Sinanju.

Remo regarded the clear African sky. "Sorry," he said to the stars.

Chiun waited a long time, as if he expected the wrath of the gods to rain fire on both their heads.

When the heavens remained silent, he turned his attention back to his pupil.

"It is not wise to tempt the gods in such a way," the old man offered, his voice a respectful whisper. His tone implored understanding.

"I'm sorry, Little Father," Remo said. And this apology he meant.

The tiny Asian nodded. "As for Batubizee, he looks as he does because he is chief. He was not chosen because he did not perspire on television and another would-be chief did, or because females wished to lay with him more than some other or because he was an inch taller or lied about experiencing the pain of his subjects. He is chief because he was born to be chief. I do not expect you to understand, but as the future standard bearer of our House, it is important that you at least *feign* understanding."

It was as if he were trying to will Remo to understand.

Remo nodded tightly. "I know my obligations."

Chiun could sense his pupil's heavy heart.

The old Korean suddenly held out a bony hand to all that was visible of the once mighty Luzu nation. Moonlight dappled the savannah. Nearby, the toppled foundation of an ancient building jutted from the wind-worn dirt.

"Remember that the worries of those who made this empire have long since turned to dust. The woes that burden you will one day be the same. You flutter here and there, hoping that each moment will bring you happiness. But a mere moment cannot be so powerful. It is but the lost blink of an eye, forever locked in time. True joy comes from within. Do not struggle so hard to find it, and perhaps it will find you."

"Sometimes I've thought I had," Remo admitted gently. "But every time things seem to get okay for me, the world comes along and kicks me in the nuts."

Chiun offered a flickering smile. "At those points, my son, it is always important to kick back harder." His eyes darted over his pupil's shoulder. "Your ride is here."

When Remo turned, curious, he saw that Bubu was picking his way around the broken baobab. The young man had changed back into the suit he'd worn at the airport.

Remo noted that Bubu was lean, but not emaciated. His stride was that of a confident feline. There seemed a quiet grace to him as the young man stopped beside the rock on which sat the two Sinanju Masters.

"If you wish to return to Bachsburg tonight, Master Remo, the chief has said I may take you," Bubu said with a polite bow. "Provided you are staying, Master Chiun."

Remo turned to his mentor. "Chiun?"

The old man shook his head. "I cannot go," he said.

"Okay," Remo said, scampering down the rock. "You're on. Name's Remo, by the way. You can cut out that Master stuff."

The Luzu offered another short bow. "I am Bubu."

Remo's eyes took on an amused glint. "You're kidding."

The native seemed puzzled. "No, that is my name."

"Well, make sure you stay away from my pick-a-nick basket," Remo warned.

"Do not embarrass me," Chiun hissed, scurrying off the rock.

To Bubu, he said, "Pay no attention to my son. Although he considers himself a wit, he is only half-right."

Remo wondered why Chiun would worry so much about the feelings of a common Luzu native.

As the three men started back through the village, Remo leaned close to the Master of Sinanju.

"I don't know the customs around here," he ventured out of the corner of his mouth. "Should I pay my respects to the chief before I go?"

"I will do so for you," Chiun droned. "With the tact you have displayed since arriving, one goodbye from you and the House of Sinanju will be at war with the Luzu Empire."

20

The big bulletproof limousine with its black-tinted windows stole like a sleek, silent panther through the streets of Bachsburg. In the rear seat, a lone figure sat.

Bachsburg was alive, vibrant.

A million lights washed over the modern miracle of a city that man had carved out of the inhospitable African wilderness. To Mandobar, it seemed almost possible to reach out and feel the night pulse of that great metropolis. The world's new crime mecca.

At a streetlight, Mandobar lazily scanned the activity taking place beyond the limo's smoky windows. There were whores down the block. Nearer, a man had been stabbed in the belly by a mugger. The sound of an ambulance swelled in the distance.

All of this would end soon. Soon, this city would be ruled with an iron fist. Petty crimes would cease as the energy of a nation was directed outward. With a vengeance, East Africa would foster *real* criminal activity. All around the world.

The next day, the remainder of the crime lords would descend on the city. In the late afternoon— under twenty hours away—they would be whisked off to the village of bungalows that had been constructed at the periphery of Luzuland. For safety's sake, they would be told. Little did any of them know that they would never return.

Mandobar smiled at the thought.

So many dead. Massive piles of charred corpses. No. Less than that.

Mere stains in the sand. Like the ash left in Russell Copefeld's wake.

The leading criminals of the world. All dead. Crime syndicates everywhere with no one to command them. A power structure already in place in Bachsburg, with Mandobar at its helm. Of course, not without help.

On the phone earlier this afternoon, Don Giovani of the Sicilian Mafia had been quite anxious. Don Vincenzo of Camorra had insisted that Don Giovani be in Bachsburg for the inaugural festivities. Giovani knew what was going to happen in that little village on the outskirts of the dead Luzu Empire, and so did not wish to be anywhere near East Africa. But Vincenzo had said that Camorra would not attend if the Sicilian Mafia did not. Giovani had relented.

Mandobar had done a good job soothing the Mafia leader's concerns.

Camorra would come, Mandobar had said. It couldn't afford not to. And well before the appointed time, Mandobar would personally see to it that the Mafia was safely out of the area. After all, they were going to be future business partners in the new East Africa.

The car phone buzzed to life. Outside the limousine, insects danced around streetlights. Eyes on the flitting bugs, Mandobar answered the phone.

The coolly efficient voice of L. Vas Deferens spoke without preamble. "I have received word from Nunzio Spumoni that Don Giovani will be attending after all," East Africa's defense minister announced.

In the dark of the back seat, Mandobar smiled.

"I know."

Deferens did not attempt to hide his surprise. "You do? May I ask how?"

"I have spoken to Don Giovani today."

"Ah..." A hint of confusion. Concern?

It was nice for Deferens to be confounded on occasion. Until that moment, the defense minister had known nothing of Mandobar's private conversations with the Mafia leader.

"What about Don Vincenzo?" Mandobar asked. "Giovani is concerned that Camorra will back out."

"Nunzio assures me that he can convince him to come," L. Vas Deferens said. "I believe in the end he will. After all, he cannot afford not to."

"What about the Luzu?" Mandobar asked. "I don't need that headache now, too."

"I've sent men to Luzuland to neutralize Batubizee. I expect them back with good news by tomorrow morning. As far as today's incident at the palace, it has been contained for now. I cannot promise that word will not leak out, however. There were too many killed and too many involved in the cover-up. We have a couple of days at best."

Mandobar sat back heavily in the car seat. "This is all the fault of that aborigine Batubizee. Things were going perfectly up until now."

An image of the Luzu chief came to mind, a flaming, gasoline-filled tire around his fat neck. As quickly as it came, it went. The streets of Bachsburg again stretched out beside the gleaming black sides of the speeding limo.

"I want him dead, Deferens," Mandobar said menacingly.

"The man I hired for the job is a real find," the defense minister said with uncharacteristic enthusiasm. "He actually wished to go to Luzuland with only one guide. I insisted that he take a few more men."

"Alone against those savages? He sounds a bigger fool than Batubizee."

"You have not met him," Deferens said with irritating confidence.

"The Luzu may boil him in a pot to feed their starving bellies for all I care. Just as long as Batubzee is dead by tomorrow. Keep me informed." Mandobar hung up the phone.

One man against the entire Luzu nation. Alone in the back of the limousine, Mandobar snorted derisively. Deferens could be so limited sometimes.

That had been the defense minister's problem since the outset. Deferens was ambitious, but not creative. He would never think beyond the initial plan to turn Bachsburg and eventually all of East Africa into a haven for crime.

Mandobar, on the other hand, was not limited like

the prim little defense minister. The plan to get the crime leaders to gather here was just a ruse.

Leaning back in the car seat once more, Mandobar realized that Chief Batubizee would most likely be dead by the following day, one way or another.

If the explosion didn't get him, the fallout would.

Picturing mound upon mound of whimpering, screaming Luzus covered in sheets of bleeding, peeling radioactive flesh, Mandobar's smile returned.

The grin never left the fat face for the entire ride back to the tiny bungalow village.

21

Savannah faded to shanty villages, which in turn eventually became the outskirts of Bachsburg.

Remo had remembered the carved stone figure in his pocket only when they'd passed the spot where he had seen the young Korean boy. He had no idea why he had forgotten to mention something so important to Chiun. It sat in his pocket now, next to baby Karen's crucifix.

Depression swelled anew as he thought of both children and what each represented. By the time they reached the city with its tall buildings, windows gleaming in the early-morning sun, he felt more miserable than ever.

Bubu steered the Luzu chief's Suburban through the spotty postdawn traffic.

"Where does Master Remo wish to go?" Bubu asked agreeably as they headed into the heart of the city.

Remo had tried a number of times during their long night's drive to get the native to drop the "master," but the younger man seemed determined to remain respectful.

"You can drop me off at my hotel," Remo said. "They should have the floor mopped up by now."

Bubu apparently knew his way around town. When Remo gave him the address, the Luzu native didn't need to ask directions.

"Looks like most of the delinquents are sleeping it off," Remo commented as they drove past empty sidewalks.

"Soldiers began clearing the streets last night. I have heard that this is an important day for Mandobar," Bubu said seriously. "According to Luzu who have fled their ancestral land to live in this place, today is the day that the wicked chiefs descend on this city for some great meeting."

Remo raised a surprised eyebrow. "No kidding?"

Bubu nodded. "May I tell you something for your ears alone?" he asked.

Remo was struck by the native's innocence. He barely knew his passenger yet he was already willing to trust him.

Remo nodded. "What's on your mind?"

"Our chief feels that the problems Luzuland now faces were created by Mandobar here in Bachsburg. But the danger this city poses existed long before Mandobar. It has been such since the whites came here centuries ago. Even with Mandobar gone, I fear that the threat from Bachsburg to our way of life will live on."

Remo knew he was right. The world had long ago moved away from the simple life the Luzu once lived. Times had changed. And the tribe hadn't kept up with that change.

Bubu's face was deadly serious. "There are times I wish the Luzu gods of old would reach down from on high and crush this wicked city in their hands," the native intoned.

Remo's jaw clenched. "That wouldn't be such a bad idea right around now," he admitted.

"You agree with me?" Bubu asked, surprised. His eyes darted from the road. "But you are from the West."

"I don't mean we should stomp out the whole Western world," Remo explained. "Your problem is with the modern age—mine's with the rats who are ruining the world for decent people. The guys responsible for a lot of the misery going on out there are here in Bachsburg. If this one city was wiped out today, we'd be a long way to curing the troubles of the whole world."

Bubu studied Remo's troubled profile. "No matter the reason, we both wish for the same thing," the native said with quiet sadness. "That which is impossible."

The silence remained between them for the rest of the ride to Remo's hotel.

Stopped at a traffic light one block from the hotel, Bubu made a sudden surprised exclamation.

"It is one of them!" he barked. Eyes wide, the native was looking down a side street.

Remo glanced down the narrow lane.

A city truck was parked near the curb. Yellow hazard posts slung with matching tape were positioned around a hole in the roadway next to the truck. The heavy flat disk of a manhole cover sat nearby.

Bubu was looking at neither truck nor hole, but at the three men loitering nearby. Each wore matching powder-blue coveralls and hard hats. Tool belts were slung around their waists. On their backs, an oval patch identified them as Bachsburg city workers.

When the streetlight changed, Bubu didn't even see it.

"One of who?" Remo asked, peering at the workers.

"The men Chief Batubizee spoke of," Bubu whispered excitedly. "Those who we followed into the sewers, only to have half of our party slain."

"*We?*" Remo asked. "You were there?"

Bubu wasn't listening. He threw the truck into park, fumbling over the seat. When he spun for the door, spear and machete were in hand.

"Whoa," Remo said, grabbing the native's wrist before he could spring the driver's-side door.

"Release me!" Bubu cried. "I must avenge my tribesmen!"

"Think you could avenge a little louder?" Remo griped. "I don't think they can hear you in Liberia."

Over Bubu's protestations, Remo slipped the truck back into drive. As he flicked Bubu's foot off the brake, the big truck rolled forward. Once they'd passed through the intersection and were out of sight of the city workers, Remo took his toe off the gas.

"You sure it's the same guy?" he asked, slipping the truck back into park.

Bubu nodded. "He was there that day. He once worked for the defense ministry."

"Defense ministry to sewer workers?" Remo asked. "Remind me not to look for temp work through his agency."

When Remo popped his door, Bubu jumped out the other side. Luzu weapons in hand, he hurried after Remo.

The truck was still there, but the sewer workers were gone. Hurrying to the roped-off manhole, Remo cocked an ear.

The distant echoing sounds of the men carried back through the stone tunnels.

"I don't suppose I can convince you to stay topside?" Remo asked.

Bubu's jaw was firmly set. "I owe my brothers vengeance," he insisted. His hands clenched weapons.

"Didn't think so." Remo sighed. "Okay, but stay out of the way and keep the dying to a minimum. Chief Jabba the Hut doesn't like me enough already without having his favorite guard buy it on my watch."

At this, Bubu seemed about to say something more, but Remo didn't give him a chance. Snapping his ankles together, Remo slipped like a silent shadow down into the inky well.

Grabbing his spear and machete close, Bubu scurried down the ladder after him.

THE REAL East Africa was dead.

For F. U. Gudgel, the country of his birth had

fallen victim to internal meddlers and international do-gooders.

East Africa was now a zombie. It stumbled around wrapped in its familiar geography and name, but inside it was rotten to the core. A dead country with a *mooka* president.

Mooka. The *mookas* wouldn't even let you use that word anymore. Because the *mookas* ran the country. Because the gutless whites had caved to *mooka* pressure and turned it over to them. F. U. Gudgel fervently wished all the *mookas* would join old East Africa in its grave.

Before the collapse of the old structure, Gudgel had been a member of the defense ministry. But sometime around the point when the last white president, O. C. Stiggs, handed the reins of power over to Willie Mandobar, someone in the new government had gotten it into his fool head to make East Africa nuclear free. The nukes were ordered dismantled. And almost the entire defense ministry was summarily tossed out in the streets. Replaced by *mookas*.

When the transfer of power was complete in the early 1990s, F. U. Gudgel became a former government official with no experience in the job market. Gudgel had been forced to find work—not an easy task for a man who had risen from enlistee in the East African army to a position with the Advanced Projects Agency of the Ministry of Defense.

When he was faced with chronic unemployment, Gudgel's savior had come in the unlikely form of Minister L. Vas Deferens.

Deferens had been the ultimate boss of Gudgel and the others at the A.P.A. He was thought by most to be a slippery bureaucrat who had betrayed his race by cozying up to Willie Mandobar when the former political prisoner became president of East Africa. When Mandobar retired and Kmpali had assumed the presidency, Deferens had remained in place. The defense minister had the cold outward appearance of a typical *mooka*-lover. But as F. U. Gudgel learned, the pale man in the perfect white suit was more complex than he seemed.

Deferens had to have had this planned right from the start. As the old East Africa was in its death throes, the man charged with the defense of the nation was working diligently to endanger it like none other before him.

In the months following its dissolution, Deferens had reassembled many of the old Advanced Projects Agency personnel. Some were experts in the field of nuclear technology, while others, like Gudgel, were men with strong backs and strong opinions. All of these men were of the same mind when it came to Mandobar and the rest of the *mookas*.

A.P.A. was not dismantled after all. It merely went underground. Literally.

As F. U. Gudgel and his companions made their careful way through the sewers beneath the heart of Bachsburg, Gudgel wished that ''underground'' meant the old Luzu diamond mines and not these slime-filled catacombs.

This early in the day, the water level was low. The system had been flushed from the night before, and chemicals for decomposition had been pumped into the old aqueducts.

Gudgel kept his breathing shallow as he picked his way along the slippery walkway. The plain white masks he and the others wore did little to ward off the stench of shit mixed with chemicals.

One of the smooth rocks of the walkway had come loose. The first man, a scientist, kicked it into the river lest someone trip and fall. It struck water with a mighty splash.

"Watch it!" Gudgel growled as sewer water flew up, staining his pant cuffs.

Cursing, he shook his leg in disgust as the small group made its way up a side tunnel.

Gudgel's anger faded when they stopped before an alcove.

Nuclear technology in East Africa had developed further than the world community knew. Although the world was led to believe that the entire East African nuclear arsenal was dismantled, such was not the case. The proof was right before their eyes.

The scientist in the group pulled a Geiger counter from his tool belt. He ran it up and down the stainless-steel device secreted in a fissure in the wall. The handheld counter let off a series of crackling pops.

The scientist tsked unhappily. "I figured," he commented to the third man in the group. "Leaking."

Behind the others, Gudgel's ears instantly perked up. "Radiation?" he asked, worried.

"Nonlethal levels," the scientist assured him.

"Should we seal it?" the third man asked.

"Not necessary. In eighteen hours, a radiation leak this small will be the least of Bachsburg's problems."

"Maybe we should ask Deferens," Gudgel suggested. He had taken a few steps back from the leaky hydrogen bomb.

"No," the scientist said. "It will work." Gudgel missed the wink he gave the third man. "Of course, there is the slight risk of impotence after short-term exposure."

Gudgel didn't stick around long enough to see if the man was joking. Hands pressed firmly to his lap, he turned and ran down the tunnel.

The remaining two men laughed and shook their heads.

"Let's catch him before he accidentally sets one of them off," the scientist said.

Leaving the first nuclear bomb in its cranny, the two men hurried after their panicked comrade.

THE BACHSBURG SEWER system was a confusing labyrinth. Plastic-encased droplights were strung like weak Japanese lanterns along the slippery walls. The yellow glow sickly illuminated the stream of sewage that ran beside the path.

As soon as he'd entered the tunnel, Remo had found three soggy sets of footprints pressed into the black moss that sprouted along the platform walkway.

Once he'd come down from the street, Bubu had scampered out before Remo. Trailing the native,

Remo was impressed with the way the young man carried himself. The Luzu moved confidently through the catacomb-like sewers.

Bubu's keen eyes had detected the footprints in the moss as well, which was unusual for someone of normal vision.

Only once did Bubu hesitate. At two intersecting tunnels, he glanced back in confusion. When Remo jerked a thumb right, Bubu struck off in that direction.

That was it. No hesitation. No questioning. He simply looked to Remo for direction and then went.

Watching the native in action, Remo wondered if Chiun's gods might not have brought him to East Africa at this time for their own purpose. While pondering a possibility that the day before would have seemed preposterous to him, Remo became aware of the three men closing in on their position from an adjacent tunnel.

One was ahead of the others. All were far enough away to not be a problem. Remo was moving to overtake Bubu to get him out of harm's way when a shout issued from out the long tunnel far away.

"Gudgel, slow down!"

That was all Bubu needed. Without looking back to Remo, he ducked around the corner and raced down the tunnel.

Remo flew into a full sprint, racing after the native. By the time he tore around the corner and into the gaping mouth of the tunnel, he was too late.

A man stood far down the platform, automatic in

hand, face angry. The explosion from his barrel cracked off the stone walls of the sewer.

Between Remo and the gunman stood the young Luzu native.

The bullet struck Bubu with a meaty thwack. One hand sprang open as he spun in place. His spear clattered to the stone walkway.

For a moment, his eyes met Remo's. Where there should have been a look of shock or fear, there seemed only calm acceptance. He blinked and was gone.

Momentum whirled him off the ledge. Still clutching his machete, Bubu spun into open air and plunged into the river of waste, disappearing below the water without a trace.

Remo didn't slow his pace. Loafers gliding over stone, he ran down the passage.

Far down the tunnel, F. U. Gudgel whipped his gun up. Leveling it on Remo, he fired.

He was stunned when the bullet missed.

Before he could squeeze off another round, Remo reached Bubu's dropped spear. He scooped it up in one hand.

To F.U., it looked as if the primitive weapon leaped off the ground and onto Remo's fingertips. No sooner had it brushed the pads of his fingers than it was airborne.

The impulse to flee could not hope to match the rocketing speed of the spear. As the first sense of danger sparked in the limited brain of F. U. Gudgel, the weapon found its mark.

With a speed and accuracy far greater than any mere bullet, the spear slammed the East African in the dead center of his chest. Feet left the ground, and he was carried back on the shaft. When spear point met wall, the wooden tip buried itself in the mossy stone.

Gudgel hung slack from the quivering shaft of the spear, his toes dangling to the catwalk.

And in his brain's last functioning moment, as the blood from his shattered chest cavity filled his mouth and lungs, F. U. Gudgel recognized the irony of his being killed with a *mooka* weapon. He almost laughed. Instead, he died.

Farther back, Remo saw the other two bogus sewer workers frozen in shock. They had watched all that had just transpired with mounting astonishment.

As Gudgel twitched his last, they seemed to find sudden focus. Spinning, the two ran back in the direction from whence they'd come.

Remo had taken but one step toward them when he heard a noise to his left. When he glanced into the river, he was just in time to see Bubu break the surface.

"Master Remo!" the native gasped before slipping back below the greasy waves.

Remo could hear the two fleeing men in the distance. They slipped on rock as they ran. There came the sudden hollow metal scraping of a manhole cover being pushed away.

Remo spun back to the river.

"Damn, damn, double damn," he groused as he kicked off his loafers.

He was still cursing when he dove from the platform. He struck the water without so much as a splash.

22

Night shadows had long since engulfed the East Coast, yet Harold W. Smith was still at his post.

A half-empty foam cup of chicken broth, scavenged from the Folcroft cafeteria, had been pushed to one side of his desk. The soup was cool now, as was the mournful breeze that carried in off Long Island Sound. World-weary eyes studied the latest information from East Africa.

They were coming from all over the world. Japan, China, Russia. North and South America. Representatives of criminal groups from around the globe were either en route or were already on the ground in Bachsburg.

In its nearly four-decade history, CURE had encountered at various times different attempts to consolidate crime in a particular location. Bay City, New Jersey and the small nation of Scambia, most notably. But this latest enterprise in East Africa put all others Smith had seen to shame.

His computer automatically pulled the names of those with criminal affiliations currently in Bachsburg, dumping them into a single file. Setting the automatic-scroll function, Smith watched the three columns of names slip through the electronic ether that was his monitor. Like a stone thrown in a pond, the ripples of their evil reached out to encompass the entire planet.

He didn't know how long he watched the list go by. Eventually, he pulled his exhausted eyes away from the screen. As the names continued to roll beneath the surface of his desk, Smith removed his rimless glasses. He let his tired hand drop beside his worn leather chair.

So many names. An ocean of crime.

Smith felt like the captain of a sinking ship, trying desperately to spoon out water even while saboteurs punched more holes in his riddled, rusted hull.

During their time together at CURE, it was Remo who battled cyclical bouts of depression. Smith had come to his job with a level of professional detachment that had served him well in his battle against the evils of the world. Yet at that moment, alone in his shadowy Folcroft office, Smith allowed a creeping sense of doubt to invade his thoughts.

Maybe Remo was right.

Smith was not a young man any longer. From the OSS to the CIA to CURE, he had given his life for ideals that seemed to no longer matter to the current generation. In his three-piece gray suit, locked away in his austere office with his unwavering patriotism and selflessness, Smith was an anachronism. And if he could no longer understand the world he was in, perhaps it was time to turn the reins over to those who did. Let the younger men of this generation take up the cause.

There was no doubt that CURE had enjoyed many successes during its history. But could he say that America was a better place than when he'd started?

When he first came to Folcroft, most of the cars in the employee lot were left unlocked. By the 1970s, if a car wasn't locked it was generally by accident. Today, the annoying electronic whoop of car alarms issuing occasionally from the sanitarium parking lot was demonstration enough of how far downhill America had gone. A minor symptom of a much larger disease. And the infection spread to the world.

Lost in dark thoughts, Smith hardly heard the muffled jangle of the telephone. Feeling his fatigue deepen, he reached into his bottom desk drawer to answer the special White House line.

"Yes, Mr. President," the CURE director exhaled.

"Smith, what do you know about the situation in East Africa?"

The familiar hoarse voice of America's chief executive held an irritated edge. Smith knew why.

Over the past two years, this president had on multiple occasions attempted to use CURE in his political self-interest. The incorruptible Smith had steadfastly refused. As a result of his unwavering ethics, Smith had lately been treated to a steady diet of hostility from the chief executive. His relationship with the current president had deteriorated greatly over the past few months.

"There is an attempt to consolidate criminal interests there, Mr. President,'' Smith replied, puzzled. ''Frankly, I'm a little surprised that you even know of it.''

''I have my sources,'' the President answered vaguely. ''What about those guys who work for you?''

Smith frowned. ''I have dispatched my people to look into the situation,'' he admitted.

''Whoa,'' the President rasped angrily. ''They're already *there?* Dammit, why didn't you tell me you were on this?''

Smith carefully replaced his glasses on his patrician nose. ''I did not see the need, sir,'' he replied cautiously. ''I remind you that assignments are decided on at my discretion. You have no oversight of CURE beyond suggesting assignments and disbanding this organization, should you deem it appropriate to do so.''

''Stop doing that all the time,'' the President snapped. ''I'm sick of you telling me what I can and can't do with your group. What have they done there so far?''

''Not much,'' Smith answered truthfully. ''It is a complicated situation made all the more so by the involvement of certain key government figures.''

The President exhaled relief. ''Then I caught you in time. Thank God. Smith, I don't know what you have planned for the folks in charge there, but there are a few little people who should remain off the list when it comes time to…you know.'' He rattled off a short list. ''Indonesians, South Americans…hell, a whole shitload of Chinese. They're, well, FOBs that need to be taken care of. I'd appreciate it if your people were hands-off on them. I'll fax you the names. What's your number there?''

Smith closed his eyes, calling up reserves of patience that were nearly tapped out. ''Mr. President—'' he began.

''Now don't take that tone with me, Smith,'' the President snapped, already knowing where the CURE director was heading. ''I'm looking at legal bills up the yin-yang when I leave office, plus the banks won't trust me with a loan and I want a West Coast house. A *nice* one. With separate bedrooms, wall-to-wall shag and maybe a mirror or two on the ceiling. You know, tasteful. Those folks are just friends—*generous* friends—who somehow took an unlucky turn and wound up in East Africa at an unfortunate time. So before you unleash those two corpse-making machines of yours, I'm ordering you to shepherd my poor, wayward friends and their house-buying wallets out of harm's way.''

Alone in his office, Smith shook his head. ''I can only reiterate that which I have told you before,'' he said flatly. ''CURE does not exist for your personal use. And I might add, Mr. President, that I am tired of having to tell you so.''

He could almost feel the hot breath of the President hissing through the receiver. When he spoke, his voice was a low threat. ''You won't have to tell me much longer.''

That was it. No further arguments. The line went dead in Smith's hand.

With a deep breath, Smith replaced the cherry-red receiver in its cradle, sliding the drawer slowly back into place. His cracked leather chair creaked protest as he straightened. At least the call had been short.

Thinking of America's current chief executive, Smith could not help but realize how out of touch he actually was. Smith was a relic from another age, locked behind the protective glass of his Folcroft display case. In this new age, it was easy to lose one's idealism.

Tired eyes found his cursor, winking like a subterranean orb beneath the surface of his desk.

The list of names had stopped scrolling. Visible on the screen were dozens of names beginning with Z. Nearly all the men were connected with some Russian Mob group or another. All brought together by one man.

Smith had been one of the millions around the world who had greeted with optimism Willie Mandobar's release from prison and election to the East African presidency. Although he hadn't governed well, he had done so to the best of his abilities. He was by all accounts a decent man. Now this.

Of course, Mandobar wasn't the sole author of this plot. With the former East African president away, Defense Minister Deferens seemed to be running the show. Mandobar's trust in his subordinate had to have been absolute, for the two men hadn't been in contact the entire time Mandobar had been in China. Indeed, the bulk of the calls coming back from the presidential mission were from President Kmpali's staff to the Ministry of Foreign Affairs and other official government arms. On the surface, there was nothing untoward that could be connected to official East Africa.

It was all just a weak cover. And with his supporters in the international press, Willie Mandobar might just make it stick. After all, he was no longer president. He could not be blamed for the extracurricular activities of current renegade government officials.

Although Smith had initially rejected the idea of sending Remo after Mandobar, he was beginning to question his decision. But Mandobar wasn't there. And for now, there seemed to be one man in charge.

Remo had been seen in public with L. Vas Deferens, but as yet Smith hadn't heard a single account of the incident. Remo was probably right. There would be no risk to security were he to take out the defense minister.

And in a moment of tired decision, in the dark of his Folcroft office, the amber light of his monitor casting skeletal shadows across his gaunt, gray face, Harold Smith decided to send Remo against Deferens after all. With him neutralized, perhaps this insane scheme would collapse.

Decision made, Smith backed out of his computer, shutting off the system. He blinked as the light winked out.

With a gnarled hand, he found his leather briefcase in his desk's footwell. Tired bones creaked as he rose to his feet and crossed to the light switch. His back ached.

Feeling every bit his age, Harold W. Smith quietly left his office.

23

The instant he arced below the surface of the filthy water, Remo extended his senses to their maximum.

Momentum had already carried him partway downstream. He found Bubu farther ahead. The native's heartbeat was strong. He seemed to be clinging to something jutting from the smooth bottom of the aqueduct.

The water was slick against Remo's skin. Trying not to think about what he was swimming through, he frog-kicked, hard. Eyes screwed tightly shut, he shot through the water with the focus of a laser-guided torpedo.

When his hand grabbed the Luzu native's collar, Bubu began to struggle viciously. The sharpened steel of his machete sliced through the water.

Impatiently, Remo caught the blade, knocking it out of Bubu's hand. It shot to the surface. Remo pulled Bubu away from the twisted metal bar he'd been holding on to. With a kick, he tugged the native up through the weak current.

The Luzu thrashed in his arms only until they broke the surface and he was able to see who it was who had dragged him from the river bottom.

"Master Remo!" Bubu spluttered, blinking greasy water from his eyes.

"Who the hell'd you think it was?" Remo griped as they pulled themselves up the slippery stone wall. He had to help Bubu along. "And you've got a lot of nerve not being dead. Why'd you yell to me like that?"

Kneeling on the platform, Bubu's face beamed innocence. "I was warning you of the man with the gun," he replied. "And I did not know if the men would come in after me. They have killed Luzus before."

"Don't tempt me," Remo grumbled. His body had automatically shut down his pores before he hit the water, but his clothes were a dripping mess.

Bubu climbed to his feet beside Remo. A tear of the fabric at his shoulder showed where the bullet had grazed him. He was looking around the platform.

"Oh, my," Bubu announced all at once.

Remo tracked his gaze to the spot where F. U. Gudgel hung slack from the wall.

Bubu hurried over to the dead East African. When he tried yanking his spear free, it failed to budge. Awed eyes searched for his missing machete. He found it half-buried in the ceiling of the cavern.

"Do you possess skills greater than the Master of Sinanju?" he asked in wonder as Remo came over to him.

"Lesson number one," Remo snarled as he

pulled Bubu's spear from the wall. *"No one* possesses skills greater than the Master of Sinanju."

F. U. Gudgel dropped to the mossy floor.

"What does this mean, 'lesson number one'?" Bubu asked.

"Nothing." Remo sighed. "Lemme get your steak knife."

Still on bare feet, Remo padded to the edge of the platform. The instant his toes curled over the edge, he launched himself forward.

Spinning in air as he sailed across the river, he hit the far wall with the soles of both feet. Before gravity could take hold, he used his momentum to propel himself up the wall and around the broad arch of the ceiling. He plucked the machete from where it jutted at the apex and continued his sprint down the far side to where Bubu waited on the platform.

When Remo presented him his blade, an amazed smile cracked the young native's dark face. "How is it possible for a man to do such things?" he asked.

"Gimme twenty years and maybe I'll show you one day," Remo replied. "For now, we should see what these guys were doing down here." He nodded to Gudgel's body.

At this, Bubu's expression became abruptly urgent. His amazement at Remo's abilities had made him forget why they were there.

"There were two more," Bubu announced. "We must give chase."

"You give chase if you want to," Remo said,

picking up his shoes. "Thanks to your shit swan dive, they're long gone."

Spinning, Remo headed down the tunnel. Bubu trailed behind. The native held his weapons in one hand, rubbing his injured shoulder with the other.

"Don't fool around with that," Remo called without turning. "As it is, you've probably got typhoid fever and about fifty different kinds of V.D."

Remo followed the clumsy footprints Gudgel and the others had made in the moss to the end of the tunnel. Down another short corridor, the prints stopped abruptly.

Remo didn't need to see the nuclear device to know it was there. His body had detected the radiation leaking into the cavern before he and Bubu had even turned into the tunnel. Luckily, it wasn't bad enough yet to damage a body trained in Sinanju. The shiny silver bomb was tucked neatly away in a dank alcove at the tunnel's far end.

As Remo stood in silent contemplation of the hydrogen bomb Deferens's men had planted directly below the heart of Bachsburg, Bubu stole up behind him. The Luzu native stared in wonder at the bomb casing.

"What is it?" he whispered.

To the native, Remo's answer was chillingly calm. "A nuclear bomb," he said, biting the inside of his cheek in concentration.

It was all suddenly clear. Deferens ran the department that controlled East Africa's nuclear arsenal, and had kept the bombs after they were supposedly destroyed. Either on his own or at

Mandobar's insistence, the defense minister had planted this bomb at the time when the most criminals would be in East Africa. Mandobar and Deferens intended to kill the very men they'd invited here—the criminals who were even now stirring from their restful night's slumber in fancy hotel suites far above Remo's head.

"Should we not do something?" Bubu whispered fearfully. His Luzu weapons were out before him, as if they would be enough to ward off the most awesomely destructive force human technology had ever harnessed.

Remo nodded slowly. A glimmer sparkled in the depths of his dark eyes. "You're right," he said. "We *should* do something."

And throwing back his head, Remo laughed out loud.

"Master Remo?" Bubu asked worriedly.

But Remo didn't hear. He had already turned from both bomb and native. Rubbing tears of mirth from his eyes, he marched back down the tunnel.

His sinister laughter faded in the distance.

When L. Vas Deferens stepped through the main door to his government suite, the offices of the Ministry of Defense were abuzz with activity. Much of the excitement spilled into the rest of the presidential palace, as harried workers labored to coordinate the events scheduled for the day.

Pagers buzzed and rang. Directions were barked into cell phones. Keyboards clattered relentlessly as computers connected to those at the airport recorded arrivals, adding them to the growing list of foreign dignitaries.

Everywhere, people were talking, running. Conducting the business of the new East Africa. It was a thrilling chaos, barely controlled.

Through it all, L. Vas Deferens strode, cooler than the air-conditioned marble beneath his feet.

The defense minister had been inspecting his troops. As he walked from office to office, from floor to floor, the thing he was most proud of was the fact that the faces of all who worked for him were like his own: white.

It was an amazing thing to be able to get away with in this current *mooka*-loving East Africa, especially in the presidential palace of all places. After all, this wasn't like the old days.

Deferens had been born and raised in the whitest of white Bachsburg suburbs. His father had been a judge under the old system. In an irony that resonated with his son to this day, the older Deferens had been on a panel that had twice denied parole to political prisoner Willie Mandobar.

His mother had been the grande dame of the lily-white East African society set. Before he could even walk, Deferens had long grown used to her daily abuse of the black help.

From his father's knee, straight through Bachsburg University, Vas had been conditioned to accept his superiority. So ingrained was it, it wasn't even an issue. He fervently believed in the Kipling theory that care of the dusky-skinned races was the burden of the white man.

But unfortunately for Deferens, the caste-system world of his parents would not last for his lifetime.

Unlike most racists, Deferens had seen the way the wind was blowing. Back in the 1970s he had guessed correctly that the old regime was unsustainable. Already a low-level government functionary by this time, Deferens was risking all when he threw in with Mandobar's African Citizen Caucus.

At the time, his parents had disowned him, his wife had divorced him and his friends had abandoned him. But in the end, all the personal costs were outweighed by the benefits.

After the white government structure was dismantled, Deferens was one of the few nonblacks kept aboard. After all, he had a public track record of racial tolerance going back almost twenty years.

Deferens was the reed that bent in the wind. And because of his pragmatic flexibility, he had prospered.

The public face of the ice cold defense minister was one of great liberal open-mindedness. But in that private part of himself that he dared not share with anyone, his racism blazed.

L. Vas Deferens was white.

L. Vas Deferens was proud to be white.

L. Vas Deferens hated anyone who was not white.

And yet the world mocked him by forcing him to throw in with one of the most famous black faces on the planet.

No matter. Deferens had just made a deal that would guarantee insulation from nonwhites for the rest of his natural days. And Bachsburg would be a smoking crater. A final stab at the *mookas* who had led his nation to ruin.

A soft smile brushed Deferens's perfect white face as he headed down the hallway to his private office.

In the small lobby, his white secretary informed him that there had been an urgent call while he was away. When Deferens picked up the note, he found that it was from one of the scientists working on his special project.

Frowning, he carried the scrap of paper into his office. The soundproofed door clicked shut on all the noisy activity outside. Deferens bolted it securely.

He crossed to his desk. The minister was just sinking into his seat when the door popped open again. When he looked up, the door was closing gently once more.

Remo Williams stood before the East African defense minister, a thin smile on his cruel features. He wore a clean set of clothes.

"Remo?" Deferens said, masking his surprise. "I was not informed you were on your way up." He looked beyond his guest, to the door he was certain he'd locked.

Remo seemed to enjoy the minister's thin discomfort. "Didn't check in at the front desk," he explained. As he crossed the room, his feet made not a sound.

"I see." Deferens sat up more straightly. He placed his secretary's note carefully on his desk.

He was getting a strange sensation from this man—something Deferens himself had been accused of giving everyone all his life. An icy chill ran up his rigid spine.

"I trust Batubizee is dead," he ventured.

Remo shook his head as he sat on the edge of the desk. "You're too trusting," he said. "Now me, on the other hand? The only thing I trust in is man's limitless capacity to be a two-timing asshole to his fellow man. So far, Elvis, I haven't been disappointed."

A cloud crossed the defense minister's face. "What is the meaning of this disrespect, Remo?" he asked, feeling the first stirrings of fear in his chest. "I hired you because you led me to believe you were competent. Now you break into my office—yes, *break*—and tell me that Batubizee is still alive. On top of that, your rudeness is inexcusable. Get off my desk," he ordered.

Remo didn't move.

"Gee, I hope I don't have to give up my job as East Africa's official assassin," Remo mused. "I already ordered the stationery. Course, I could always get a job as a sewer worker. You gotta watch your step down there, though, what with all the alligators and thermonuclear warheads people flush these days. But I hear the benefits are good."

When the grin broke full on Remo's face, Deferens was already diving in his desk drawer. A delicate hand wrapped around the butt of an automatic.

The gun turned to brittle ice, shattering into a hundred metal shards. When he looked up, Remo stood above him. Panic spread wide across Deferens's face.

He grabbed for the phone. It seemed to explode on contact with his flesh. Shards of black plastic scattered across his spotless desk surface. When he tried to bolt from the room, a strong hand pressed against his chest.

Coaxing the East African official back into his well-oiled chair, Remo leaned against the edge of the desk.

"Okay, all the nukes weren't dismantled when they were supposed to be," Remo ventured. "That's pretty clear. So I'm guessing you and Mandobar planted one of them beneath the city for what, blackmail? Because if it's just to unclog some backed-up pipes, you're really overcompensating."

Deferens stiffened in his chair. Screwing his mouth tightly shut, he stared defiantly at the wall.

His defiance lasted only until the pain began.

Remo pressed but two fingers into his shoulder. To Deferens, it was as if someone were pouring molten metal into the joint. He gasped in pain.

"No," he breathed. The pain was too great for him to shout. "I brokered a deal with Camorra to destroy Bachsburg. Mandobar doesn't know."

Remo eased back the pressure, a puzzled look on his face. "Isn't Camorra that big turtle that's always trashing Tokyo? Shoots fire from his ass?"

Deferens shook his head. His green eyes watered. "It is a rival of the Mafia. Based in Naples, not Sicily."

"Never heard of them," Remo said.

"Few have in this century," Deferens said. "That is why they wished to destroy Bachsburg. World crime will be crippled at midnight tonight when the bombs go off. Afterward, Camorra will dominate the global scene."

"And you swear Mandobar doesn't know?"

"No," Deferens insisted. "The plan is the result of lengthy negotiations between myself and Don Vincenzo."

Remo's fingers dug into his shoulder. "Elvis wouldn't lie to me?" he cautioned.

The pain was excruciating. "No!" Deferens gasped.

He was telling the truth. When Remo's hand retreated to his side, there was a thoughtful look on his face.

In his seat, Deferens rubbed at his aching shoulder.

"I suppose you're some sort of American agent," he snarled.

Remo shook his head. "Actually, I consider myself more of a conscientious world citizen," he replied. "Aside from me and Ted Turner, we're a dying breed."

The pain was rapidly becoming a distant memory. Already the gears were turning as Deferens tried to figure a way out of this. If he could just get Remo outside, he could signal the guards. Yet, he realized, Remo had apparently gotten in here without anyone seeing him.

"I suppose you wish to deactivate the bombs," Deferens suggested.

"Bombs?" Remo asked. "There's more than one?"

Deferens nodded. "And since I am the only person who knows the precise location of *all* of them, I will have to lead you to them. If you will allow me to summon my driver, we may begin deactivating them."

When he called his bodyguard driver, a prearranged signal would flood the office with palace guards.

Deferens stood. Remo shoved him back in his chair.

"Gimme a minute," Remo said. "I'm thinking."

In his entire life, the defense minister of East Africa had not once perspired. But as Remo stared off into space above him, the first prickly hint of a rash began to form beneath Deferens's white shirt collar.

The East African dropped his voice low. "Remo, I can see you are having difficulty with this," he said. "Perhaps I can make things easier. I will double your retainer if you come to work exclusively for me. One million dollars per year." His eyes were crafty.

That got Remo's attention. He glanced down at the defense minister. "Three million," he countered.

A hopeful smile twitched the corners of Deferens's lips. "Done," he nodded.

"Too quick," Remo said. "I want six million. In gold. Up front."

The smile tightened to a flat line. "That would be more difficult," Deferens said.

"Nonnegotiable," Remo insisted. "I know you've got it, and I'm sick of being yanked by everyone all the time. Six million in gold or no dice."

Deferens considered deeply. His Camorra position in East African after the destruction of Bachsburg would net him much, much more than that. And given the abilities he had displayed, Remo would make a powerful ally when Deferens made his inevitable move against Don Vincenzo.

At last, the minister nodded. "Agreed," he said crisply.

Remo smiled tightly. "Sorry," he said, shaking his head. "Just wanted to prove I wasn't as big a schlemiel at negotiating as some people think. Besides, you look like an even bigger fusspot than the guy I work for now." He hopped down from the desk.

Deferens recoiled. The back of his chair struck the wall. When Remo reached out a thick-wristed hand, Deferens shrank fearfully.

"Think this through, Remo," he warned, sweat trickling down his back. "There is no way to deactivate all the bombs without my help."

And Remo's smile was as icy cold as Deferens's own black heart. "Who said I wanted to deactivate them?" he asked.

Deferens didn't have time to consider Remo's surprising words. Before he even knew what was happening, Remo had reached out and tapped a spot in the perfect center of L. Vas Deferens's pale white forehead.

For the shocked East African defense minister, all thoughts of his bombs or this madman in his midst dissolved in an instant. The entire world of L. Vas Deferens collapsed into a single bright white dot that vanished into a sea of inky blackness.

25

Chiun sat in a lotus position on the floor of Chief Batubizee's hut, the hems of his pale orchid kimono tucked neatly around his bony knees. The steamer trunks he had brought from Castle Sinanju were stacked against one wall, a colorful contrast to the washed-out surroundings.

On the hills around the village, sentries scanned both plain and sky. So far, the anticipated attack from Bachsburg had not yet materialized. Chiun assumed that this would change once the failure of Remo's expedition was learned. Until that time, all the Master of Sinanju could do was wait.

Although he had not let it show, the news of Remo's visions had disturbed the old Korean. They betokened a future that, in truth, Chiun had hoped was far away.

Deep in meditation, he was attempting to seek the guidance of his ancestors when he became aware of an urgent conversation beyond the thin walls of the hut.

He had not detected the engines that would bring more men from Bachsburg. Only the sound of Batubizee's own truck returning a few moments before.

Since no one called to him, Chiun remained seated. Eyes closed, he continued meditating.

His concentration was shattered a minute later by the anxious appearance of Chief Batubizee and Bubu.

Eyes flitting open, Chiun crinkled his nose in displeasure at the odor that clung to the young native's soiled clothes.

"Master Chiun, I bring grave news," Bubu said excitedly.

Chiun resisted the urge to pinch his nose between his fingers. "Have the invaders arrived?" he asked.

Batubizee shook his head. "It is far more serious than an attempt on my life," he intoned. "Bubu and your son found one of the men who slew my warriors in the Bachsburg sewers. The young Master of Sinanju dispatched the villain."

A puff of pride swelled Chiun's silken kimono. "He is a good and faithful son." The old man nodded. "True to his House and our traditions." He suddenly noted the bandage tied over Bubu's sleeve. "You are injured." He frowned.

"Master Remo saved my life," Bubu offered.

The chest of his kimono expanded further. "He is an ally of both the present and future Luzu Empire." Chiun smiled.

"I am not so certain," Batubizee intoned seriously.

Chiun allowed the air to slip slowly from his lungs. "What do you mean?" the Master of Sinanju asked, praying Remo hadn't done anything more stupid than usual. He was stunned when the truth was far worse than he could have imagined.

Bubu quickly related all that had occurred in Bachsburg. The story ended with the discovery of the nuclear device.

"You are certain this is what it was?" Chiun asked thinly once the breathless native was finished.

"I cannot say," Bubu replied, shaking his head. "I can only tell you that which Master Remo claims to be true."

"And what did my son do about this device?"

Bubu glanced anxiously at Batubizee. "Nothing, Master," he admitted to Chiun with some reluctance. "He merely laughed and left it where it sat."

Frowning deeply, Chiun said nothing.

"This is terrible if true," Batubizee interjected. "I know well of these devices. When one explodes, death rains down many miles away. Luzuland would not be spared."

"I cannot believe that Master Remo would allow that to happen," Bubu insisted.

But on the floor, Chiun slowly shook his head.

"You do not know him as I do," he said quietly.

"Then he *would* do this?" Batubizee demanded.

"I cannot say," the old Korean replied. "Remo's emotions are not his own. There is no telling what he might allow at this fragile state." He rose to his feet. "I must leave your side and hie to Bachsburg," he told Batubizee. "For to protect your land, I must see to it that this device of wicked consequence is destroyed." He marched to the door.

Bubu hurried after him. "I will take you," he insisted.

As the three men left the hut, Batubizee and Bubu hoped there was time enough for the ancient Master of Sinanju to stop the bomb.

For his part, Chiun hoped there was time enough before they left for the eager young native to bathe.

26

Plastic fruit adorned the brim of the big straw hat. Strawberries, grapes, an orange and two bananas nestled neatly on the crown. As a dark-faced assistant opened the door, Mandobar stopped beside the overly muscled young man, first checking the hat's reflection in the shiny glass panes at the front of the huge auditorium.

Perfect. Almost.

Mandobar tipped the brim of the plastic-fruit-covered hat ever so slightly.

Now it was perfect.

"All right, all right!" Mandobar snapped. A fat hand waved angrily.

The man dutifully drew the door open fully. Mandobar breezed inside.

The great foyer with its crystal chandeliers and rich imported tapestries was chilled to an icy sixty-five degrees. A great change from the hundred-degree weather outside.

Feeling gooseflesh rise across exposed arms, Mandobar hurried to a rear office.

As Mandobar settled into a wide chair, a fat finger stabbed in the speed-dial number for the office of the defense minister. It rang several times before the voice of a male secretary finally answered.

"Minister Deferens's office. How may I direct your call?"

Mandobar leaned forward. The farthest rounded end of a well-fed belly brushed the edge of the desk.

"Get me Deferens."

"I am sorry," the secretary replied. "Minister Deferens is unavailable at the moment."

It was already a risk to be speaking to someone other than Deferens directly. Mandobar's voice was recognizable.

Hoping that the five syllables already spoken would not be enough to alert the secretary to the caller's identity, Mandobar broke the connection. A chubby hand continued to rest on the phone long after it was back in its cradle.

Where was Deferens? This was the most crucial phase of the operation. Nearly all of the dignitaries would be in Bachsburg now. Deferens should have been coordinating with them from his palace office. Those had been Mandobar's instructions.

After a long time, the hand finally left the phone.

Mandobar would have an underling at the village make the necessary calls to Bachsburg. The criminal leaders still needed to be told when and where to come. The men who had been brought here so far were always blindfolded. Even Deferens didn't know about the village. He had always been too busy with his work to ask or care where Mandobar's secret meetings were being held.

Of course, there would be no risk of exposure by

having someone else call. After all, everyone here in the bungalow village already knew who their employer was. Not that this knowledge would do them any good. Unlike the coordinators in Bachsburg, all of the people in the village would be dead by tomorrow.

Mandobar stood. The fruit hat reflected smartly in a glass picture frame on the opposite wall. Beneath the mound of fruit, a plump face scowled back at Mandobar.

One thing was certain. If an AWOL Deferens ended up torpedoing this deal so late in the game, Mandobar would make certain his death would not come as painlessly as those in the bungalow village. After all, there were still plenty of tires lying unused around East Africa.

Gaily colored burnoose trails swirling wildly behind an ample derriere, Mandobar stormed from the office.

27

When he pulled open his hotel-room door, Remo found the Master of Sinanju waiting inside. The old man was fuming.

"Is this where it ends for us?" Chiun accused hotly. "You fleeing with your wretched life while you leave your father in spirit to the mercy of radioactive booms and toadstool clouds?"

"Do I look like I'm fleeing?" Remo asked, perturbed, as he closed the door.

"Worse," Chiun snapped. "You would make yourself a martyr to a cause no one but you understands."

"Nope," Remo said. "Not in the martyr biz. Actually, I was just gonna go get you. I'm glad you're here. You saved me another trip out to that dump."

Chiun's face hardened. "Do not dare speak ill of Luzuland, American. Yes, *American*," he stressed, as if employing the most vile of curses. "Those simple people have something you will never have."

"Cholera?" Remo suggested.

The tiny Korean stomped his feet in anger. "Respect for their elders," he hissed. "Bubu would never abandon his chief to an idiotic boom device."

"There's more than one bomb, Little Father."

"Worse still," Chiun accused. The anger seemed to drain from him all at once. "Oh, Remo," he lamented. "Have these visitations so hardened your heart? Do you now covet the title of Reigning Master so greatly that you would not even give me time to at least make peace with my ancestors?"

It was an accusation Remo had endured before. This time, however, it took on special meaning.

"Don't say that, Chiun," he said quietly. "And I *was* coming to get you. The bombs aren't due to go off until midnight. We'll get out of here in plenty of time."

He headed for the bathroom. Chiun trailed him inside.

"We are not going anywhere," Chiun insisted.

"Well, we're sure as hell not staying at ground zero," Remo replied. Running water in the basin, he splashed some on his face.

As he stood in the door, Chiun saw Remo's sewer clothes stuffed in the toilet. Some water had spilled over onto the tile floor. His nose rebelled at the stench.

"What is this?" he demanded.

"Didn't Bubu tell you?" Remo asked, drying his hands.

"He mentioned some misadventure the two of you shared in a cesspool. I assumed you were on yet another quest to root out other ancestors of yours who are not of Sinanju."

"Lay off," Remo griped.

Flinging down the towel, he left the room. Chiun followed him into the living area of the suite.

"Very well," the Master of Sinanju replied. "I will not speak ill of your mongrel heritage or your quixotic search for the ragpickers who hatched you, but if I am going to be that nice to you, you must give something to me in return. The location of the boom devices."

Remo shook his head firmly. "You've got a lot to learn about sucking up," he said. "And I'm not telling."

Chiun pulled at the tufts of hair above his ears.

"Stop this madness!" he demanded, jumping up and down. "Do you care nothing for the Luzu? If these devices go off, they will be destroyed, as well."

"You don't know that," Remo said, his brow furrowing. "Luzuland is pretty far away from Bachsburg. If the cloud blows the right way, they could come out of this fine."

Chiun threw up his hands. "Woe to the Luzu that they must risk their futures on *your* feebleminded guesses."

"Well, why don't *you* go back and get them the hell out of there?" Remo snapped, color rising in his cheeks. "Chiun, if these bombs go off, the whole world wins. Don't you think I haven't thought about the people here? I *have*. But when I weighed them against the whole rest of the planet, I'm sorry. They lost."

"I cannot believe what I am hearing," Chiun gasped. "You have truly gone mad."

"I was mad before I got here," Remo said. "Mad that we were losing the fight. Mad that I wasn't making a difference. Now I've been given a chance to do what I couldn't do on my own. When the bombs go off, we sweep the planet clean of nearly every bigwig bastard there is. We can start again with a clean slate."

"Oh, *why* did you have to be afflicted with Master's disease?" Chiun wailed. "Could I not have a pupil who was blind? Or lame?" He stabbed a sharpened fingernail at Remo. "You say you are worried about the entire world. Tell me, Remo Williams, what has the world ever done for you?"

Remo's shoulders sank imperceptibly. Only the Master of Sinanju would have seen the subtle motion.

"Not much, I guess," he answered quietly

"How dare you!" Chiun shrieked, his shrill voice rising ten octaves. Stemware in the hotel bar twelve stories below rang in protest. "The world has given you *me!* And what have I ever asked from you? Nothing! I give, give, give while you take, take, take. Well, I am asking for something now. I *command* you to tell me where those booms are!"

When Remo spoke, his voice was small. "I'm sorry, Chiun. I *can't.*"

Chiun studied his pupil's face for a long moment, his thin lips fading into an invisible rictus of disgust. Remo refused to meet his teacher's penetrating gaze.

"Pah!" Chiun spit all at once. "You are an obstinate fool." He spun away from Remo, his kimono swirling wildly at his ankles. He marched into the bedroom, calling angrily over his shoulder as he went, "If you will not listen to true reason, perhaps you will give ear to the idiot logic of another block-headed white."

"You *WHAT*!?"

The voice of Harold W. Smith over the international line was a mixture of shock and horror. Remo could actually hear the crack of Smith's arthritic knuckles as they tightened on the receiver.

"Aside from his overuse of the word 'lunatic,' Chiun got it about right," Remo replied thinly.

The Master of Sinanju had placed the call to Smith from the bedroom. He was on that extension now as Remo spoke on the living-room phone.

"It is the waning days of his illness that has made him do this thing, Emperor," Chiun interjected. "The Master's disease I told you about many years ago has nearly run its course. He has decided to mark the occasion of his recovery with an act of utter lunacy."

The old Korean had mentioned Remo's illness when first he called Smith. It had been so many years since he had heard of it that it took the CURE director a moment to remember.

"Illness or not, this is totally unacceptable, Remo," Smith insisted.

"Accept it," Remo said flatly.

"How many bombs are there?" Smith begged.

"I don't know," Remo replied honestly. "I only saw the one. But Deferens said there were more."

"You must find out their exact locations," Smith said, trying to inject a reasonable tone into his lemony voice. "They must be disarmed."

"No way," said Remo. "I didn't decide on this on a whim, Smitty. We've been presented with a real opportunity here. Think about all the skunks who are in this town right now. We could get them *all*. No more of this nickel-and-dime water-treading crapola we've been doing all these years."

Smith did not allow his own earlier doubts to invade their conversation. "That cannot be a factor," he said.

"Why not?" Remo pressed, his voice passionate. "These creeps are like weeds. We pull one out, and another five sprout up. We've been giving the world's problems an ounce of CURE all these years when what they've really been screaming for is a pound of prevention. We can do that here. *Today*. Think about it, Smitty. We'll finally have the upper hand after all these years. That's got to be worth one crummy city."

Smith remained unmoved. "And what of the innocent people in Bachsburg?" he asked. "Have you given them any thought at all?"

"Yeah, as a matter of fact, I have," Remo said. "What's the population of Bachsburg?"

Smith hesitated. "About one hundred and fifty thousand, including the wider metropolitan area," he replied slowly.

"And how many people are victims of crime every year?"

He saw now where Remo was headed. "On a global scale, those statistics are not available," Smith insisted.

"You don't have to tell me," Remo said. "I know it's more than the population here. A *lot* more."

"You would not stop *common* criminals, Remo. Everyday killers, pushers and rapists would still exist."

"But we can cut off the *head* of crime," Remo stressed. "Local police can mop up the rest. The guys who are here today are the ones running the show. They have the network that gets the drugs to the addict who has to steal to feed his habit. You *know* I'm right, Smitty."

"I know nothing of the sort," Smith answered tartly. "And if you will not follow orders, let me speak with Chiun alone."

"Don't count on him to do the heavy lifting," Remo said. "I think his Luzu gig's turning into a full-time job."

"Silence, madman," the Master of Sinanju snapped in rebuke. "I am here, Emperor," he said to Smith. "It is as I warned you. Remo is not given to many thoughts, so when one roots in his granite skull, it is difficult to dislodge."

"Sweet-talk me all you want," Remo warned. "It ain't gonna work."

"Remo, hang up," Smith ordered.

"Look, Smitty," Remo said. "Why don't I save you both some grief. Deferens is the only one who knows how to turn them off, and Elvis has left the building. He's out cold someplace safe, and I'm the only one who knows where he is."

"You did not eliminate him?" Smith asked, his sharp tone growing puzzled.

"No. Listen, Smitty, I have to go. Chiun and I are gonna need tickets out of here before the fireworks start."

After he hung up the phone, he heard Chiun speaking in hushed tones a few moments longer. The old Korean made it impossible for Remo to hear either side of the conversation. When he was through, he hung up the phone and padded back into the living room, a dull expression on his wrinkled face.

Remo was loitering near the door.

"Smith is not pleased," Chiun said flatly.

"He'll get over it."

"Perhaps," Chiun said. Like a collapsing parachute, he settled cross-legged to the living-room rug.

"What are you doing?" Remo asked.

"Waiting," the Master of Sinanju said blandly. "Thanks to you, there is nothing else for me to do."

"You're just gonna sit there?"

"There is time. You have said so yourself."

"But don't you want to go back to Luzuland and get your stuff?"

Chiun shook his head. "Bubu has already returned with the chief's vehicle. I doubt a taxi would take me there. I am content to wait." With his long tapered nails, he fussed with the robes at his knees.

"If you're waiting for me to change my mind, don't bother," Remo warned. "I'm not going to."

"Of course not. The seed has already germinated in the sidewalk that is your brain. And because of this, an entire city must be made to suffer. Perhaps more."

"Guilt won't do it, either," Remo said. "I'm right and that's that. Case closed." He turned for the door.

"But consider," Chiun called after him.

Remo had his hand on the doorknob. "Consider what?" he asked, turning warily.

"The lesson of Nuk," Chiun explained. "For although it is written that his sole purpose in this land was to exploit the rich diamond mines of the Luzu, there has always been a sneaking suspicion among later Masters that he had more esoteric reasons. A paternal fondness for the Luzu people."

Remo's face fouled. "Chiun, I don't give a wet fart in a windbreaker about those people."

"No," Chiun agreed, his eyes flat. "Your concern is far greater. You care for the entire world. You are Remo Williams, the Great Preserver of Peace and Justice for all Humanity. And because of your great caring soul, hundreds of thousands will die this day."

And having delivered his final word on the subject, the Master of Sinanju closed his papery eyelids.

Across the room, a scowl formed deep on Remo's face. And in the furthest recesses of the cruelest lines, the shadows of doubt appeared. He refused to entertain them.

"Put a sock in it," Remo growled, flinging the door open. The hotel door slammed violently behind him.

meeting here.

28

The helicopter grew from a tiny black speck in the pale white African sky. It swept across the plains to the south, cutting up over the bungalow-lined street in the small village at the outskirts of Luzuland.

Standing on the great, flat roof of the huge meeting hall, Mandobar watched the helicopter close in.

The rear wall of the big auditorium was set into the side of a rocky hill. The hill itself was a natural plateau that had been made perfectly level. The helipad would soon be filled to capacity. A few helicopters were already there, rotor blades sagging inert.

Mandobar held a knot of fabric from the billowing skirts of the burnoose to keep it from blowing immodestly up. Another fat hand held the big fruit hat in place.

Almost time...

"THERE ARE NOT enough houses here," Don Giovani complained over the radio headset. He was a portly, white-haired man of seventy with a tomato-garden tan.

The chopper was flying over the last of the bungalows.

"Perhaps there are more elsewhere," Nunzio Spumoni suggested over his own slender microphone.

"I see no others," Giovani scowled. "If I am expected to sleep out in the desert, you will return me to my hotel in Bachsburg immediately."

"Amen, Marlon Brando!" shrieked another voice over the headset. "And if you've got bread, you can count me in. 'Course you gotta promise I won't wake up with a horsie's head in my bed, luv! Shudder!"

Don Giovani and Nunzio Spumoni had endured the endless interruptions of the Seasonings for the entire ride from Bachsburg. The singers were crammed like a row of garishly painted dolls on one of the helicopter's broad back seats.

Pushed in tightly, the huge bellies of the four women were wrinkled and buckled at inhuman angles. Nunzio swore at one point that Trollop's stomach flesh had come apart and that she had refastened it. Of course, that was impossible.

The Camorra man tried to ignore the annoyingly distracting women as he spoke to the rival Mafia leader.

"Please, Don Giovani," Nunzio pleaded. "I did not know of this place until an hour ago. I was asked by the office of the defense minister to bring you here."

"Why did Defense Minister Deferens not bring me here himself?" Giovani demanded.

"Perhaps he is busy elsewhere," Spumoni suggested. Even as he spoke, he felt the first cold trickles of sweat.

The truth was, Spumoni wished he knew where the East African defense minister was. He had been trying to contact L. Vas Deferens for much of the day. The man had vanished.

As far as he knew, the nuclear bombs were still hidden beneath the streets of Bachsburg. However, they would do little good if the crime leaders were to be brought out into this wilderness. Nunzio had only just learned of this change of plans from the defense ministry. His own boss, Don Vincenzo of the Napoli Camorra, would not be pleased if this costly plan of Spumoni's were to fail at this late stage.

Nunzio was sweating and twitching by the time the helicopter soared up to the roof of the grand glass-and-stone structure at the end of the village's only street.

Nunzio saw the familiar fat face smiling up from the auditorium roof. He still couldn't believe it.

Most still thought that the former president of East Africa was behind all this. Until today, Nunzio had been one of them.

He should have known. If Willie Mandobar were the true architect, he would never have been able to leave his country at such an important time.

Nunzio was amazed at the coy act L. Vas Deferens had been playing all this time. The minister had led Nunzio to believe that the beloved former East African politician was playing an active role behind the scenes. Pulling the strings of this great plan. But now it was clear. It was entirely *her* plan.

The plastic-fruit hat was nearly thrown from Nellie Mandobar's head by the downdraft from the big rotor blades. The chopper settled to its skids in the wide landing area.

Servants rushed over to open the doors.

Don Giovani and Nunzio Spumoni were helped out onto the helipad. Behind them, the Seasonings hopped out.

"Find me a loo, pronto!" Slut Seasoning screeched to one of Nellie's men. "Either that or me and baby're gonna break yellow water all over your roof!"

"Girl domination over the johnny closet!" agreed Ho.

The singers were ushered quickly away.

Grateful for the relative silence of the pounding rotor blades, Nunzio Spumoni escorted the Don to the former first lady and ex-wife of Willie Mandobar.

"Mrs. Mandobar, Don Giovani," Nunzio shouted over the helicopter noise.

Nellie Mandobar smiled broadly. "Welcome to the new East Africa, Don Giovani," she shouted. Still holding her fruit hat in place, she leaned forward, kissing the old Italian lightly on the cheek.

"I must get back!" Spumoni called.

Nellie Mandobar nodded. "Thank you for giving our first guest a ride. It was most kind of you. How soon will your Don Vincenzo be arriving?"

"I'll get him now," Nunzio replied. He tried not

to show his reluctance. He was thinking of the bombs under Bachsburg, and of what his Don would do to him if this expensive plan failed.

Bowing a polite goodbye, Nunzio hurried on long legs back to the helicopter. As soon as he climbed aboard, it ascended, roaring back across the savannah toward Bachsburg.

The landing pad grew blessedly quiet.

"Forgive the arrangements, Don Giovani," Nellie Mandobar apologized, taking the Mafia man by the arm. "My man in Bachsburg has taken a few hours off before the event for personal reasons. When I learned the Camorra helicopter was available, I assumed you would not mind."

Don Giovani allowed the plump woman to lead him across the roof. "Is one of those mine?" Giovani asked. As he shuffled along, he pointed to the row of helicopters already at the edge of the broad airfield.

"Yes," Nellie Mandobar replied. Her broad smile had not yet left her fleshy face.

Giovani's tan face was humorless. "Make certain it is ready to leave at a moment's notice," he ordered. "I am not staying here one second longer than is absolutely necessary."

"Both of our helicopters will be ready long before tonight's festivities—" she smiled broadly "—wind down."

And Nellie laughed the laugh of a woman for whom death was an old friend.

The Mafia man's hand rested in the crook of her

arm. Clapping her own fat mitt atop it, she ushered the old Don into the chilly interior of the huge auditorium.

Her joyful laugh echoed hollowly up from below.

29

Pedestrians cut a wide swath around Remo. It was as if his dark inner mood projected an invisible charged field around his body. As he prowled, unmolested, through the streets of Bachsburg, he was a thing to fear and avoid.

After leaving the hotel, Remo hadn't gone to the airport for tickets out of East Africa. Wandering alone, he was deep in thought, wrestling with an inner conflict he thought he'd already put to rest.

There shouldn't have been any turmoil. He had made up his mind. But both Smith and Chiun with their carping and calls to duty had chipped away at the rock of his certainty. Now, though he would never admit it to either the CURE director or the Master of Sinanju, Remo did not know.

He wandered aimlessly.

With the discovery of gold in the late 1800s, Bachsburg had become a boomtown. Peeking out through the present-day city were remnants of its nouveau riche past, evidence of the frontier town that had made good.

Many of the hotels Remo passed were of a variety of different styles. Baroque, Gothic and Byzantine architecture were interspersed in a matter of two city blocks. Remo's own hotel, which dated back to just after the turn of the century, looked like a cross between the Pantheon and a New York skyscraper. Somehow, the sharp contrast of styles worked.

In spite of himself, Remo had begun to look at Bachsburg as a city where actual people lived and not as an abstract model in which an untold number of faceless criminals would die.

His face growing hard, Remo started walking with more purpose, as if by hurrying he could outpace his own doubts.

Although it was barely midafternoon, midnight had begun to loom large and real as Remo headed from the hotel district. As he crossed one street after another, his mind could not but go to the bombs beneath his feet.

Just outside the modern business district, the largely played out and abandoned gold mines of Bachsburg's past had become tourist attractions. There were men and women there now, dressed in vacation clothes, cameras slung around their sweating necks.

On the sidewalk in front of an information center, Remo had to avoid a busload of chattering tourists who were crowding excitedly down to street level.

Even though the East Africa they were in wasn't the one from their glossy tourist brochures, these people were oblivious. They were insulated, hiding in hotel rooms and restaurants, only venturing out by bus to whatever local sites their package tour had picked for the day. It was very likely they had no idea at all what kind of city they had come to.

Remo kept his eyes locked on the sidewalk as he walked past the happy band of tourists.

He would not be blamed for their bad timing. Was it his fault they'd picked now to come to East Africa? And anyway, if they wandered into the wrong part of town, they'd likely end up shot or stabbed. By the end of the day, they'd wind up just as dead.

And it wasn't as if it would be painful. The bombs would incinerate them in an instant. Boom, flash, gone. And as the radioactive dust settled on the twisted ruins of Bachsburg, the world of their families would have become a better place. If anything, the whole planet should be thanking him after tonight. He had seen an opportunity to do good and had seized it. He alone had it in his power to cleanse the earth of an infectious disease. How many criminal generations were represented in Bachsburg right now? Men from twenty to eighty. Three generations, gone.

Behind him, several tourists started laughing at some private joke. The sound was a dagger in Remo's back.

He skulked quickly around a corner.

Sure, the innocent people in Bachsburg probably wouldn't thank him if they knew. But if they could just step back and see the big picture like he did—if they only knew the sheer number of people he'd killed in order to make their lives a little better—

then they'd understand. He was making a better world for their kids.

It popped into his head before he could stop it. Children. He instantly regretted thinking it.

How many children would be without parents after tonight? How many parents would lose sons and daughters?

According to Smith, there were a hundred and fifty thousand people in and around Bachsburg. The blast would claim them in an instant. Beyond that, no one but L. Vas Deferens could say for sure. He was the only one who knew how many bombs there were, and the yield of each.

As he walked, Remo gauged the direction of the wind. At the moment, it was blowing from west to east. If it shifted direction after midnight, Luzuland would be swept by the radiation cloud. All of the people Remo had seen there would die—from Chief Batubizee to Bubu to the women and children who sat in the bone-dry dust. All dead.

And the deaths of the Luzus wouldn't be painless. For the people of Luzuland, there would be sores and radiation poisoning and cancers of every kind. A slow, painful process that would take years to finish.

But it was *worth* it, wasn't it?

Wandering from one street to the next, Remo hadn't been paying attention to the sounds around him. Vaguely, he became aware of a noise coming from somewhere up ahead. It had filtered up from his unconscious into his conscious mind as he crossed from yet another strip of black asphalt over to an area of well-tended lawn.

Still walking, he looked up. And blinked.

His aimless meandering had brought him to the edge of a city park. All around the lawn, dozens of small children were running and laughing. The oldest couldn't have been much more than eight.

Skirting the edge of the park, he tried to force his eyes down. But as he walked, his troubled gaze was drawn to the activity.

He had decided that the bombs of Minister Deferens should be harnessed as a cleansing tool. But as he watched the children at play, the seeds of guilt sprouted full bloom.

As he circled the park, he tried imposing on the people nearby the same negative emotions he felt for Mandobar's criminal guests.

In the park, black and white were still largely separated.

Racial hatred. From *both* sides. Would that be enough to doom an entire city?

Fighting his own doubts now, Remo wanted more than anything to believe that *everyone* in Bachsburg was evil. But as he crossed the narrow footpath that sliced through the wide lawn, he found not evil, but hope.

On a wrought-iron bench, two women talked, one black, one white. Other racially mixed groups pushed strollers through the park or sat on blankets spread out on the grass.

The children seemed to care less about skin color than the adults. They disregarded race entirely, playing loudly and happily together. Sometimes a parent—mostly whites—would pull a child away from a group of mixed-race children, but by and large this was the exception.

The thing that had thrust East Africa into the international spotlight was hardly visible in this place. All around him was the joy and contentment of youth. Tomorrow it would all be ashes.

Stopping near a chain-link fence, Remo stuffed his hands into his pockets. His fingertips brushed a pair of familiar objects.

He had switched them from the pants he'd ruined in the sewer. At the time, he didn't know why he'd bothered.

In one hand, Remo held the cross given him by baby Karen's great-grandmother. In the other, the tiny stone figure that had been a gift from the child apparition.

He had been furious at the news accounts of the infant's death. He had wanted more than anything to bring her back to life, to be there to stop Brad Miller from murdering her in the first place.

The Master Who Never Was had spoken of Remo's destiny. Of the day he would bear the terrible, wonderful burden of the proud history of Sinanju on his shoulders.

And in that moment, Remo knew that no matter how he tried to rationalize it, this could not be his future.

In one palm, sunlight glinted off the shiny silver crucifix. In the other, the carved stone face no longer seemed flat. In the details of the mouth and eyes there seemed a quiet hope.

He stared at both objects for a long time.

Thank you, Remo.

No one ever said that to him. No one would ever say it.

Thank you. It was something he longed to hear. But never would.

So many years. No difference...no change...

By the time he looked back up, many of the parents were packing up their families and getting ready to leave.

How many hours had passed?

Slowly, with infinite care, he folded his hands shut. He replaced crucifix and carving delicately in his pocket.

When Remo turned his back on the park, his eyes were rimmed in red. He struck off across the street, heading slowly toward the hotel district. Not once did he look back.

30

"Sometimes I really hate you."

The Master of Sinanju was sitting in the same spot where Remo had left him. His hazel eyes were knowing as Remo slammed the hotel-room door shut.

"Did you get our plane tickets?" Chiun queried.

"Cut the crap and get up," Remo snarled. "We've got work to do."

From the hall, he'd sensed someone else inside. Bubu stood from the couch as Remo crossed into the living area.

"Do you get a nickel every time you drive in and out of Luzuland?" Remo asked the native.

Bubu hesitated. "I do not mean to interrupt," he said, confused. "Master Chiun has told me that you were about to begin destroying the devices beneath the city."

Remo shot a glance at Chiun. "Did he," he said blandly. "Well, it was iffy for a while, but I guess it's made it onto the 'to do' list."

The Luzu smiled. "I am glad you have changed your mind, Master Remo," he said. "I was worried that you had taken my wish for the destruction of Bachsburg to heart."

"No fear of that," Remo replied, his face sour. "This town will stand as a testament to vice for years to come. Get a move on, will you, Chiun?"

The Master of Sinanju rose to his feet. "Bubu has something to tell you," he intoned.

"If it has something to do with the ranger shipping me off to a zoo, I'm not interested," Remo said.

"Listen," Chiun insisted. There was an urgency to his tone that Remo could not ignore.

"Okay, what? And make it snappy."

"After I left Master Chiun here in the city, I returned to my village. On the way, I encountered many aircraft. They flew above me across Luzuland."

Remo instantly thought of Deferens and his murder plot. "Were they going after Batubizee?" he asked.

Bubu shook his head. "At first I thought this, as well. I assumed the villains here had learned of the departure of Master Chiun and were hoping to attack before his return. I made haste back to my village only to find things as I left them. The helicopters from Bachsburg were not flying there, but to the evil city at the edge of Luzuland." The native nodded to the Master of Sinanju. "Master Chiun saw it on our way to the Luzu treasury."

"It is a small settlement," Chiun interjected.

"There are a few dozen homes, as well as one very large building."

Bubu nodded eagerly. "I led an expedition to the hills above this place. Many of the helicopters were there, as was the fiend Mandobar."

This got Remo's attention. "Mandobar?" he asked sharply. "Isn't he still in China?"

"The *husband*," Bubu stressed. "Not his wife, Nellie. She is bringing many of the evil chiefs to her right now."

Remo scrunched up his face. "Nellie Mandobar? I thought she faded away once Willie ditched her."

"No. She is here. Many are loyal to her still. The men from the helicopters embraced her."

In an instant, it all made sense.

"Nellie Mandobar," Remo said, nodding. "That's why he could be away now. He doesn't have anything to do with it."

And in a very quiet part of himself, Remo felt relief. He was glad that a man who was a hero to so many people wasn't involved in something so sinister.

"This does not make sense," the Master of Sinanju said. "Why would this female plot the destruction of this city only to remove her victims from it beforehand?"

"She doesn't know about it," Remo explained. "Caving in Bachsburg was a side scheme Deferens cooked up. And speaking of Casper the GQ Ghost..."

Spinning, he hurried into the hallway. Chiun and Bubu followed, the Luzu jogging to keep up.

Marching down four doors, Remo entered the suite. When they crossed to the bedroom, they found the sleeping form of Minister L. Vas Deferens stretched out on the sheets.

"*This* is where you hid him?" Chiun scowled.

"I'm getting slicker in my old age." Remo grinned.

Reaching down, he tapped one knuckle against the minister's forehead. The pale man's eyes sprang open wide.

"Wakey-wakey," Remo said.

It took Deferens a moment to get oriented. When he did, panic set in. "Where am I?" he demanded, jumping to a sitting position. "What time is it?"

"Bachsburg, premidnight," Remo said. "And unless your shorts are lead-lined, you've got some bombs to deactivate."

"We were in...my office," Deferens said as he looked around the hotel room in amazement. Remo's words brought his wandering mind back into focus. "The bombs," he gasped. "What *time* is it right now?"

"Almost seven."

"Seven? But they are going to go off at *midnight!*"

"So you'll have to work extra fast," Remo said sweetly.

"No, no, no," Deferens insisted. "We have to get out of here."

When he tried to push his way past the trio, Bubu stepped forward to stop him. A bony hand got there first.

Chiun flung Deferens back to the bed.

"How long will it take to pull the plug on all of them?" Remo pressed.

"What? *No!* We have to—"

He gasped in pain as a pair of talonlike fingernails squeezed the fleshy part of his earlobe.

"Four hours," Deferens yelped. *"Five* if traffic is bad."

"Let's hope the lights are with us, Little Father," Remo said as Chiun released his grip on the minister's ear.

He spun to face Deferens. "This is just for my benefit, but Willie Mandobar doesn't know anything about all this, right?"

"That senile old *mooka?"* Deferens scoffed. "He and Kmpali are fools. I engineered it all beneath their very noses."

"So it was all Nellie's idea?"

His hesitation was precursor to a lie. But when a long-nailed hand appeared before him, the truth spilled forth.

"I told you before, she knows nothing of the bombs," he insisted.

"You knew it was her before?" Chiun demanded of Remo.

"Hey, he said Mandobar. So sue me for not pinning him down on a gender."

"She came to me with the crime-capital idea

when her husband was still in office,'' Deferens continued. "I crafted it. She considers herself a leader, but she is nothing more than a homicidal maniac."

"Not like you," Remo said, his tone flat.

"I was killing for a *purpose,*" he spit. "That fat *mooka* sets fire to people for sport."

"Dead's dead," Remo said thinly. "How many bombs we looking at?"

Deferens didn't even try to bluff. "Six," he admitted glumly.

"I'm no nuke expert, but that sounds like overkill to me," Remo said. "Not that any of the guys you wanted to off are even in town anymore."

"What do you mean?" Deferens asked.

"Your mistress has taken them to her city outside Luzuland," the Master of Sinanju intoned.

"City?" Deferens frowned. "What city?"

Sensing truth from him, both Masters of Sinanju exchanged a quick glance.

"Guess she doesn't tell you everything, white man," Remo said. "Shake a leg." He dragged Deferens up by the arm.

"Wait!" the defense minister insisted. His eyes were calculating. "If this is true..." He looked to Remo. "May I make a phone call?"

"Um, let me think. No," Remo said. He began hauling the minister to the door.

"It could help you!" Deferens cried. "If you wish to know what she is doing, I can find out!"

Remo stopped. When he looked to the Master of Sinanju, the old man nodded.

"Chief Batubizee would no doubt be curious to know why she is there," Chiun said.

Sighing, Remo scooped up the phone and tossed it to Deferens. "Knock yourself out," he said. "But make it quick. 'Cause if we're late, anyone sitting on the john at midnight's gonna get a nuclear-powered prostate exam."

31

"Where have you been?" Nellie Mandobar demanded.

She was in her office at the great meeting hall in her bungalow village. The noise of a raucous party pounded in through the vibrating walls. Her dark, blubbery face was bunched into an angry knot.

"I was unavoidably detained," the precise voice of L. Vas Deferens said, his words faint over the phone. They were nearly drowned out by the nearby revelry. The Seasonings were screeching absurd lyrics at their captive audience.

"This is a very important day," Nellie Mandobar warned. "You have disappointed me greatly, Deferens." Her words were slurred. She raised a big glass of frothy pink liquid to her lips.

"Why did you not tell me of this village near Luzuland?" Deferens asked, agitated.

When she lowered her fruit-filled drink, the smile behind it was pleased. Deferens always considered himself so superior. Even to her. Nellie was delighted that she had been able to keep a secret from him.

"I must have some secrets, Vas." She giggled,

then hiccuped as she again raised her drink. Some of the pink liquid sloshed over the edge of her glass, landing with fat splats on her desk.

"You are bringing the dignitaries there?"

She nodded to her empty office. When her fruit hat dropped in front of her eyes, she shoved it back in place.

"Most are here. Only a few have yet to arrive. It is a party, Vas. To celebrate our great enterprise."

She raised her glass in a toast. Beyond the wall, the Seasonings ended their song. The walls resumed their rattling protest when an even more discordant bashing of instruments began. The women sounded as if they'd each swallowed whole a pair of squabbling cats.

"I should have been informed," Deferens insisted.

"You *would* have been if you were in your office today. But I will not be angry at you, Vas. You have been very helpful to me. You stood by me even when that husband of mine deserted me. And for what did he leave? A few burned nobodies." She pondered the popping pink bubbles in her drink. "As East Africa's first lady, I told him I should be allowed to set fire to whomever I wish, but he would not hear it." A dark finger stabbed a mound of foam, bringing it to her broad lips. "Willie is a coward. But I've shown him, haven't I?" She licked the foam viciously away.

"I cannot believe you kept this from me," Deferens said.

"Do not pout," Nellie Mandobar admonished.

"You are still invited. Your office knows the location now. You may take one of the helicopters. They are leaving from the Bachsburg airport at regular intervals."

In the ensuing pause, Nellie thought she could hear the sound of another voice beyond Deferens.

"Who have you invited there?" Deferens asked abruptly.

"Just the dignitaries themselves. No bodyguards or staff. It is a demonstration of trust. Now, I must get back to my party. I hope to see you soon." Her voice suddenly steeled. "And, Vas...do not disappoint me again."

It took Nellie Mandobar three tries before she managed to hang up the phone. As she slurped pensively at her drink, she considered the fate of L. Vas Deferens.

The defense minister had been extremely helpful to her, but the organizational phase was now over. He and those under him would soon meet their fates. When the time came, Nellie Mandobar wondered how large would be the smear in the sand that would mark the passing of Minister L. Vas Deferens.

When she pulled herself to her big feet, she lost her footing and bounced off the vibrating wall. Giggling at her clumsiness, she staggered back out to join her party.

32

"I can't believe it," L. Vas Deferens said, shaking his head incredulously. He was sitting on the edge of the hotel bed, phone in his lap.

"Yeah," Remo said without sympathy. "The best laid plans, huh? C'mon, peaches." The phone banged to the floor as he pulled Deferens to his feet.

"How may I help?" Bubu said as they hurried to the door.

"Return to your village," Chiun commanded. "Tell Chief Batubizee to gather all of his Luzu warriors. When we are finished here, we will strike the demon harpy in her lair."

"Give us time to finish here first," Remo said as he shoved Deferens into the hall. "We've got five hours to disarm the bombs, max. Plus an hour out to Luzuland. We'll meet you at about 1:00 a.m. Where's a good spot, Chiun?"

"The road to the Luzu treasury. It is near her village, yet far enough away that we will not be seen."

Remo nodded as he pushed the elevator button. "Sounds like a plan. You got all that, Bubu?"

"Yes, Master Remo," Bubu said, worried. "But

perhaps you do not realize that it takes longer than one hour to drive out to the place you have chosen.''

The elevator doors slid open, and all four men hurried onto the car.

''Let me worry about that, Bubu,'' Remo said as the doors rolled shut. ''Remember, I'm smarter than the average bear.''

33

The temperature in the sewer had risen as the day's hot sun baked the asphalt above. The goggles of Nunzio Spumoni's gas mask were fogged from humidity and anxiety. He had to pull the mask up to the top of his head to speak. His cell phone was slick in his palm.

"I don't know, Don Vincenzo," Nunzio said worriedly. "I have tried him, but he has not returned my calls."

The Camorra agent had explained all of this already.

Minister Deferens had disappeared. Not even his office knew his whereabouts.

The bombs were still set to go off at midnight. After Deferens vanished, Nunzio had come down here to check. Except now none of the men who were supposed to be caught in the blast were in Bachsburg. They were all at that damn party of Nellie Mandobar's.

Over the phone, Nunzio could hear the muffled roar of the raucous gathering. When he spoke, Don Vincenzo's voice was a rasping echo. The head of

Camorra had been forced to place his call from the men's room.

"I am *not* pleased, Nunzio," Don Vincenzo said menacingly. It was the tenth time he'd said so that evening.

His tone gave Nunzio a rare shiver.

"Don't worry, Don Vincenzo," he promised. "I'm certain he will call."

"Whether he does or does not, I am leaving this party by eight o'clock," the old don snarled. "My head is already pounding from this noise."

"You are not returning to Bachsburg?" Nunzio asked, trying to ingratiate himself by showing his great concern.

"Do you *want* me to die?" Vincenzo snapped. "Has *that* been your wish all along? Of *course* I am not, fool. I am flying to Victoria to rendezvous with my jet. Dammit, I should not even be here. That *anitra cervello* Giovani was dancing with a whore a moment ago." Low menace flooded his tone. "For *your* sake, he had better not be alive tomorrow."

Nunzio gulped. "We will make alternative plans," he vowed, his voice a croak. "We will reset the bombs for tomorrow, when Giovani and the rest have come back to the city."

"*If* your Minister Deferens ever contacts you," Don Vincenzo said, sneering. "I am very, *very* disappointed in you, Nunzio." With that, he broke the connection.

Shivering visibly, Nunzio snapped the phone shut.

Where was Deferens?

Don Vincenzo was already planning to leave the country. If L. Vas Deferens didn't call soon, Nunzio Spumoni wouldn't be far behind.

In the underground tunnel, the Camorra man pulled his protective mask back on. So nervous was he, Nunzio had hardly noticed the stench.

Like Don Vincenzo, Nunzio had his own doomsday plan. If Deferens didn't arrive by 8:30 p.m. sharp, he would drive like hell to the airport and take a nine-o'clock flight out of East Africa. It didn't matter where he flew to. Just as long as he wasn't in Bachsburg for the explosions.

He would worry about the personal fallout later.

Nunzio paced back and forth on the slimy catwalk, his arms crossed, phone in hand. His suit was drenched with sweat.

He had left more than two dozen urgent messages with Deferens's office. There were Camorra men with cell phones stationed at every bomb site. If the defense minister showed up at any one of them, his men would call.

Nunzio and a handful of men were waiting at the primary site, beneath the Bachsburg hotel district. Most of the crime lords, as well as much of the city, would be taken out with this one bomb.

Six bombs. Six timers counting down to zero.

Nunzio checked his watch. Barely five-thirty. Still, midnight was looming large for Nunzio Spumoni. As he dropped his hand to his side, he froze.

A sound. Coming up the distant tunnel.

"What was that?" Nunzio hissed hopefully.

He waved frantically at the four men he had brought down into the sewers with him to come forward. They came to him, guns drawn. All five men peered down the dimly lit tunnel.

And as Nunzio Spumoni strained to hear, the first sounds of argument carried to his ears.

"Don't bellyache to me. I told you to watch where you were going."

"He *pushed* me," insisted the voice that Nunzio knew could belong to none other than L. Vas Deferens. The East African sounded strangely cowed.

"Oh, *I* am to be blamed for your clumsy clubbed feet?" sniffed a third, singsongy voice.

"You *did* push him, Little Father."

"Surprise me one day, Remo, and take *my* side for once."

When the men broke into view at the end of the tunnel, Nunzio didn't know whether to be relieved or even more concerned. Defense Minister Deferens was flanked by an old Asian and a young white man. The East African's trademark white suit was dripping wet and stained gray.

Nunzio remembered the white as the man who had caught Deferens's attention at the Bachsburg restaurant.

"This isn't about choosing sides," Remo griped. "It's about me having to fish Himmler here out of Shit Creek."

"I think I am going to be ill," Deferens offered.

"Shut up," said Remo and Chiun.

Nunzio was stunned when Deferens actually fell silent. He merely trudged along, his hands clutching his belly, a queasy expression on his sagging model's face.

"Is everything all right, Vas?" Nunzio ventured as the men closed in. "I tried to call...."

When Deferens and his companions stopped before Nunzio and his Camorra entourage, Remo's face was a scowl. He appraised Nunzio's reed-thin frame.

"Who's the praying mantis?" he asked Deferens.

"An agent of Camorra," Deferens said, defeated.

Nunzio's eyes grew wide beyond his steamed-up goggles.

"Deferens, what is the meaning of this?" Nunzio demanded, taking a cautious step back. He was comforted by the appearance on both sides of his armed men.

"Do we need him?" Remo asked, ignoring Nunzio.

"What? Deferens—"

"No," the minister said glumly, interrupting the Camorra agent.

Remo turned to Nunzio. "Wanna see something I saw in a really bad movie once?" he asked.

Nunzio's eyes didn't have time to register confusion before Remo's hand shot forward, index and middle fingers extended.

The plastic of his right goggles lens surrendered to the stiffened fingers. Cracked plastic shards shot back through Nunzio's shocked eye, burying themselves deep in his brain.

Nunzio Spumoni's legs buckled, and he fell, slipping over the side of the platform. The body struck water with a mighty splash.

Before the first ripples from Nunzio's bobbing corpse reached the stone walls, the four remaining men opened fire.

Deferens dropped to his knees, frantically cradling his head in both hands.

Near the gunmen, Remo launched a toe into the groin of the closest. His pelvis cracked in a sideways smile straight up to his navel. As entrails splattered to stone, Remo shouted to Chiun.

"Get him out of the way!" he called over his shoulder.

Deferens only knew that he was the "him" being referred to when he felt a bony hand latch on to the back of his neck. In the next instant, he was airborne. He landed in a spray of filthy water next to Nunzio Spumoni's lifeless body.

"I hope you are happy," Chiun complained, whirling up beside Remo. He had to avoid a dozen fat automatic slugs. "I had to touch that disgusting creature."

The flat sole of one sandal lashed out, catching one of the gunmen square in the chest.

It was as if the thug were struck by a speeding car.

The man's feet left his shoes, and he rocketed back into the mossy wall of the tunnel, pounding stone with bone-crushing ferocity. When he slid to the floor, a perfect outline of his body was visible in the stone.

"Don't complain to me," Remo warned.

"You're the one who pushed him in in the first place."

Remo brought his hand across the face of one of the two remaining men in a sharp sideways slap. With a tearing pop, the man's jaw sprang free. It skipped across sewer water a half-dozen times before sinking from sight.

The Camorra agent was all panicked eyes and flapping tongue. Remo finished him with a knuckle to the nose. Bone splinters found brain, and the man fell to the catwalk.

Realizing that the battle was lost, the fourth and final man tried to run past the Master of Sinanju. His body managed to run a few yards along the platform. His head, however, hit the water just below Chiun with a brain-dead splash.

When Remo turned, the old Korean was flicking a single dollop of blood from one long fingernail. He kept his hands away from his silken robes.

"We must find a place where I can wash my hands as soon as possible," the old man insisted.

"First things first," Remo said tightly. "Let's go see if our brown fish floats."

He hurried past Chiun to the edge of the platform.

The current was stronger than it had been that morning, the water deeper. Nunzio Spumoni's body had become wedged on a rusted run-off pipe. Deferens was clinging to the body like a flotation device as filthy water splashed all around him.

Squatting at the river's edge, Remo frowned. "You gonna fish him out?" he asked the Master of Sinanju.

"I fished him out last time," Chiun sniffed.

"*I* fished him out last time. And besides, you pushed him in last time."

"Do not bother me with technicalities," Chiun said.

Deferens heard them bickering. He looked up helplessly, his pale face now ashen. "Save me!" he cried. He retched as a crashing wave filled his open mouth.

"I'm sick of always having to do all the heavy lifting around here," Remo griped under his breath.

He was about to climb down and grab Deferens when he was struck by a flash of inspiration. Jogging to one of the dead gunmen, he stripped off the man's suit jacket. Trotting back down to where Chiun waited above Deferens, Remo dangled one sleeve in front of the defense minister.

"Grab on tight," Remo called down. "Because I am *not* coming in after you."

Blinking greasy water from his eyes, Deferens latched onto the jacket with both hands. Remo hauled him up, depositing him to the catwalk. He was careful to stay out of dripping range.

As soon as he was safe, Deferens fell to the platform and started vomiting.

"Bombs or no bombs," Remo said to the Master of Sinanju, ignoring the retching minister. "Next time he goes in the drink, *you're* pulling him out."

He dropped the jacket into the dirty water.

"I make no promises," Chiun said blandly.

On the floor, Deferens made a violent puking sound.

"Oh, knock it off," Remo complained, kicking the defense minister in the side of the head with the heel of one loafer. "You're an East African government official. You should be used to swimming in shit."

Still retching, Deferens pulled himself to his feet. Clutching his belly with sick fingers, Deferens led the two Sinanju Masters down the tunnel.

For Remo, the area was becoming more familiar. Both he and the Master of Sinanju detected the radiation in the air even before they came to the entrance of the tunnel down which Remo and Bubu had discovered the first nuclear device.

The bomb casing had been leaking throughout the day. There was not enough for a lethal dose, yet neither man wished to risk it. Remo and Chiun paused at the mouth of the tunnel as Deferens ducked down it.

Alone, Deferens hurried to the bomb. The first reckless signs of hope were thudding in his chest.

These two men had displayed remarkable abilities, yet something about this bomb was keeping them back.

His queasiness was fading, rapidly being replaced by calculation. With shaking hands, he popped open the plastic panel on the side of the casing. The LED counter was still ticking remorselessly down to 12:00 midnight.

They wanted him to shut it down, but they were far enough away that they couldn't see exactly what he was doing.

Without even touching the panel, Deferens

moved his fingers, making a show of disarming the bomb. While he pantomimed, the display continued to race to zero.

He blinked excitedly, swallowing a rank clump of bile-fueled saliva.

He would leave this one armed. If he could somehow get away from these two, he might yet be able to flee the city. Thank God that Don Vincenzo had insisted on more than one bomb. At the time, Deferens had thought it foolish, but now...

Any thought of salvaging his original plan was gone. Nellie Mandobar had inadvertently taken all of his targets to safety. But this was no longer about mere money or power or racial insulation. It was about revenge.

Maybe he could escape—maybe not. But in the end, it would be L. Vas Deferens who would have the last laugh. For though these two had displayed amazing abilities, Deferens doubted either of them could withstand a nuclear explosion.

And if he *did* manage to escape, abandoning these two to the city-leveling blast, Deferens intended to pay Nellie Mandobar a visit. He would teach that *mooka* bitch a final lesson for ruining his brilliant scheme.

As he pretended to work, visions of a dead Mrs. Mandobar dancing in his fevered brain, L. Vas Deferens suddenly felt a sharp pain in the side of the head.

He toppled sideways to the floor, blinking bright stars from his eyes. When he pulled himself to his knees, feeling at the sticky blood in his hair, he glanced down the tunnel.

Remo was still standing next to Chiun, another small rock clutched impatiently in his hand.

"We know what you're doing, crap-bag, so quit jerking us around and get to work," Remo said threateningly.

Hope drained away; despair flooded in behind it.

Deferens turned woodenly back to the bomb. Soul gutted, he began dutifully punching in the proper disarm code.

34

The lone sentry patrolled the edge of the dusty bungalow village, a rifle slung over his shoulder.

Savannah had been chopped back a dozen yards from the last straggling houses, the better to see approaching enemies. While this worked well in daylight, when the inky darkness of night drew its shroud over Africa, all the world was consumed by menacing shadows.

The moon was a cloud-masked memory as the guard made his careful way along the well-worn perimeter path.

Weak spotlights illuminated the distant main street of the village. Insects danced merrily in the glow.

The sounds of revelry from the far end of the street carried back on the humid air.

The last of the helicopters had landed nearly three hours ago. Everyone who was supposed to be at Nellie Mandobar's party was already there. As the evening progressed, a few of the guests had retired with hired women to the small houses behind which the guard now walked.

To break the tedium as he walked the circuit

around the bungalows, he had been listening for the sounds of lovemaking. Near the house where he was certain he'd seen Trollop Seasoning enter with three of the caterers, the guard heard the sudden sharp sound of a twig snapping.

He froze.

Lifting his boot, he looked down and saw the small brittle branch he'd felt crack beneath his thick sole.

Of course the sound had come from him. Only Luzus ventured this far out into the wilds of East Africa these days. And even they were miles away.

When the guard looked back up, his eyes barely registered the flash of metal from out of the night. Somewhere behind it, shadows on a painted face.

The blade struck his neck, and the world turned briefly upside down before growing completely and eternally black.

As the guard's body joined his severed head on the dusty African ground, Bubu slipped forward, machete in hand. He made a soft clicking sound with his tongue.

More armed Luzu natives appeared from the darkness, dressed in the simple loincloths of their ancestors. Among them was Chief Batubizee, his broad face drawn in somber lines.

No words were spoken.

On swift silent feet, the Luzu war party moved stealthily into the village, away from Nellie Mandobar's headless guard.

In the distance, the party roared on.

A Friend of Persuasion   311

around the bungalow, he had been frantically for the grounds of lovemaking. Soon the house where he was contenting's own Truly had someone enter with their of the entrance, the grabbed and the so then strain bound of a twig snapp——

His bone.

Inking the noot, he rolled down and saw the small bring bdanch he'd fell crack beneath his thick sole.

35

Their tour of the Bachsburg sewer system at last brought them less than half a city block from the presidential palace. Many of the defense minister's minions still toiled above, oblivious to this particular aspect of their employer's plan.

Remo and Chiun had met resistance at the first three bomb sites. But as the clock crawled closer to the midnight deadline, the Camorra men assigned by Nunzio Spumoni to keep watch for the defense minister had bolted. By the last bomb, the two Masters of Sinanju found themselves racing down an empty tunnel.

Deferens had been finding it impossible to keep up. As a result, Remo and Chiun had clamped onto his arms—one on each side. As they whisked him through the tunnel, the stone walls a blur, Deferens held his breath in fear.

"I'm gonna have to boil my hands for a month after this," Remo griped as he ran. He held Deferens as far from his own body as possible.

"Must I remind you that we would not need to rush had you not frittered away much of the day?"

Chiun replied tightly. His kimono skirts billowed as his pumping legs kept perfect time with his pupil's.

Remo held his tongue.

His internal clock told him that it was past eleven-thirty. Thanks to the unexpected resistance they'd encountered at the other sites, they were half an hour later than expected by the time they reached the last bomb.

Brackish water pooled in the secluded dead end.

Remo and Chiun dumped Deferens in front of the rusted gate through which peeked the stainless-steel bomb casing.

Deferens didn't need to be told what to do. Grabbing the corroded grate, he pulled it free, leaning it against the stone wall. He squatted in front of the bomb.

"I hope those Luzu buddies of yours don't jump the gun," Remo commented as the East African worked.

"The Luzu are a patient people," Chiun replied. "They lived one hundred years in desperation before invoking the contract of Nuk."

"Maybe," Remo said. "All I know is they had itchy machete fingers yesterday. And if there's a buffet at that party, Batubizee'll lead the charge with a knife and fork."

"They will wait," Chiun insisted knowingly. "It seems all they are suited for these days."

Hunching on the floor, Deferens punched out the disarm code on the touch pad as the two men spoke.

Though the East African was shivering, it was not due to cold. Deferens was ill. It had been three bombs since the last time either Remo or Chiun had thrown him in the water, yet he had been growing sicker as the night drew on. His soiled clothes were damp.

Over soon. All of it.

There was no longer any hope for escape. These two were like no one he had ever met. He was left with but one option. If he was to die, they would go with him.

Once he had disarmed the bomb, the digital counter shut down. Moving like an automaton, he reset it.

The least amount of time the bomb's processor would accept was a minute. He set it for this. As soon as he did, the red LED counter winked down to 00:59:00. The tenths of seconds raced by in a blinding flash.

While the last seconds of his life drained away before his eyes, Deferens woodenly feigned work. He shielded the counter with his body.

"Smith will be relieved to find out Willie Mandobar wasn't behind this," Remo commented absently.

"He will be more relieved that you did not allow this city to be destroyed," Chiun replied.

"I guess so," Remo mused thoughtfully. "It was still tempting, though. Our work would have been done for at least a year or two while the bad guys regrouped."

As he spoke, he reached into his pocket. Remo took out the stone-carved figure. He was studying the remarkably detailed image when he heard a gasp beside him.

When he glanced over, Chiun's mouth had formed a shocked O.

"Where did you get that?" the old man demanded.

Remo glanced at the figure. "Oh, yeah," he said. "I forgot to show you. That little Korean ghost kid gave it to me. You want to see it?"

When he tried handing it over to his teacher, the old Asian took a startled step back. He bumped into the still squatting Deferens, knocking the defense minister to the ground.

For an instant, Remo pulled his eyes from his teacher's uncharacteristically bewildered expression.

He saw the LED counter racing down to zero.

"What the hell did you do?" Remo snapped.

Deferens scampered back up, plastering his back to the face of the bomb. Sweat covered his pale forehead.

"*Nothing,*" he promised desperately.

For Remo, the Master of Sinanju's strange behavior was instantly forgotten. Dropping the stone figure quickly back into his pocket, he shoved Deferens out of the way.

There were only twenty-five seconds left.

"Dammit, he screwed with this thing, Chiun," Remo said urgently.

"You're too late!" Deferens barked triumphantly, his eyes burning hatred. "You're both *dead!*" He wheeled to Remo. "You are an *idiot!* I would have hired you both for twenty times what I paid you!''

He shook visibly—terror, exhaustion and victory pummeling his rattled senses.

Before Remo could take even a single step toward him, a new expression overcame his triumph.

Deferens gasped in pain, clutching at his stomach where a red incision had abruptly slithered across his abdomen.

Remo alone saw the flashing nail as it exited the wound. As Deferens's organs slipped through the yawning opening, Remo wheeled to the Master of Sinanju.

The old man's hand was returning to his side.

"Chiun, are you nuts?" Remo snapped.

The display was down to ten seconds.

The Korean's shocked expression upon seeing Remo's gift from the Master Who Never Was had steeled.

"Move," Chiun commanded, sweeping past Remo.

Crouching before the bomb, the Master of Sinanju's hands became a blur over the control pad.

"This isn't your VCR," Remo warned.

With only six seconds to go, Chiun shot his pupil a single glance. "You have yet to learn how to program that, too," he said thinly. Without turning back to the control pad, a single tapered index finger reached out and entered a final number.

The countdown halted with three seconds left.

The display panel on the side of the nuclear device winked to multiple zeroes and then slowly faded to black.

Standing beside his teacher, Remo blinked amazement. "How did you do that?" he asked.

"*I* have been paying attention all evening," the Master of Sinanju answered. He still seemed vaguely unnerved. His tone grew serious. "Someday, Remo, you will be required to use your eyes and I will not be here."

Remo didn't have time to respond.

On the floor, even as his grimy hands struggled to hold on to his dying organs, a waxy smile had formed on the perfect face of L. Vas Deferens. But when he saw the display grow dark, he began to slowly shake his head.

"No," the minister panted weakly. A thin trickle of watery blood gurgled up between his model's lips.

"Sorry, Elvis," Remo said with not a hint of sympathy. "Guess you're just shit out of luck."

A toe kick sent the East African defense minister into the stagnant pool. Trailing organs, he hit with a splash.

"What did that one say about paying you?" the Master of Sinanju asked as the sewer water accepted the gutted body.

Remo shook his head. "We'll talk about it later. Right now we've still got an army of Luzus to meet, and if Batubizee's got one whiff of the dessert cart, he's probably already led the charge." Spinning from his teacher, he hurried down the platform.

For an instant, a troubled flicker passed across

Chiun's wrinkled face. As quickly as it came, he banished it.

On steady, gliding feet, he raced to follow his pupil.

Behind them both, the body of L. Vas Deferens bobbed on silent ripples in the water of the stagnant pool.

36

Through a boozy haze, Nellie Mandobar watched Don Giovani approach. She staggered over to him, throwing a huge flabby arm around his shoulders. The Mafia leader shrank from both her touch and her alcohol-fueled breath.

"And how are you enjoying our party?" Mrs. Mandobar belched. She lowered her voice to a stage whisper. *"Partner,"* she added, giggling.

His dark tan paled. Giovani strained to keep his horror from showing. "Keep your voice down, *fool,*" he whispered. An unnatural smile that did not match his words was plastered across his weathered face. He tried to twist from her embrace, but her big arm was stuck fast to his shoulders.

"No one hears us," she grinned. She waved to the stage where three of the Seasonings cavorted in Lycra and Spandex. Their massive pregnant bellies bounced to the beat. "They're too busy enjoying the last party anyone here will ever have. Everyone but *us,* that is." Winking broadly, the former first lady of East Africa took a slug from her omnipresent glass.

"Shut up," Giovani snarled. He glanced around. "Have you seen Vincenzo?"

Nellie was exchanging her empty glass for a foamy green concoction from a passing waiter's tray.

"Hmm?" she asked, oblivious to the question.

Don Giovani exhaled quiet disgust. He had thrown in with this woman, whose only motivation seemed to be revenge against her husband. The Mafia leader was stuck with her. For now.

The old Italian glanced around, scanning for Don Vincenzo of Camorra. It was nearly 12:30 a.m., and the party was still going strong. Some men had disappeared a few times during the evening, always in the company of one of Nellie's hired whores or one of the Seasonings. They always returned, smiles plastered on their faces. From what Don Giovani had seen, the Seasonings seemed to be taking on more action than the professional prostitutes.

As his sagging eyes searched the sea of faces in the huge meeting hall, he did not see his Camorra rival.

"He had better be here," Don Giovani grumbled to Nellie. "I am leaving. If you do not wish to be incinerated in four hours, I suggest you sober up and do the same."

Turning on his heel, the old man marched away.

Alone again, Nellie Mandobar sipped her drink.

Although she knew she was very drunk, she was still lucid enough to know that he was right. It was time to think about leaving. A shame. It was quite a good party. And she had certainly earned this time to celebrate.

Willie Mandobar would be ruined. Short of hanging a gasoline-soaked tire around his scrawny neck, this was the best revenge she could hope for.

Her plan had been timed to come to a head while her ex-husband was away. It was her own sympathizers in the Kmpali government who had requested his presence in China.

The explosion here would prove that East Africa's claims of being a nuclear-free zone were a lie. The government of her husband's party would be discredited. And without his leadership as president, the new East Africa would have to turn to another Mandobar to lead.

Nellie Mandobar would succeed. And she would crush utterly the weakling man who had failed to stand by her at her time of greatest need.

Nellie struck off around the edge of the crowd, sipping her drink as she walked.

The band screeched on. Wails that passed for singing attacked the crowd from the speakers positioned at angles just below the bordering skylights. On stage, there were now only two Seasonings left. As she walked, Nellie thought she saw a pair of white go-go boots sticking up in the air behind a vibrating amplifier.

Nellie returned a few smiles as she weaved her way out to the main hallway. The high glass doors of the grand foyer muffled the cacophony from inside. Mrs. Mandobar's ringing ears were just starting to relax when she became aware of a fresh sound.

Pop-pop-pop.

Listening to the muted noises, Nellie frowned.

For a moment, she thought it was static from the sound system. But it seemed to be coming from outside.

When she pushed open one of the thick front doors, she was instantly assaulted by the hot African night. Stepping onto the vast patio, she let the door swing shut behind her. The party sounds grew softer still.

Taking a deep, cleansing breath, she searched the immediate area for the source of the popping sound.

It came again. Louder now than before. A sharp slap that echoed out across the savannah. It was followed by another. Then another.

Worry immediately knotted Nellie's ample belly. Gunshots.

Even as this shock was registering, Nellie heard the screams. A moment later, men and women in various states of undress appeared, running up from the village.

Trollop Seasoning—her pregnant belly bouncing to beat the band—led the pack of crime figures and whores.

As she ran, she tugged at her sides. With a rip of spirit gum, her stomach prosthesis came free. Like her bandmates, she only wore it for media attention. The faux stomach was trampled beneath frantic stomping feet.

"My God, they're *attacking!*" the pop singer

screeched as the first of the crowd stampeded up the auditorium stairs.

Mrs. Mandobar didn't need to ask who. When the first Luzu natives appeared down the road, Nellie's drink slipped from her pudgy hand. It shattered into splattering green fragments on the flagstone patio.

Far away, the natives fell upon the stragglers, machetes slicing the night. Running bodies surrendered heads and arms.

Trollop and the others pounded past the stunned Nellie Mandobar.

"Girl domination, my ass!" Trollop was screeching as she clawed past a pair of hookers on her way through the door. "Get me men with big bulging biceps and guns! I mean—God, this is worse than that mall opening we did in Detroit!"

As the men and women streamed inside, more gunshots rose from the village.

Nellie finally got her bearings. Spinning from the rampaging Luzus, she raced back inside.

It was coming apart. All her planning, all her dreams. But none of that mattered now. Suddenly safety was her overriding concern.

When the door closed on her ample derriere, it was torn open a minute later by the first charging Luzu.

The natives swarmed the building.

And as the band stopped dead, their rehearsed shrieks supplanted by cries of pure terror, high on the roof the first of the helicopters coughed to life.

37

Simple persuasion was all it took to convince one of Nellie Mandobar's pilots at the airport in Bachsburg to ferry Remo and Chiun to the site near the secret village. The man was still spitting out bloody tooth fragments as Remo and Chiun's helicopter rattled in over the area of savannah where they were to rendezvous with Batubizee's Luzu natives.

An undercarriage searchlight revealed nothing but empty ancient road and mile after mile of barren savannah.

"I thought you said they'd wait," Remo commented tightly as they swept over the treasury road.

As he scanned the path, a spark of optimism lit the Master of Sinanju's youthful eyes. "We are late. Perhaps they have decided not to wait for fate to come to them."

"Well, good for them and the Boston Braves," Remo griped. "Why couldn't they decide to carpe diem on their own damn time?"

The Master of Sinanju gave a flickering nod of approval. "It is a start," he said.

Remo directed the pilot to take them to Nellie Mandobar's village. They spotted the fleeing helicopters the instant their own chopper skirted the rough black hills.

There were dozens of them, flying up out of the distant night, one after another. The helicopters raced out in every direction, desperate to put distance between themselves and the glass-and-stone auditorium that rose up like a glistening, illuminated diamond from the arid black earth. Remo and Chiun's pilot had to swoop and dive to avoid three midair collisions.

The choppers clustered back together far out over the savannah. As they raced off in the direction of Bachsburg, more fleeing helicopters roared in behind them.

When they arrived at the village, it was still far too dangerous to land on the busy plateau airfield. Remo instructed the pilot to set down on a dusty stretch between bungalows and hall.

There had been sporadic flashes of light as they approached, indicating spotty gunfire. The shooting had dwindled to next to nothing by the time their helicopter touched ground.

As soon as they landed, a dozen panicked guards swarmed the craft.

Remo popped the rear door into the faces of two of the charging figures. With a crunching clang, the men collapsed to the dust. As the first guards fell, Remo and Chiun sprang out into the night.

One guard tried to shoot Chiun, while another managed to get one leg aboard the helicopter. Chiun's flashing nails sought legs and hands. The gunman was left with two pumping wrist stumps while the other guard found himself pitching forward in the dirt onto his own severed legs.

When Remo planted a single rifle barrel through two consecutive heads, the remaining guards seemed to get the lay of the land. The six men tore away from the helicopter they'd hoped to commandeer. They had no sooner vanished in the darkness behind the nearest bungalow before Remo and Chiun heard the swish of machete blades through air.

Screams cut the night.

"Guess there's no doubt who the party crashers are," Remo said aridly as he slammed the helicopter door closed.

The instant he did so, the chopper lifted off. Flying fast, it joined the mass migration back to Bachsburg.

At a full sprint, the two Masters of Sinanju raced for the huge auditorium, which sat in a blare of lights at the far end of the street. They met up with Chief Batubizee and Bubu on the sprawling flagstone patio.

"And what part of 'wait' don't you understand?" Remo asked the young native after he and Chiun had vaulted up the front steps.

"I am sorry, Master Remo," Bubu apologized.

"*I* ordered this attack," Batubizee intoned. His massive sagging belly nearly obscured his loincloth. "Bubu has told me that it is Mandobar's woman who has brought East Africa to ruin and ordered you to kill me. I will have my revenge."

At the chief's side, the Master of Sinanju nodded

approval. "It is good at times for men to fight their own battles," he said. "At others, it is prudent to enlist aid. A worthy leader understands the difference."

Batubizee's sweating face showed deep understanding. "You are truly a worthy successor to Nuk," he replied.

Remo and Bubu stood together near the frosted doors. The fighting inside seemed to be dying down.

"If we're through with the life lesson, can we please get inside before all the good heads are taken?" Remo asked.

The Luzu chief and the Master of Sinanju exchanged a sharp nod. Hurrying across the patio, all four men ducked through the door and into the air-conditioned hall.

WHEN WORD of the Luzu attack first broke, most of the village guards had fallen back to the auditorium. It was during the skirmish there that many of the crime leaders had found the time needed to flee. Of the many dead around the hall, nearly all were guards.

Remo, Chiun and their two Luzu companions avoided pools of blood and severed limbs on their race across the big room.

"You see Nellie anywhere?" Remo called over his shoulder.

Batubizee and Bubu were scanning the area. It sounded as if the final skirmish was being fought somewhere near the kitchen.

"She could be anywhere," Bubu said. "Perhaps she has already fled."

The steady rumble of helicopters above their heads had nearly died. "Let's try the roof," Remo suggested.

The stage near the open door was littered with bodies. While the band had been slaughtered where they sat, there was no sign of the Seasonings.

The four men mounted the stairs to the roof. They broke out onto the helipad just as two of the last four helicopters were lifting off.

A fat woman in a fruit hat and flowered burnoose was running desperately away from the spot where the two choppers had lifted off. She thundered over to one of the last two as it was preparing to take off.

"Let me on!" Nellie Mandobar cried, grabbing at the door frame.

A hand wielding a four-inch fluorescent lime-green clog appeared in the door.

"Let go, fattie!" Ho Seasoning snarled as she smacked the former East African first lady's thick fingers. "There's a two-ton weight limit."

For emphasis, she hurled her other shoe at Nellie. It struck Mrs. Mandobar square in the forehead.

As the stunned woman staggered back, the helicopter took off. Regaining her senses, she ran for the last chopper.

It was already rising from the platform by the time she arrived. Fat fingers grabbed for the skids. They missed.

"I will have you necklaced!" Nellie Mandobar screamed furiously at the helicopter.

Overloaded, the chopper dropped from sight beside the plateau. It appeared a moment later in the distance, struggling to pull into the air.

"You are all dead!" Nellie screeched, waddling to the edge of the platform. Fat hands waved menacingly in the air. "I will burn you alive! Do you hear me! Listen to me!" She stomped a fleshy foot. Her fruit hat dropped over one eye. "Come back here this instant!"

But no amount of jumping or screaming would bring the helicopter back. Continuing to fly low, it headed off across the savannah toward the city, rotor noise fading.

"I am going to stop payment on your *check!*" Nellie yelled after the long-gone Seasonings.

Furious at wasting four hundred dollars on the washed-up girl group, she wheeled in a desperate search for alternative transportation. Only then did she see Remo, Chiun and Chief Batubizee walking toward her. Spear raised, Bubu walked protectively next to his chief.

Nellie's bugging eyes collapsed to instant tunnel vision. The others were nothing; mere shadows. Seeing only the Luzu chief—the man whose attack had brought her to ruin—Nellie's eyes ignited beneath the mound of plastic fruit. A crazed serpent's hiss issued from deep within her ample bosom.

"*You!*" she exclaimed.

And like a bull from a gate, she charged.

Long nails were talons. Bared white teeth were

angry fangs as she raced across the helipad toward Batubizee.

Bubu sprang out to hurl his spear. Remo held his arm.

"Watch and learn, kid," he suggested quietly.

The young native's worried eyes darted to Chiun. The Master of Sinanju had faded back, allowing Nellie a clear shot at the chief.

Batubizee stood motionless, raising himself to his full height. For the first time, Remo glimpsed the dignity of the ghosts who had built the Luzu Empire.

Nellie's head was tipped so that she could rip out Batubizee's throat with her chomping teeth. Growling, she was about to clamp down on his Adam's apple when a big fist lashed out.

Batubizee punched Nellie solidly in the chest just above her massive bouncing breasts. The wind whooshed from her lungs, and the former first lady of East Africa dropped backward onto her ample padded rump.

When the chief reached two clutching paws for her throat, a bony hand restrained him.

"In due time," the Master of Sinanju said softly.

Nellie scurried from broad bottom to dimpled knees. Her rage collapsed once more to panic.

"You have to get me out of here!" she begged.

Her demented eyes were pleading as she looked at each of the four men above her.

That she would beg for help from the men who had led the attack on her party was evidence enough that there was more here than met the eye.

"Okay, Carmen Miranda," Remo said, his tone wary. "Why the big rush to leave?"

"I will tell you on board your helicopter," she promised. "Where is it? We must hurry!" Unblinking eyes darted in search of an invisible helicopter.

"Will I be as upset as you're gonna be when you find out our pilot took off on us?" Remo asked.

Nellie's shriek sent sleeping birds a mile away fluttering into the dark sky.

"I'd say that's an 8.5 on the yes scale." Remo nodded to the others.

Nellie pushed herself upright on thick ankles. "A car will not get us far enough," she said, her mind reeling.

"Far enough from what?" the Master of Sinanju demanded.

She wheeled on him. "There is a nuclear bomb planted in a cave near here!" she cried. A plastic banana fell in front of her eye. She tore it loose, flinging it away. It landed near a pair of hollowed-out Seasonings bellies.

"Not Deferens again," Remo groused. "What, did he plan on blowing up the whole continent?"

"What are you talking about?" Nellie spit. "Deferens had nothing to do with this."

"Then everyone in this dingdong country made the same deal, 'cause we just spent half the night defusing six bombs Elvis and Gamera planted around Bachsburg."

Nellie was trying to wrap her brain around what he was saying. "Camorra?" she asked. "But I made a deal with Don Giovani of the Sicilian Mafia to destroy this village. He and I were the only two meant to escape."

"I guess there's no such thing as an original plot," Remo said, "because that's just what he had in mind."

Confusion turned to cold rage. "I will kill him," Nellie menaced. She grabbed Remo by the arm. "Come, we will take your car. Do you have a spare tire? Oh, and we'll need to stop somewhere for gas."

She tried marching back across the helipad, but before she could take a single step a broad hand swept in, slapping her on one fat cheek. Nellie Mandobar's fruit hat sailed off as she fell to the ground, clutching her face in pain.

Chief Batubizee towered above her, rage painted large on his moon face.

"Where is this bomb, woman!" the chief bellowed.

Bruised flesh stinging, she cowered from the Luzu leader.

There was nothing she could do. Her only hope of escape was with these men. When she spoke, her voice was small.

"I will show you," Nellie Mandobar said.

38

Even in its heyday four decades ago, the mine had yielded few diamonds. Several scraps of rotted lumber and some corroded chunks of metal were all that remained beside the scrub-lined path that led up to the black cave mouth.

"It was close enough to obliterate the village but far enough away to escape detection," Nellie Mandobar explained as they hiked up to the cave opening. Her dark face was slick with sweat.

Remo, Chiun, Bubu and Chief Batubizee accompanied her. Coming up behind them all were three hundred Luzu warriors.

The stars above were starting to fade.

"How far in is it?" Remo asked as he eyed the lightening sky.

"Perhaps a hundred yards," she replied.

"Does it use the same code as the others?" Chiun asked.

Nellie scrunched up her face. "I do not know," she said. "Probably not. I acquired it several years ago from an East African scientist just before the program was disbanded. If Deferens got his afterward, he could have changed the code."

"Where's the scientist?" Remo asked.

Nellie pointed sheepishly to a dense thicket. Sticking out from beneath the wild shrubs were two charred legs that ended in a pair of burned boots. They appeared to have been there for some time.

"Have you ever met anyone you *didn't* set fire to?" Remo asked, disgusted. He continued before she could answer. "Can you shut it off?"

"He only showed me how to arm it," Nellie replied. "I did not think I would have to disarm it."

"Great," Remo muttered. He turned to the Master of Sinanju. "What do you think, Little Father?"

"For the future of our House, I would ordinarily insist you find a safe haven while I deal with the boom," Chiun said. "But since neither of us could flee in time, we will go in together."

Chief Batubizee and Bubu stepped forward. "We will accompany you, as well," the Luzu leader insisted. "If I am to meet my ancestors this day, I will do so while laughing in the face of the beast."

"I won't ask if you mean Nellie or the nuke," Remo muttered. "The rest of you fellas stay here," he called to the Luzu army. "And if you see a really bright flash, run like hell."

Propelling Mrs. Mandobar before them, the small group entered the black cave opening.

INSIDE WAS LIKE an abandoned Western gold mine. Ancient wooden support beams ran up to the rock roof where overburdened lintels strained to keep the ceiling in place.

At the cave mouth, Nellie found a bag with flashlights and other supplies she had left during her earlier visits. She and Bubu each took one. The washed-out white beams cast eerie shadows far down the man-made shaft.

"This way," the former first lady said.

She led them far down the tunnel.

About seventy yards in, an alcove opened up on their right. Although it was short, Remo got a sudden sense of vast emptiness beyond, as if the world collapsed into nothingness at the end of the small side tunnel.

Peering through the darkness, he saw the opening of another tunnel in the rock face at the far end of the alcove.

"What's that?" he asked.

"Nuk wrote of them in his accounts," Chiun supplied. "They are passages without end. Nuk thought they led to the Great Void."

The thought, as well as the sense of infinite emptiness from the tunnel, gave Remo a chill.

"The geologists from Bachsburg call them kimberlites," Bubu whispered in explanation. His flashlight beam found the opening. "They occur naturally. Some are many miles deep."

The native's beam aimed forward once more, and they continued down their own tunnel. Eventually, the flashlight beams fell across the by now familiar shape of an East African nuclear warhead.

Remo and Chiun stooped to examine the bomb.

The flashing red timer was set for 5:00 a.m. An hour and a half away.

"Wanna start ripping wires out?" Remo asked Chiun.

"Given your inability to screw in a lightbulb without first consulting General Electric, it would not be my first choice," the Master of Sinanju replied.

Remo looked to Nellie Mandobar. She licked her broad lips. "I would not try it," she said anxiously.

Chiun studied the bomb casing. He ran a hand along the stainless steel, as if measuring its circumference.

"Okay, who's for making Broom Hilda here eat this thing?" Remo asked. He raised his own hand to drum up enthusiasm.

"*She* cannot eat it," Chiun said, stroking his beard thoughtfully.

When Remo met his teacher's gaze, silent communication explained his meaning. The younger Master of Sinanju nodded, taking up the thread.

"It'd have to be pretty deep," he warned.

"Did you sense a bottom?" Chiun offered.

"This would all have to come down, too," Remo said, waving a finger to the ceiling.

It was Chiun's turn to nod.

"All right, we've got a plan," Remo announced.

Reaching out, he slapped his hands on either side of the nuclear device, lifting it from the mine floor as if it were papier-mâché.

Bomb in hand, Remo and Chiun led Mrs. Mandobar and the natives back to the alcove where the kimberlite opened up. He balanced the warhead on the rocky edge of the deep shaft. Holding the bomb in place, he turned to Batubizee and Bubu.

"You two had better scram," he warned.

Chief Batubizee hesitated. "Master of Sinanju?"

"Go," Chiun nodded. "If the end comes, you should be with your people."

With a final questioning look at Remo, Bubu reluctantly trailed his chief down the tunnel. When Nellie Mandobar started after them, Chiun restrained her.

"Hold, evil one," he said, his voice steady.

"Hold?" Nellie frowned. "Hold what? I am getting out of here."

In the yellow glow of her flashlight, Remo's smile was demon sent. "Lady, you couldn't be more wrong."

With a push, he dumped the bomb down the kimberlite. It disappeared inside the smothering blackness. As the nuclear device began its endless tumble through space, Remo spun to the former first lady of East Africa.

"Night-night, Margaret Dumont."

Her flabby face was just knotting in confusion when Remo reached out and tapped the center of her forehead. Nellie Mandobar's crazed eyes rolled back in her head, and she collapsed to the rock floor.

They left her unconscious in the kimberlite alcove.

Racing out into the main tunnel, Remo and Chiun flew down a few dozen feet. Each Master of Sinanju took a position on either side of the main path next to one of the support columns. A sharp nod and two tight fists shot out simultaneously.

The rotten wooden columns splintered at the center, bringing down the lintel above, as well as much of the cave roof. When the rock ceiling collapsed, Remo and Chiun were already gone.

They ran up the tunnel side by side, their legs harmonious blurs. Every time they passed another set of columns, hands shot out, pounding wood.

Walls and ceiling shook as if clutched in an angry fist. Even the floor seemed to buck as they raced through the rising hail of dust and stone.

Ahead, a stab of washed-out gray. A hint of starlight.

Running faster. Legs invisible, arms flashing, smashing columns to splinters of creosote-soaked wood. The dust cloud racing ahead, obliterating the cave entrance. A final rumble. Rocks collapsing above them.

A final surge propelled them through the storm and out the cave mouth. They sprang into the fresh warm air. Behind them, the cave vomited a massive burst of dust at the sky.

At the appearance of Remo and Chiun, a cheer went up from the assembly of Luzu warriors. Faces beaming pure joy, Bubu and Chief Batubizee broke from the crowd, running over to the two Masters of Sinanju.

"Master Chiun!" Batubizee whooped.

"Master Remo!" Bubu cried at the same time.

Remo held off an embrace from the young native.

"Before you bust out the champagne, maybe we

should put some distance between us and that,'' he suggested, nodding back to the tumble of rocks that obscured the old cave mouth.

The Luzus nodded. With Remo and Chiun in the lead, the triumphant natives marched down the hill, leaving the dust and rocks of the collapsed cave to settle on the final resting place of both Nellie Mandobar and her twisted scheme.

39

The explosion came in the wee hours of the morning, at the time when Nellie's party would have been winding down. Remo and Chiun alone felt the gentle rumble of earth. They sat on rocks near the dusty well in the middle of the Luzu village. All around, natives danced and sang. To Remo, what appeared to be a Luzu conga line pranced past for the millionth time. He was called to join but declined.

"Don't they ever get tired?" Remo asked.

The celebration had begun at their victorious return. Although dawn had long started to streak the sky pink, the party showed no sign of stopping.

"They have had little to celebrate for many years," the Master of Sinanju replied simply.

"I suppose." Remo nodded. The soft rumbling beneath their feet began to slow. It faded to a shuddering stop. "Looks like that shaft was deep enough to hold the blast. You think Nellie's awake by now?"

Chiun raised his shoulders indifferently. "Assuming the tunnel where we left her did not collapse, too."

"With any luck, she's sucking on radioactive dust and digging like mad," Remo commented with satisfaction.

Chiun was deeply unconcerned. He watched a dancing figure across the square.

Bubu was swaying in place, his arms waving in time with a rhythm that was being tapped out on a primitive drum. Remo was again impressed by the native's innate grace.

Chief Batubizee stood near the younger man. The Luzu leader was smiling and clapping. Around Bubu a dozen Luzu women watched him dance with giggling glee.

"What's with the belle of the ball?" Remo asked, nodding to the young native.

"As eldest son of the chief, Bubu has his choice of consorts," the Master of Sinanju explained.

Remo's head snapped around. "Bubu is Batubizee's kid?"

Chiun inspected his pupil's face. "Are you embarrassed now for making sport of his name?"

Remo considered. "Not really," he admitted. "I'm just surprised no one mentioned it."

The Master of Sinanju leaned close. "Do you realize, Remo, that you saved the life of the chief's son?"

"What, in Bachsburg?" Remo shook his head. "He was fine. I just pulled him out of the sewer."

Chiun pitched his voice low. "Do not allow silly modesty to ruin what is potentially a good thing," he said craftily. "You are now a hero to these people. For Bubu will one day succeed his father as ruler of all the Luzu. And if nothing else, the lesson of Nuk teaches us that the potential payday from the Luzu can be great indeed.''

A faint smile crossed the face of the younger Master of Sinanju.

"Did I say something humorous?" Chiun asked.

"No, Little Father. It's just that I feel kind of good. You know, by helping Bubu I sort of helped their future." He waved an arm, encompassing the entire Luzu nation. "I was worried about saving the whole world before, but maybe I just need to save a little piece of it every now and then."

As he spoke, he fished absently in his pocket. He studied the carved face of the stone figure the small Korean boy had given him.

His thoughts were on the future. On *his* future.

"May I see that?"

Chiun's hushed voice shook him from his reverie. When Remo looked up, the harsh lines of his teacher's face were smooth.

"You seemed spooked by it before," Remo said, handing it over.

As he studied the figure, a hint of an unfamiliar emotion passed across the old man's weathered face. "Surprised, that is all," Chiun replied softly. "I have not seen a carving like this in many years."

"You've seen one before?" Remo asked, surprised.

Chiun nodded. "I have many of them stored in a chest in the Master's House in Sinanju. I have not looked at them in a long, long time." His voice grew faraway. "My son Song used to carve them with his nails for the children of the village."

The old man had taken years to tell Remo about Song, his son and first pupil who had died in training. And in that moment, Remo understood the true identity of the Master Who Never Was.

"I thought you said Song was almost nine when he died," Remo said quietly. "The boy I saw couldn't have been older than six."

When Chiun looked up, there was flitting sadness in his hazel eyes. But when he beheld the deeply sympathetic face of his pupil, his smile returned. "The Void reflects your true self," he explained. "My son who died was younger than his years because I tried to force him to grow up too quickly. It gladdens me to know that, in death, he is enjoying the childhood that I in my stubbornness would not permit him to have." He started to hand the figure back.

Remo shook his head. "You should keep it," he insisted.

But the old Korean shook his head. "I told you, I have others. This was a gift from my son in flesh to my son in spirit. Treasure always this gift from your brother, Remo."

He pressed the small stone into Remo's palm. Nodding, Remo replaced it in his pocket.

For a moment, he took out baby Karen's crucifix. A small rectangle of yellow paper fluttered to the ground.

As he studied the cross, the world suddenly seemed less cruel than it had just a few short days before. With but a ghost of lingering sadness, he started to put the cross away. Before he could, there came a gasp beside him.

"What is that?" the Master of Sinanju demanded.

Remo braced himself, preparing for the usual carping about his latent Christianity.

"It's just a cross, Little Father," Remo said.

"Not that pagan idol," Chiun spit. *"That."*

An accusing finger pointed to the piece of paper lying in the dirt. Remo gathered it up.

"Oh," he said. "It's my check from Deferens for the Batubizee hit."

"You accepted a *check?*" Chiun gasped. "A mere *promise* of payment? Remo, tear out my heart that I might not feel the agony of the knife you have driven into it." He pressed a hand against his chest.

"Oh, can the bad acting," Remo said, suppressing a grin. "Besides, I had him up to six million in gold."

"A likely story," the old man countered.

Remo's face suddenly grew crafty. "While we're at it, how much did *you* get paid for all this?"

Chiun's back stiffened. "None of your business," he retorted. "And we are talking about *you,* not me. Do you not yet know that a check is even worse than government bills? It is a paper promise of more paper. Oh, the shame, Remo."

"It's not even like I ever intended to cash it," Remo said. Crumpling the check, he tossed it away.

Before it hit the ground, a long-nailed hand snatched it from the air. Chiun laid the paper on his knee, smoothing it flat.

"We will stop at a bank as soon as we return to Bachsburg," the Master of Sinanju sniffed as he secreted the check into the folds of his kimono.

"Oh, no, we won't," Remo said. "I'm not endorsing that."

"That is not a problem," Chiun replied, fussing at his kimono sleeves. "In East Africa, baboons are known to come out of the jungle into inhabited areas."

"So what?" Remo asked warily.

Chiun raised a bemused eyebrow. "I will give a pen to one of them. Surely they can duplicate the jumble of scratches that constitute your signature."

40

Luzuland, East Africa (AP)—An as yet unexplained underground tremor rocked this northern tribal homeland early this morning. Seismologists from nearby Bachsburg have been sent to investigate.

Preliminary reports indicate that the small earthquake has caused a slight shift in tectonic plates. As a result, a previously unknown underground river has broken through to the surface, flooding the man-made channels of an ancient irrigation system built during the days of the old Luzu Empire.

The inexplicable phenomenon, occurring as it has in a region not prone to seismic activity, has lent hope to the indigenous tribesmen. Chief Batubizee, leader of the Luzu tribe, has expressed confidence that this fresh supply of water will revive the formerly rich farmland of his ancient empire. When that day comes, the chief has promised that all debts incurred by the Luzu nation will be paid in full.

A journey through the dangerous frontier
known as the future...

JAMES AXLER

DEATH LANDS.

Zero City

Hungry and exhausted, Ryan and his band emerge from
a redoubt into an untouched predark city, and uncover a
cache of weapons and food. Among other interlopers,
huge winged creatures guard the city. Holed up inside
an old government building, where Ryan's son, Dean,
lies near death, Ryan and Krysty must raid where a local
baron uses human flesh as fertilizer....

James Axler

OUTLANDERS®

DOOM DYNASTY

Kane, once a keeper of law and order in the new America, is part of the driving machine to return power to the true inheritors of the earth. California is the opening salvo in one baron's savage quest for immortality—and a fateful act of defiance against earth's dangerous oppressors. Yet their sanctity is grimly uncertain as an unseen force arrives for a final confrontation with those who seek to rule, or reclaim, planet Earth.